THE WEDNESDAY MORNING WILD SWIM

JULES WAKE

One More Chapter
a division of HarperCollins*Publishers* Ltd
1 London Bridge Street
London SE1 9GF
www.harpercollins.co.uk
HarperCollins*Publishers*
1st Floor, Watermarque Building, Ringsend Road
Dublin 4, Ireland

This paperback edition 2022

1

First published in Great Britain in ebook format
by HarperCollins*Publishers* 2022
Copyright © Jules Wake 2022
Jules Wake asserts the moral right to be identified
as the author of this work

A catalogue record of this book is available from the British Library

ISBN: 978-0-00-840900-5

Printed and bound in the UK using 100% Renewable Electricity
by CPI Group (UK) Ltd

For my Champneys' swimming buddies, Jo L, Celia, Jo P, Emma, Liz, Susannah, Fiona, Susie and last, but not least, the perennially cheerful Katie who works on the front desk – all of whom brighten my mornings.

Chapter One

Ettie pushed her way through an unexpected crowd of people milling about like lost but very curious sheep, and stuttered to a halt. Damn and double damn. A police cordon on Wellbeck Road at ten in the morning. OK, ten past ten. Possibly quarter past. All right, twenty-five past. She was well and truly late. Her own fault, she shouldn't have pushed to do another two lengths during her regular swim in the pool, but Mr I'm-such-a-fantastic-swimmer-and-don't-I-look-great-in-my-budgie-smugglers had been showing off with his flashy freestyle in the lane next to her and she'd been determined not to get out of the water before him. And then she'd had to do her hair and make-up, although feasibly she could blame that on her boss, Sally, who insisted that Ettie looked the part even though she hated the bright-red matt lipstick she had to wear. Triple damn. Her boss would not be happy about opening up this late, not that you saw many customers in this part of London before midday.

She was about to duck under the flimsy black-and-yellow tape that quite frankly wouldn't have stopped an ant in its tracks, when a large, uniformed policeman loomed in front of her. He, however, might well have stopped an elephant. She stared at the fluorescent-yellow vest he wore for a moment before giving him a brilliant smile.

'Hello, officer.'

He grinned back with a decided I-know-what-you-were-up-to smirk. 'Morning.' Despite the grin, his bulk didn't move an inch.

'Can I just get through? I work down there.' Ettie found charm got you a long way in lots of situations. She pointed, trying to peer over his bulk and failing miserably. 'Do you play rugby?' she asked, examining what had to be prop forward shoulders. Her grandad was a big rugby league fan, she'd been to a game or two in her time.

'It has been known,' he said, blinking at her as if trying to remember why he was there and what he was supposed to be doing.

She beamed at him and went to step forward again.

'Not so fast, Miss. I'm sorry, you can't come through.'

'But I'm soooo late for work!' The pitiful wail unfortunately had no effect, although his face sobered.

'Where do you work?'

'Something Old. The vintage clothes shop. Just down there. Can't I just go through?' She pointed again.

Suddenly there was an almighty bang. Ettie's ears

popped as the ground shook, car alarms began to shriek and a few hundred metres away brittle glass spat out of windows, raining down on the ground.

With a horrified shock, everyone stared down the road at the rising puffball cloud of dust as a column of flames licked the air, wreathed in acrid smoke.

'That would be a no then,' said Ettie, more to herself than anyone else, her heart pounding as pieces of information clicked into place, brick by brick like Lego. If she'd been on time, she'd have already been in the shop, making her first coffee of the day in the back, checking her phone. She'd have ignored any knock on the door as she never opened up before her first shot of caffeine had hit the target. Opening times in her book were of the flexible variety. Usually when she was ready. It wasn't as if buying second-hand clothes constituted any kind of emergency.

Her knees went a little wobbly and to her utter amazement, because she wasn't a swoony sort of girl, she found herself sinking to the floor. They always said (whoever 'they' were – a question Ettie asked herself frequently) that in times of near death, your life flashes before you. Well, 'they' had it nailed. That was exactly what was happening to her as she sat on the cold pavement, her legs splayed out in front of her, the bright-rose pattern of her skirt incongruous against the pitted and cracked paving slabs. She liked this skirt. *Please don't let there be chewing gum or dog poo on the floor.*

Thirty and still waiting for her life proper to start. She lived in a crappy house with four other people she barely knew; had to write her name on her milk, which still didn't deter the midnight milk thief; couldn't so much as chill a bottle of wine in the fridge for more than half an hour because that baby would be long gone, and don't even get her started on the daily battle against the mould in the bathroom which had stained the grouting beyond saving.

As for her job – the latest in a very long line – it turned out that working in a vintage clothes shop wasn't quite as glamorous as she'd been led to believe. In truth it was more like working in a charity shop, frequented by young people without the charity element, although she did meet some interesting people and there were perks. Last month, she'd snaffled a pair of vintage Louboutin shoes from an auction job lot of accessories, having spotted the scuffed red leather soles. And before anyone should go thinking that was thieving, she had told Sally, the owner of the shop, that she'd got her eye on a pair of shoes and paid the suggested twenty quid because Sally wasn't fussed about looking at them. It wasn't as if she ever got paid overtime for all the times she stayed late at the shop or had even seen so much as reimbursement for the Mac Red Rock lipstick that Sally insisted was essential for the job. Being blonde, blue-eyed and with a magnolia complexion, it really wasn't her colour. Ettie felt you needed a brunette bob, nice thick lips and a mysterious smile to pull that look off, and possibly a trench coat that belted in the middle. She had thinnish lips that were quick and ready to smile and there was absolutely nothing mysterious about her. What you saw was what you got. Plenty of enthusiasm and not much staying power.

'Are you all right, Miss?' asked the burly police officer, crouching down on his haunches beside her, his forehead furrowing in rather admirable concern, given she was a complete stranger. Of course, he had a proper job, he was trained for this sort of thing. She gave him a weary smile and a sigh, nodding as she tried to scramble to her feet, brushing down her skirt.

'Yes. What happens now?' she asked, staring up at the roiling plume of ugly, Mordor's Mount Doom-style smoke belching from the middle of the terrace where Something Old had once been, sandwiched between a bookie's and a bakery. She surveyed the crowd and saw the guy who was always smoking outside the betting shop, standing talking to Jean and Jan, the ladies who ran the bakery, and who took it in turns to pop in and see her to scrounge a coffee in exchange for one of yesterday's leftover buns.

Jean caught her eye and with Jan in her wake, bustled over.

'My, you're a sight for sore eyes. We were worried you might be inside. Gary said he smelled gas as soon as he opened up the betting shop this morning. He called the gas board. Just as well. The police only just evacuated us in time.' As Jean spoke, Jan, paler than usual – and she was quite pale to start with – wrung her hands, the agitated movement compensating for her uncharacteristic silence. Normally it was hard to get a word in edgeways with either of them.

'Thank goodness I was late.' Ettie stared at the debris littering the tarmac further down the road, still not quite able to believe what had happened. The thoughts in her brain didn't seem to know which way to turn. She'd only done the new window display yesterday. That had been a waste of time. Would she be able to get back into the shop to retrieve the good coat she'd set aside for next month's pay cheque? Would there *be* a next month's pay cheque? Was all the stock damaged? There were too many things to think about and when she found her voice again, it was very small and defeated. 'I don't know what Sally's going to say.'

'Well, let's just hope she's got good insurance,' said Jean.

———

It turned out that Sally didn't have good insurance. She didn't have any insurance at all.

'Never seemed worth it,' she said dolefully, on the phone, when Ettie finally got through to her three hours later from the less than comforting privacy of her boxroom bedroom. The police had already delivered the bad news to her boss, as had her landlord, the neighbour's landlord, numerous friends on Instagram and a news reporter from *London Tonight*. 'Only an idiot would insure a bunch of old clothes.' While Sally had assumed that the landlord's buildings insurance covered the shop in the event of a disaster, what she hadn't factored in was the business continuity element of insurance which would have paid Ettie's salary until the shop could be opened again and would also have covered the refit and redecoration as well as the purchase of new, as in additional, stock.

'So what's going to happen now?' asked Ettie, studying the alarming shade of blue furry mould in the corner of her room and imagining her and Sally, sanding back fire-blackened woodwork, painting walls and washing all the clothes. Hard work, but it sounded quite jolly. It might bring her and Sally a bit closer.

'Wellll...' Sally paused and Ettie's heart clenched in sudden dread. 'I'm afraid you're out of a job. The shop's completely gutted and nearly all the stock burned. What's left stinks so badly, it'll have to go in the skip.'

'But couldn't we ... you know, paint it, get more stock, you know...?' Her voice trailed off, for once uncharacteristic defeat settling on her shoulders like a heavy weight. Ettie was a Prosecco-flowing-down-the-side-of-the-glass sort of girl, she always looked on the bright side of life. At least until the explosion had quite literally floored her.

'Sorry, Ettie. There's no point opening up again. Besides, I've been thinking about going away travelling for a while. Running a shop is such a tie.'

Which was laughable because Sally had pretty much left the running of the shop to Ettie. Her contribution had been going to auctions and buying shedloads of tat and leaving it for Ettie to sort through to find saleable gear.

Ettie winced as she finally hung up the call and glared up at the blue fur skirting the ceiling, thinking about Aliona, the girl who'd had the room above until last month when she'd moved out to a much swankier pad. Enough was enough. After being a chambermaid for two years, Aliona had taken an online bookkeeping course and had got a much better paid job with, as she'd told Ettie, prospects. She'd been promoted in just three months and the company were always looking for more people.

Ettie had been wondering whether it was something she should consider, not terribly seriously until now but, she sighed, perhaps she should give it a go. The thought of it bored the pants off her, but today's near brush with death told her that it was past time to get a decent job and start being a proper grown-up. Clearly trying to discover what she really wanted to do with her life wasn't working out for her.

Chapter Two

'So what you going to do now, love?' asked her mother, Sandra Merman, exhaling a plume of heavily scented white vape smoke and putting a mug of tea in front of Ettie, who'd just arrived by taxi from the station in Churchstone. Sitting in the kitchen at home with its bright-green tiles, yellow walls and newish lino floor, it felt as if she'd never left. The last few years simply melted away.

'I mean, you know you're welcome to stop here as long as you want. I never did understand why you were so keen to go off to London.' Having just shoved a tray of frozen chips in the oven along with a whole packet of fish fingers, her mum sat down opposite her with her own mug of tea.

'Thought the streets were paved with gold,' Ettie said with a sudden grin. It was good to be home (fish fingers were her absolute favourite tea), even if it wasn't what she'd planned. 'Turned out it's just chewing gum, mainly.'

'Dirty beggars. What you going to do now?'

'Not sure in the short term. I need to do something for a couple of months, but I've started a bookkeeping course.' A slight exaggeration. What she meant was, she'd signed up and opened up the first page of the first module, and promptly closed it because it looked seriously dull. 'When I've got the diploma, I can get a job in bookkeeping. Aliona, my old flatmate, is earning three times what she was before at a big accountancy practice.'

'Bookkeeping! No disrespect, our Ettie. I mean, you're a bright girl an' all, but you and numbers never did get along.'

'It's not proper numbers. Not like algebra or trigonometry at school. It's common-sense stuff. I've looked into it and I could get a decent job with the qualification. When I worked at that accountant's, I didn't mind it too much.' She winced. It had been excruciating, but even as an admin assistant the pay had been good. They were just a bit too inflexible about time-keeping and rules. There'd been a lot of policies about use of mobile phones, sick leave and dress code, but not so many about partners' wandering hands. Or about slapping one of the said partners when they touched your bum.

'When was that? I'm not sure I remember you doing that.'

'It was before I worked at the dry cleaners in Kilburn and after I worked at that hotel in Maida Vale.'

'What, the one where you had to clean that room with

all the leather whips and cuffs in? Our Lindsey told me about that one.'

Ettie laughed. 'Bondage aside, I quite liked that job. There's something quite satisfying about finishing work with nineteen clean rooms. And the bondage man was only there the once. Funny, he looked quite tame when I saw him.'

'Just goes to show, it takes all sorts.' Her mum shook her head. 'But I'm still not sure about the bookkeeping. It doesn't sound like you.'

'Thing is, Mum, I'm not sure what *does* sound like me anymore.'

'Don't be like that, love. You've got to do what makes you happy.'

Ettie sipped at her tea and sighed inwardly. Mum had worked early shifts at the mustard factory down the road as well as being a dinner lady and a cleaner at the local primary school for the last twenty years. Despite her working three jobs, money was still tight in the Merman household and Mum looked every one of her forty-five years.

Ettie wanted more out of life than poorly paid jobs with few prospects.

'Earning decent money and having a job with prospects will make me happy,' she said resolutely.

'I s'pose there's a lot to be said for that,' agreed her mum heavily, rising to her feet to check the oven chips as the back door opened.

'Look, it's Auntie Ettie,' said her sister, Lindsey, marching in with a baby hoicked on her hip. 'I hear you lost your job. Again. Honest, you should get one down the factory. The pay's not bad and you can work as many hours as you like.'

'Thanks,' Ettie said, not meaning it in the slightest and making it quite clear.

'Ooh, our Ethel! Love those shoes. Don't tell me, no please, please don't tell me they're Jimmy Choos. Let us try 'em on.'

Lindsey shoved her niece at Ettie and kicked off her own shoes.

'Don't call me Ethel,' said Ettie with a sigh.

Her sister flashed her a grin. 'Why not? It's your name.'

'Leave 'er be for a minute, Linds.' Mum shook her head and gave Ettie's feet a disdainful glance.

Sighing and breathing in the unmistakable baby smell of Tiffany Eight (yes really), who fitted herself into the crook of her arm with a gummy grin, Ettie slipped off her pale-lavender silk crepe and black suede shoes with the red soles. 'They're Louboutin,' she said rather proudly. 'Second-hand and very vintage but designer all the same.'

'Not Jimmy Choo?' said Lindsey with a pout, sliding her feet into the shoes and clomping up and down the tiny kitchen with a model-like sashay. 'How the hell do you walk in these all day?'

Mum rolled her eyes. 'Give 'em back to your sister. She carries class off a bit better than you. She's the posh one in the family.'

While Ettie didn't consider herself the least bit posh, she had to acknowledge that she had always differed from her mum and sister. Was it wrong to want more out of life; to want nice things rather than the cheapest all the time, to have a job with prospects or to want a job with some status? Her plan had been to stay on at school and go to university but everything had gone awry when Gran died, leaving Mum laid up with what they'd now probably call depression but then was a bad back because she couldn't get out of bed. Someone had needed to go out and earn a living. Her younger sister's part-time job after school at the Co-op wasn't going to pay the electricity bill.

'Charming.' Lindsey pouted again and then grinned. 'Any chance of a cup of tea round here?'

'Actually, I brought some wine with me.' One-handed, Ettie pulled a bottle of Prosecco from her bag. It had been an unexpected leaving present from Sally, who in a fit of conscience had also given her the rest of the month's pay.

'Fizzy! Yay.' Lindsey seized the bottle. 'I love this stuff. On my hen do, I'm only going to drink this.'

'Hen do? Has Darren popped the question?' Ettie shifted the baby in her arms, trying to get a look at Lindsey's hands.

'Don't be daft.' Lindsey's happy smile sagged. 'I'm going to have to hog-tie that boy to get him into church.'

'Hmm. As soon as Tiffany Eight is old enough to be a bridesmaid, he'd better pull his finger out.' Mum grumbled but there was a feral light in her eyes that left Ettie in no doubt that Darren, for better or worse, would eventually be escorting her younger sister down the aisle.

'So where's Grandad?' asked Ettie, having handed her niece back to Lindsey and dispensed the wine into three mismatched glasses.

'Down the allotment. He was muttering something about rhubarb. There's that much rhubarb crumble in the freezer, I could open a flamin' pie shop.'

'Who's opening a pie shop?'

Ettie turned, feeling a sudden burst of emotion bloom in her chest. There were silver foxes and there was Grandad, who was more silver weasel with a touch of Gandalf thrown in. With his scrawny frame, thinning, long, grey hair and lines outlining the features of his face like contours on a map, he was a testament to a life well lived. He was the one person in her life who had told her over and over she could do whatever she wanted.

'Ettie! You're home, love!' He swooped her into a big hug, and she could feel his ribs under his flannel shirt.

'Hi Grandad, how're you doing?'

'All the better for seeing you, my favourite granddaughter.'

'I thought I was your favourite granddaughter.' Lindsey waved her glass at him.

'Yeah, you were. Last week. This week it's Ettie's turn.'

Ettie grinned at her sister. It was a long-running joke but both sisters were secure in the knowledge that he shared his love and affectionate grumbling equally between them.

'What you girls drinking?'

'Prosecco, Grandad. Do you want some?'

'Aye, I'll have a drop.'

He sniffed suspiciously at the glass Ettie poured him before taking a gulp. 'By heck, it's like pop. That's not a proper drink.' He handed the glass back. 'I'd rather have a pint of Tetley's, thanks.'

'Waste not want not,' said Lindsey, grabbing the glass and upending its contents into her own.

'So, lass, what are your plans?' Grandad sat down opposite Ettie.

'Find a job. In the short term. I'm training to be a bookkeeper.'

Sandra coughed and indiscreetly rolled her eyes. Ettie ignored her and the sick feeling in her stomach. She had to make the course work. She was fed up with dead-end jobs. At thirty, she hadn't found that perfect job and was now resigned to the fact that she probably never would. At least with bookkeeping there were opportunities and the chance of promotion.

'A bookkeeper, eh. Good for you. How long's that going to take?'

'Only a few months. It's all online and then I have to do an exam at the end. I can do it in the evenings, so I can look for a temporary job while I'm doing it.'

'There's a chap down the allotment whose cousin works over on the Hepplethwaite Estate. They're turning it into a hotel. You might get a job there.'

'And how's she going to get there every day without a car?' asked Sandra, tea in one hand, Prosecco in the other.

'If you go to the back gates and walk across the estate, round the lake, it's not that far.'

'Still a good forty-five minutes, and what if it rains?'

'She's not made of sugar. You ought to pop in, see if there's anything going.'

'That's not how they do things these days,' said Ettie.

'They might not, but some folk do,' said Grandad. 'How do "they" do things?'

Ettie smiled. She and Grandad both had views on the mythical 'theys' of the world.

'Advertise, post something on social media, put something on their website.'

'Well, get looking then. You got one of them there fancy phones, haven't you? An iPhone 953, or whatever they're up to now.'

Actually, that was quite a good idea, thought Ettie, pulling her phone out of her bag. 'Any idea what they're calling the hotel?'

'Hepplethwaite Hall, I believe,' said Grandad, 'least that's what George said. Mind you, some days he can't remember his own name.'

'I've got it,' said Lindsey, who'd been tapping at her phone at lightning speed, while Ettie had been trying to keep hers out of reach of Tiffany Eight's chubby little fingers. 'They're hiring. Looking for a Girl Friday, whatever that is.' She held up her phone to Ettie, who read the job description:

We're in desperate need of a temporary assistant to run errands, liaise with suppliers, answer the phone and do general administration as we bring Hepplethwaite Hall back to life in readiness for its opening as a hotel in early autumn. This may lead to a permanent position. Please apply by email with your previous experience in either the hospitality trade or an administrative capacity.

Ettie bounced in her seat. 'I've got both. That sounds perfect for me.'

'And they're desperate,' pointed out Lindsey with a grin.

'You say that about every job,' muttered her mum, not unfairly, if Ettie was honest. The thing was, she was prepared to try her hand at anything. Admittedly, milking goats hadn't been quite her thing but it had been an experience, even if she'd lost half a trainer in the process. It was true, goats ate anything.

'So, what went wrong with the last job?' asked Lindsey, relieving Ettie of the baby and strapping her into a high chair. 'I thought you quite liked that one.'

'I did. Unfortunately, the shop blew up.'

'How the heck did you manage that?' asked her mum, expertly sliding fish fingers and chips onto four plates.

'This time, it really wasn't my fault,' said Ettie, relieved that it was true. When Jean had told her Gary smelt gas, for a horrible moment it had crossed her mind that she might have left the gas hob on after she'd made beans on toast for tea before leaving the shop to go home. Eating at the shop was preferable to facing the shared kitchen which she was convinced harboured enough germs to fell an army regiment.

'I don't know, Ettie, you're a walking disaster,' said Lindsey, blowing on a chip before handing it over to Tiffany Eight.

'Wrong place at the wrong time, that's all,' said Grandad, giving her a wink. She could always rely on him to have her back. 'Bit like that poor lad Josh.'

'Is he the one who lost his leg in that car accident?' piped up Lindsey.

'That's the one. His mum's at her wits' end. He won't go to school. Won't leave the house without her. Such a shame. As I'm right next door, it's no skin off my nose to pop in on him every day.'

'If it weren't for your grandad popping in when she's at work, he wouldn't see anyone at all.' Ettie's mum gave him a pat on the shoulder. 'You're a kind man, Dad.'

'Not sure Josh thinks so,' said Grandad with a grin, his eyes lighting up with mischief. 'I just barge right on in. First couple of times, he gave me some choice language, but now he's resigned to it.'

'It must be so tough for him,' said Ettie. 'He was hell on wheels when I used to babysit for him, never sat still.' She had wondered whether he might have ADHD. His attention span darted around like an overexcited puppy and he was the most impulsive child she'd ever known, leaping off the dining table because he wanted to see what being Batman felt like, running up and down the stairs ten times because it seemed a good idea, and refusing to go to bed before midnight. He was always in constant motion, a mile-a-minute sort of kid. Ettie didn't really know what else to say.

Losing a limb was a bit too big to comprehend. How on earth did he cope, let alone his mother? It had to be so difficult.

'Aye,' said Grandad. 'He were always such an active little tyke. A grand swimmer, but then he got into football. Never off the street, kicking a ball. He wanted to play for Leeds United. Mind you, all of 'em do.' He shook his head. 'Playing Fifa on the Xbox day in and day out is no good for any kid. If only I could get him out of the house and off that bloody telly screen, but he don't want anyone seeing him.'

'It'll take a bit of time, I guess,' said Ettie. 'Maybe you ought to take him your old football card collection.'

'Maybe give them to him,' said Mum, 'stop 'em littering up your place.'

'I'm not giving my collection away,' said Grandad, reeling back in his chair, as if his daughter were suggesting he give away both kidneys, along with his liver for good measure.

'You ought to get him swimming again, Dad. You always said he could have been a champion if he'd stuck at it,' suggested Sandra. Grandad had taught swimming for over thirty years at the local pool, and had taught Ettie and Lindsey to swim, although Lindsey lost interest a long time ago.

'I'm doing my best, love, but he's not going anywhere. I've got him teaching me football on that Xbox thing. His eyes'll turn square, he spends so much time on it. You're right. Swimming would do him the power of good.'

'You still swimming, Ettie?' asked Lindsey.

'Yes. That's probably what saved my life. I was late from the pool when I went to work that day. I'd have been blown up in the shop if I'd been on time.' In one way or another, swimming had been saving her life for most of it. When she'd moved to London the first thing she'd done was check out where her nearest swimming pool was. It wasn't quite an addiction but it had become a definite compulsion. It was something she needed to do. She missed it when she didn't do it.

Swimming gave her control and time to take charge. Her brain always seemed to be humming with ideas and thoughts, and a few lengths in the pool allowed her to switch off all the superficial, unnecessary stuff and drill down to the important things. If she'd tried to describe how swimming centred her and gave her headspace, it would have felt pretentious, the sort of thing clever, worldly people could talk about, not ordinary folk like her. Or Grandad. He understood, but it was an unspoken thing between them. When she'd had to leave school at seventeen to look after her mum and go out to work, he'd often say after tea, 'Why don't you go off for a swim, lass?' And she'd come back feeling that the blackness around the edge of her peripheral vision had receded. Being in the water pushed it back. When Granny Cynthia had died, Grandad had swum for two hours every morning for a whole year, and Ettie had understood exactly why.

'Blown up? Really?' asked Lindsey, wide-eyed.

'You didn't say that before,' accused her mum. 'See, I

told you it was dangerous in London. You should listen to me. I know what I'm talking about.'

Ettie exchanged a wry smile with Grandad. Mum always knew what she was talking about. Her word was law around here.

Chapter Three

S ummer had well and truly arrived, which was great following a week of non-stop rain, but after walking the three miles to the Hepplethwaite Estate, Ettie now had sweat patches under each arm. Not what you wanted when you were turning up to an interview trying to make a good impression.

To her delight she'd got an almost instant response to her email enquiring about the job, inviting her to an interview the very next day. She hadn't even unpacked her stuff properly, so finding a suitable outfit that was clean (because of course she'd brought all her washing home) was a challenge. Finally, she'd settled on a lavender-blue crepe dress which she'd rescued from the reject bag at work, which had ended up there because it had an unsightly stain just above the left boob. With a pale-pink felt flower strategically pinned, it was now as good as new – well, as new as a vintage dress could look. The Louboutin shoes were in her bag and on her feet she wore a pair of Adidas tennis shoes, which was just as well, because the walk was a bit further than she remembered.

As kids they'd occasionally played on the estate, larking about in the woods around the lake and dodging the estate's gamekeeper. She vaguely remembered that there'd been an old couple living in the house and that they'd died in the last five years. From Grandad she'd learned that the house had gone to some distant relation who'd since sold the land on the south side of the estate to a property developer who'd promptly built a housing estate of executive homes, backed onto a rather swish golf course, creating a hinterland between the houses and the Hall. That distant relation had died and left it to an even more distant member of the family.

Ettie cut through the woodland, the path dappled by the sunlight pouring through the green leaves of the beech trees that lined either side. Birds called in the distance as her feet crunched on the packed surface. Smiling to herself, she studied the twisted shapes of the trees, spotting an elephant complete with trunk in one and a half-moon face in another. It had always been a fanciful game of hers. There was something about the trees and the seasons that had always fascinated her and now she wondered just why she'd spent so long in London, away from all of this. All around her were colours and shapes, and she stood for a moment taking in the vibrant emerald of the moss growing on some of the trunks, the faded green of the ground elder threatening to swamp the woodland floor, and the deep, glossy dark-green of ivy twining the trees in its loving, suffocating embrace.

There was something called 'forest bathing' that she'd heard of when she'd worked in a branch of Muji in Kensington. She'd not paid much attention at the time, but maybe there was something to it. She already felt her senses settling and softening. Slowing her pace, she took a deep breath, inhaling the woody freshness of the grasses and wild flowers waving in the slight breeze. That hamster-on-a-wheel urgency of needing to be somewhere, someone, even faded. She'd adopted so many guises in her different jobs, trying to fit in, she was never quite sure who she really was anymore.

A sudden shriek of laughter, followed by a splash of water, distracted her and she took a detour off the path, cutting down through the trees to the shore of Hepplethwaite's majestic lake. Even though she hadn't been here since she was a kid, she could just about remember the terrain. She, Lindsey and a couple of school friends had sneaked up here a couple of times on hot summer days to sunbathe. None of them were willing to get their hair wet by going in the water, although they had paddled to cool off. There was actually a sandy, weed-free beach along with a little wooden jetty. The beach had been an irresistible temptation, even though they'd had to leg it a couple of times when the estate manager came upon them.

Ettie gazed out at the water where a swimming-cap-topped head bobbed up and down like a little Duracell bunny doing a speedy breast stroke. The swimmer turned and began to swim back towards her. The sun danced lightly across the water stirred by the crosswinds, like spilled silver paint rippling out across the surface. The calm serenity of the moment, with the pigeons coo-cooing in the woods and the soft breeze tugging at her hair, stoked an instant desire to be in the water. To feel the cool slide of liquid over her body and the soothing calm in her head. She hadn't swum for a few days and she felt the absence of the physical activity like a dull ache.

As she looked at the water, she wondered why it had never occurred to her to swim here before. She supposed she'd always had access to the pool through Grandad, but that had been all about training and competitive swimming. It was only when she moved to London that swimming became more about 'me time' and less about exercise. Gazing at the gentle ripples streaming her way, she could imagine the motion of her arms pulling through the water, the kick of her legs and the roll of her body as she took her in-breath, and immediately she wanted to be in the water. With a longing gaze, she stared at the water, wanting to shake the anxious fidgetiness out of her limbs that had taken up residence since the explosion. Unemployment didn't suit her. Neither did not having a regular routine. She really hoped she nailed this interview.

As Ettie was pondering the sort of questions she ought to ask, the swimmer, a woman, reached the shore and rose to her feet, casting wary glances towards Ettie, despite the defiant tilt of her chin and the broad shoulders which were thrown back.

Ettie gave her one of her best brilliant smiles, wanting to put her at her ease. 'Hello, that looks wonderful. Is the water very cold?'

'Not too bad once you get in,' said the woman, now striding out of the water, yanking off her cap and shaking out short, bright burgundy-coloured hair, her initial suspicion immediately vanishing as she scooped up one of the towels hanging from one of the nearby bushes. Ettie hadn't noticed the natural towel rail earlier and it tickled her. 'Neat idea.'

'You have to use what you can find when you wild swim.'

'I've never tried it,' said Ettie. 'It looks … peaceful.'

The woman tilted her head as if giving the word careful consideration.

'That's a good word for it. There's nothing quite like it. It wakes everything up. Makes your whole body tingle; it's like plugging yourself back into nature's life force. Sixty per cent of our bodies are made up of water, so it makes sense. Or at least I believe so.'

It was clearly good for *her* body. The woman, who was probably in her mid-fifties, had a lean and lithe body and was just a little taller than Ettie. She eyed Ettie's clothes. 'You're clearly not here to swim.'

'No. Job interview.'

'What, here?'

'Up at the house.'

'Ah. Him.'

'Who?'

27

'The owner. I'd better be off before he catches us ... again. This is private property.' She gave Ettie a sudden naughty smile. 'You can probably tell from all the notices.' With a nod, she indicated one of several wooden boards. *Private Property. No Swimming.*

Ettie grinned. 'It always has been. Never bothered us when we were kids. We used the place as our private playground.' She stood on tiptoe and pointed to the slope at the end of the beach where the grass came right down to the water. 'I don't think you can see this part of the lake from the house. We were always being chased off by the estate manager. It's not like you're doing anyone any harm.'

'Exactly,' said the woman. 'It's not like I'm causing any trouble.' She sounded slightly defensive. 'Anyway, I'd better go. No point hanging around to be caught. My car is on the other side of the woods in a layby.'

'Oh, I know,' said Ettie. It was the way she'd have come in if she were coming by car. Back in the day one of her friends had a work van that they would all pile into the back of, completely against every rule and regulation in the highway code, no doubt, but it hadn't bothered them.

'I'm Ettie, by the way.'

'Hazel. Will I see you here again?'

'Depends on whether I get the job or not.'

'What's it to do?'

'Not sure. Secretarial, I think.'

Hazel pulled a face. 'Not my cup of tea.'

Ettie shrugged, she needed a job.

'Well, good luck.'

'Thanks,' said Ettie, as Hazel slipped on flip-flops and began to stride towards the woods. Standing alone on the beach, she felt oddly bereft. For a moment she looked longingly at the water and considered stripping off, and then gave an impatient laugh. Seriously? And turn up to the interview with sopping-wet hair and damp underwear – or, worse, no underwear at all. Chuckling to herself at that thought, she turned and headed towards the house.

The imposing big double front doors were open when she approached the steps to the porticoed entrance. She sat on the bottom step, quickly changing her shoes as she wondered what etiquette dictated when you were coming for an interview at a stately home? Should she cross the marbled floor hall or look for a tradesmen's entrance around the back somewhere?

As a child she'd always wondered what the house was like inside but had never even got close enough to look through a window. Even though Grandad worked on the estate, he'd only been inside the house on the odd occasion. He'd said it was quite shabby and run down but that wasn't her impression this morning. The entrance hall was light and airy, with sunshine flooding through the rows of sash windows on either side of the door, creating shadows on the black-and-white marble-tiled floor. The room was dominated by a beautiful wide-planked, conker-coloured wooden staircase which wound around the walls, with barley-twist spindles holding up the glossy banister. She liked the fact that the uncarpeted steps looked worn and faded, a testament to all the people that had lived here at some time. But everything else looked smart, the walls crisp and clean as if they'd been painted recently.

'Hello, can I help you?'

Ettie whirled round. She hadn't heard the man walk up behind her.

'Hi,' she beamed at him. Firstly, because she was a beaming sort of person and secondly, because he was the sort of man that deserved a beam. Deep-blue eyes studied her with interest, framed by long lashes that Ettie immediately envied. He had proper cheekbones that didn't need any highlighting and a strong firm chin, covered in dark bristles. There was also the matter of a rather nice wide, kissable mouth, but despite all this there was nothing pretty-boy about him at all. With broad shoulders, a deep-blue shirt and lean hips, there was a ruggedness to him that, combined with the tanned skin, suggested that he spent a lot of time outdoors. Her smile broadened because, yes, he really was one hottie.

'Hi,' he said, and her heart did an odd salmon leap in her chest as she saw that brief infinitesimal pause, as if he needed a moment to take her in.

'I'm Ettie Merman, here for the interview.' She held out her hand.

His eyebrows rose as he gave her a quick, surprised up-and-down look. She noticed a pale white scar bisected one of them. 'Ettie?'

She sighed. 'Ethel.'

'You're Ethel?'

''Fraid so.' She shot him a mischievous grin. 'I prefer Ettie, for obvious reasons.'

His mouth crimped as if he were holding back a laugh.

'Understandable.' He gave her a nod before saying, 'I thought you'd be … older.'

Oooh, smooth-as-chocolate voice. Ettie wanted to fan herself, and her pulse was having a funny turn.

'That's very polite. You don't need to be. Most people expect to see an OAP. My mum's fault.' Ettie rolled her eyes, deliberately eliciting his sympathy. 'She thought she was being dead clever, what with our surname being Merman.' The great irony was that Mum thought she was paying tribute to the famous swimming star in honour of Grandad, who was a champion swimmer. Unfortunately, she'd got muddled up between Ethel Merman and Esther Williams. The former was a musical star, the latter a star of 'aquamusicals' in the forties and fifties. Ettie would far rather have been called Esther.

'I see,' he said politely, although his eyes danced with amusement.

'No, you don't. It's ridiculous. Hence Ettie for short, which you have to admit is a marked improvement.'

'So why did you put Ethel on your application?'

'One, because it's official and two…' She paused and gave him a twinkly smile which was most definitely reciprocated. Unless she was mistaken, there was quite a frisson sparking through the air between them. 'It's a great icebreaker.'

He burst out laughing, a lovely rich sound. 'It certainly is. Come on through and meet my partner, Gracie.' The happy dance tripping through her system slammed to a halt. He was taken. Of course he was, a good-looking bloke like that. She'd clearly misread those flirty, instant-attraction vibes. What a terrible shame, it had been a while since she'd felt that quick tug of recognition. It wasn't like her to get it wrong, either.

She followed him through a high, wide, wooden-framed doorway through to a long … well, *corridor* wasn't quite right, because it was too wide, but then again, it was too long to be a room. For a moment she felt like Goldilocks. Perhaps *gallery* was a better name for it, although there were no pictures in here. A shame, because this would have been the ideal space – lots of light, and there was just enough room to step back in appreciation of a fine composition. She grinned to herself; she still had the lingo. Ettie had worked in a gallery for a little while. Another job she'd enjoyed, even though she knew bugger all about painting – which was what had led to her downfall. In a misplaced fit of enthusiasm, she'd got a bit carried away and unknowingly critiqued a painting to the painter himself. She bit her lip at the memory. Perhaps describing it as looking as if the painter had dunked a couple of tea bags in a pot of paint and chucked them at the canvas hadn't been her finest hour. He should have been grateful that she'd been quite circumspect. The painting was dire. Unfortunately, what she had said had been enough to get her fired.

As they walked she noticed he had a slight limp, but that was the last thing on her mind because she was doing her best not to ogle the very nice bum in blue chinos, because seriously, Ettie, that was objectification and it was just plain wrong, but it had to be said, the man had a certain something about him. Perhaps it was that laid-back confidence. He struck her as extremely self-assured. The sort of person who knew exactly what they were doing in life, like one of those super-organised hikers with a waterproof map pocket and that innate sense of direction, who could always pinpoint exactly where they were on a map. She'd be lucky to find her way with a compass implanted in her wrist. Probably because she didn't have a clue how to use one.

'This is a beautiful place. Does it belong to you?' she asked. 'Sorry, I don't even know your name.'

He stopped, a chagrined expression on his face. 'Sorry. How remiss of me!'

Remiss. Posh as well as handsome.

'I'm Dominic Villiers. I don't know how I didn't introduce…' A small crease appeared on his forehead as if he couldn't quite fathom the oversight.

'You're a relative. I remember Old Mr Villiers died a few years ago.' He'd been her grandad's employer and a mean old bugger.

'Extremely distant relative. I inherited by default a

couple of years ago. It took the executors a while to track me down. I have to say, it was quite a surprise.'

'I bet it was.' Ettie looked up at the grand plasterwork ceiling. 'Suddenly becoming lord of the manor.'

'No!' he said with sudden comical horror. 'I'm most definitely not lord of anything. This place needs to earn its keep and I need a job.'

'So, it wasn't you who sold the land on the east side off to the developers. That's not gone down so well locally. All those big executive houses.'

He held both hands up. 'Not guilty. That was my predecessor, my third cousin twice removed or something.'

'I like you better already.'

'Thank you. Am I supposed to be grateful?' He raised a teasing eyebrow.

She pinched her mouth as if she were weighing up the question and giving it due consideration.

'Yes. I think you ought to be. A lot of people weren't happy about the new estate.'

'People need houses.' He lifted his shoulders in an unconcerned shrug.

'Yes, but they also need doctors' surgeries, school places and houses that local people can afford.'

'It's the same everywhere, but people still need somewhere to live. And to be fair, if Ansell Villiers hadn't done that, this place would be falling down. That deal paid for significant renovations to the Hall and ultimately I plan for the place to create jobs for local people.'

'Yes, I heard you're turning it into a hotel.'

'News travels fast. That's the plan.'

'It does in my family. My mum and grandad know everything.'

'I'll bear that in mind.'

'And it did say in the job ad.' She grinned at him again.

'Ah, you have top-notch detecting skills.'

'I have lots of other skills besides reading,' she said with another cheerful grin, selling herself. She was here for a job interview after all. A second later, when his eyebrows rose in amusement, she realised her words could be misconstrued. 'Work-place skills,' she added, which probably only made things worse.

'I never thought otherwise,' he replied, obviously hiding a smile, as he ushered her into a study with two desks and panelled walls along with several Chesterfield armchairs and a sofa.

She almost didn't see the small bird-like woman perched in one of the chairs. She sat on the very edge as if she might take flight at any moment, although her eyes lit up with beady interest when she saw Ettie.

'Ettie, this is Gracie. My business partner.'

'Hello.' She immediately crossed to shake Gracie's hand, feeling buoyed up by the unexpected relief in the words *business partner*. Gracie bobbed up and then down again and then up again, reminding Ettie of a small robin.

'Er, hello.' Gracie held out a hand. 'Nice to er … er, um, yes.' She frowned. 'I thought…'

Ettie waited a minute before finally saying, 'Ethel.'

'Yes, that's right, dear. You don't look like an Ethel.'

'Thank goodness for that,' said Ettie. 'Although I'm sure, once upon a time, Ethels looked like anyone else. I mean in the forties or something, when the name was current.'

'I guess they probably did.' Gracie gave her a diffident smile. 'They can't have all been born old, can they? I do like your dress. I'm sure I had one very similar when I was about your age.'

Ettie pulled out the skirt and swished it from side to side. 'Vintage. Pretty, isn't it? I love the colour.'

'Yes, and your shoes. I never had a pair like that,' the older lady said a little wistfully, brushing her pale, wispy, golden hair from her face. Ettie guessed she was probably in her late sixties. Gracie reminded her of a faded photograph with all the colour leached out. There was something a bit sad about her.

'Would you like to take a seat?' interrupted Dominic, just a tad sharply.

Ettie shot him one of her trademark smiles before saying in a loud conspiratorial whisper to Gracie, 'Bored with the talk of shoes and dresses, I'm guessing.'

Gracie gave her a sudden, unexpectedly impish smile but didn't say anything. Instead, she waved Ettie towards the big heavy desk that sat in front of the Georgian paned sash window. Dominic held a seat out for Gracie before sitting down next to her in an upright dining chair.

Gracie looked towards Dominic and he nodded.

'Thank you for coming, Miss Merman.'

'Oh, please, call me Ettie. *Miss Merman* makes it sound as if we're on a film set.'

His blue eyes danced with suppressed amusement.

'Shall we get started?'

Ettie nodded, realising that she ought to be on her best behaviour. She really needed a job to tide her over – anything she could contribute to her mum's household would help – while she was studying for her bookkeeper qualification.

'Hi.' She sat down primly, legs crossed at the ankle, her hands resting on her lap with a bland, I'm-terribly-interested look on her face, all the while wondering at the unlikely partnership in front of her. Dominic and Gracie were a world apart. Everything about them was the exact opposite. He looked vigorous and strong, she looked frail and pale. He was dark, she was fair. She looked drab as if her clothes were a matter of indifference. Whereas Ettie was pretty sure that shade of cobalt blue had been selected by someone to enhance the shade of his eyes.

While she was musing, or, as her mum would say, drifting off with the fairies, Dominic had asked a question.

'Sorry?' Eek, how not to interview.

'I asked if you'd like a tea or a coffee.' He indicated a tray on the side.

'Oh. Coffee. Yes, coffee would be lovely.'

Before Dominic had managed to stand up, Gracie had jumped up and scurried over to the tea tray like a small, determined hamster.

'I'll get it,' she said and Ettie got the feeling that she was escaping and that looking after people was much more her natural milieu than sitting behind a desk conducting an interview. She saw impatience cross Dominic's face and wondered at the relationship between them.

'So, hotel,' she said. 'What sort of hotel?'

She ignored Dominic's look of surprise; she hated uncomfortable silences. He clearly expected to lead the interview and for her to follow, but that wasn't her. 'You've got a great spot. You must be very excited. All this land.' She waved her hand towards the window. 'And this gorgeous building. I bet it's going to look fantastic.'

'Yes,' said Dominic, looking towards Gracie, urging her to speak. When she didn't, he added, 'We're planning to open a … well, a hotel. As you know already.'

'A nice hotel. Where we really look after people,' piped up Gracie, suddenly getting the message a second too late. 'You know, where people come in from a walk and want to sit down by the fire and have some home-made shortbread, or on sunny days have cucumber sandwiches with fresh lemonade out in the garden. Just like your granny's.' Ettie bit back a smile, wondering if Gracie would throw in a few hugs too. That would make it novel. Could you be employed as a professional hugger? There was a lot to be said for hugging. She'd really missed it these last few years she'd been in London. Her mum was big on hugging.

'Our plans are still evolving. Perhaps we can talk about the role.'

Gracie gave Ettie a small smile. 'It'll be a lovely job for the right person.'

Ettie turned her face away so that Dominic couldn't see and gave Gracie a quick wink. She was rather adorable and he was suddenly taking himself far too seriously, and then she realised he'd been speaking and she'd tuned out for a second.

'... The role will entail everything from opening the post, dealing with suppliers, printers, builders, invoices. Liaising with delivery companies. Accepting deliveries. Answering the phone. Taking notes at meetings. Supporting Gracie. Basically, running the office for us while we set up the hotel.'

'We just need a spare pair of hands, really,' said Gracie. 'We're run off our feet and another person would be so helpful, wouldn't it, Dominic? Especially dealing with suppliers.' She gave Ettie a wan smile. 'I don't really like doing it and Dominic, bless him ... well, he needs someone a bit more...' She waved a hand. 'Someone who knows how to do things. I'm afraid I make him a bit impatient.'

Dominic shot her a very quick irritated glance, which he managed to hide equally quickly. 'That's not true, Gracie. It's just ... well, it's new for both of us and we realise we need more help on the ground.'

'Right,' said Ettie.

'We're looking for someone who is efficient, a self-starter.'

Ettie nodded vigorously. She still had no idea what the heck a self-starter was; in her head she imagined a small man with a starting pistol at the athletics and her taking off with the other runners.

'Someone who is literate, numerate, good on the phone,

conscientious and trustworthy. Honesty and integrity are extremely important.'

'And so is being good with people. And I think you're probably very good with people,' said Gracie, reaching over and patting Ettie on the hand. 'You've got such a lovely sunny smile. I bet it cheers people up no end.'

Dominic pursed his lips and then picked up a print-out of the email application she'd made.

'What makes you think you'd be suited to this job?'

Ettie smiled at him. 'I'm a fast learner. You can see from my GCSEs that I'm literate, numerate and a bit sciency. Although the RE was a bit of a fluke, getting an A* in that. And I'm a qualified lifeguard and I've had first-aid training, although I think I might need a refresher before I'd feel up to doing CPR on anyone.' She was talking too much, it happened when she was trying to impress someone. The job sounded quite interesting and Gracie was a darling.

'Mmm.'

'And of course, I've got experience of the hospitality trade and admin experience.'

'Yes,' he said dryly, looking back at the sheet of paper. 'You seem to have had rather a lot of experience.' He frowned, scanned the sheet and turned it over to carry on reading.

She caught her lip between her teeth.

'You were a chambermaid and left after four months.'

'Personality clash with the manager, I'm afraid.'

Dominic's mouth twitched. 'You were the manager of an art gallery for two months.'

'I realised I'm not a fan of contemporary art. More of an Old Masters sort of girl.'

He nodded gravely.

'You worked in a bar for three months.'

'It was taken over by an American franchise and it turns out I'm not very good at roller-skating.'

Gracie giggled. 'You'd spill the drinks all the time. That sounds a terrible idea.'

'Aside from the bruises, yes. I think they went bust not long after.'

Dominic drew in a breath. 'And the last job you had, as the manager of a vintage clothes shop? What happened there?'

'The job went up in smoke. Quite literally. There was a gas explosion and the shop caught fire, burned and ruined all of the stock. The owner didn't want to start again. So I was out of a job.' She didn't say the word *again*. She didn't need to. From the brief frown, she could guess Dominic was thinking it.

'And you're now training to be a bookkeeper.'

'Which is perfect,' said Gracie. 'Because I'm no good at that sort of thing. You can take over the books. I do get in a muddle with the invoices coming in. I can never remember whether to file them in alphabetical order or date order. And then I can't remember which ones we've paid.'

'Yes, our books do need a bit of attention. I've been keeping an eye on things, although we do have an accountant,' said Dominic, his mouth tight, clearly trying to retain a bland look on his face. Ettie wanted to laugh. He was ready to brain poor Gracie.

'Yes, and you hate it, dear. Ettie will be able to do it for you.'

'I've worked in an accountant's office before, so I know what I'm doing already. I just needed the qualification,' Ettie lied glibly, smiling at Gracie. She'd actually been fired from that job for misfiling important papers that should have been registered with Companies House. The problem was, when she got bored, she stopped concentrating and started daydreaming, which invariably got her into some sort of trouble, even without bosses with wandering hands who needed putting in their place.

Dominic sighed. 'This is just a temporary post, just a couple of months, so it might suit you.' He reeled off the hours and pay, which were no worse than any she'd had before.

'Do you have any questions?' he finally asked.

'No, I don't think so.'

'Well,' he rose and held out a formal hand. 'Thank you very much for coming. We've had a number of excellent candidates—' Gracie tutted and shook her head. He narrowed his eyes and shook his head back. 'And we have a few more interviews to do. So, we'll let you know in the next few days.'

Ettie had been to enough unsuccessful interviews to know that, in this case, 'let you know' translated as 'don't give up your trips to the Job Centre anytime soon.'

She shook his hand. 'Nice to meet you,' she said with a

cheeky smile at him because they both knew he wasn't the least bit impressed by her chequered career history. 'Good luck with the hotel. It sounds a lovely idea.' She turned to Gracie and held out a hand, giving her another one of her lovely sunny smiles. 'And it *was* a pleasure to meet you, Gracie. I hope people appreciate being looked after by you when the hotel opens. It sounds wonderful.'

'Thank you, my dear, and thank you for coming today. We'll be in touch very soon.'

Ettie held onto her smile. If the decision were down to Gracie, she probably *would* be in touch soon, but it was obvious that Dominic was in charge here. Hell could freeze over on a sunny day and she could bet he still wouldn't employ her.

She tip-tapped out of the Hall in her Louboutin shoes, following Dominic, head held high, refusing to acknowledge what they both knew. He wouldn't be in touch anytime soon.

Chapter Four

Once she was out of sight of the front door, she kicked off her shoes and, rather than put her trainers back on, walked barefoot over the grass. That had been a waste of a couple of hours. The sun had now peaked and the heat belted down. She undid a couple of buttons on her dress and fanned herself. By the time she got home, she was going to be cooked. The cool silver of the lake's surface shimmered in the bright sunshine and she was drawn to the lakeshore, trying not to feel too dispirited, wanting a moment alone.

A few drops of sweat inched their way down her spine and she raised her face to the blazing-hot sun as she stood at the water's edge. The trees on this side of the lake crowded right down to the shore, some of them almost tumbling in. Away to her left, the terracotta-tipped chimney pots of the house were just visible from here. Above her, the cloud-dappled sky was mirrored on the glassy-smooth surface of the lake, streaked by the occasional flash of a bird flying overhead. A family of moorhens pootled in the shallows to the right of the tiny knoll, puttering this way and that, oblivious to her presence. She watched them, envious of their indifference to the world, unaware of the problems of humans, jobs, earning money. Being human was so complicated. This job would have suited her down to the ground. She liked the idea that every day would be different and it sounded an exciting project, but she could tell that Dominic Villiers hadn't exactly been wowed by her sketchy employment history. She didn't so much have a track record as an unable-to-get-out-of-the-starting-blocks record.

It wasn't her fault. Ask anyone. She was a hard worker. The problem was, she didn't suffer fools gladly, and without qualifications she could only get jobs with fools as bosses. She envied the moorhens the simplicity of their lives. All they needed to worry about was where the next worm or bug was coming from and, admittedly, whether a predator might snatch up their babies, which actually was quite a big worry when you came to think about it.

The longing to assuage a nagging sense of failure consumed her. The lake was just too tempting. She needed to swim, to power through the jumble of feelings knotting her stomach up in anxiety as her body sliced through the water. On the outside she was always able to put on a brave face, but inside the insecurities were having a field day. Dominic's questioning of her career history had brought all her secret fears to the surface. Was she ever going to find a job that she could stick with?

She swallowed hard and looked at the water. Could this really be as good as that woman Hazel had said? Trepidation tingled at the thought of wading into the unknown. She didn't even know if she'd be able to see the bottom or how deep it was or whether there were fish in there. Or even a Loch Ness-type monster.

But dithering wasn't going to get her anywhere. She was hot, sweaty and really wanted to swim. *Come on, Ettie. Are you a woman or a mouse?* The next second she'd stripped off her dress and hung it on a nearby shrub. She looked around and decided that going in in just her bra and pants wouldn't offend, should anyone appear.

The first lap of water around her ankles was cold and she paused at the edge, feeling its icy bite. When silty, sandy mud oozed through her toes, she scrunched up her nose at the unwelcome sensation and thought about turning back. There was a reason they put chlorine in pools, it kept them clean and sterile ... but the urge to swim was stronger than her squeamishness and she took another few steps, the cold water clouding around her calves as she disturbed the floor of the lake. Something touched her leg and she squirmed, realising thankfully that it was just pond weed drifting across the surface of her skin. *Get a grip, Ettie. You weren't this much of a wuss when you were a kid.* Dominic's face appeared in her mind, looking critically at her CV. There was only one way for it. Go for it! Gritting her teeth, she forced herself to take a few running steps through the shallows, remembering where the lake became deeper, and threw herself into the water. The cool liquid enveloped her and the shock of the cold took her breath for a second, before she began to plough through the water with a determined breast stroke, and almost immediately she felt the calm peace that swimming always brought her. That delicious sense of her muscles stretching and working in tandem as the water flowed across her body.

She swam towards the small grassy knoll that protruded from the lake about a hundred metres away. It wasn't quite big enough to be called an island but was big enough to have a tiny beach and room for three or four people to sit side by side. It was an obvious target. As always with distance over water, it was further away than it first seemed, but with a determined push she swam on and finally reached it, floundering out of the water in her underwear. Chest heaving, she sat down on the tiny sandy beach to catch her breath, watching rivulets of water running from her body, before surveying the view. She could have been the only person in the world. This was heaven and she couldn't believe she'd never done it before. The sun dappling through the cool, green water, hearing the birdsong and feeling the breeze ripple across the surface, stirred something deep inside her. Something that made her smile all the way down to her soul.

The swim back didn't seem as far and she would have swapped to freestyle but with her hair loose and flapping across her face like seaweed, it wasn't really an option, especially as she couldn't see where she was going and she hadn't quite got her bearings here. Next time she came to swim, she'd come prepared. And there would *be* a next time, she decided as her feet touched the bottom and she walked up the silty, sandy bank. Why hadn't she done this before?

'What do you think you're doing?' asked a posh, commanding voice.

Oh no! She looked up to find Dominic Villiers standing at the top of the rise in front of the beach with his hands on his hips, his face grim.

'Er, hello again,' she said, attempting a blasé smile, looking down quickly and realising that her bra had turned completely see-through and she didn't dare squint down at her knickers. At this very moment she couldn't decide whether she was pleased or dismayed that she'd put her best underwear on for the interview. Although 'best' was a moot point, Primark rather than La Perla, but she was wearing a matching set.

Dominic Villiers glared at her, his eyes dark and flinty, nothing like the twinkly, flirty eyes of earlier. 'I could have sworn on your CV you mentioned a good standard of literacy.'

She stared blankly at him.

'You can read,' he added.

'Of course I can read,' she said scornfully, lifting her chin despite feeling totally at a disadvantage, but she had to give him credit that his eyes were staying up top.

'Then you'll know the signs say *Private property. No*

swimming.' He pointed to one of the signs to underline his point.

'Ah yes. Would you mind?' She pointed to her dress hanging from the tree. Abrupt changing of the subject had served her well over the years, but she had a feeling that, on this occasion, he wasn't going to be side-tracked very easily.

Giving him one of her best sparkly, apologetic, I'm-lovely-really smiles, she took the dress he'd retrieved for her. Originally her plan had been to strip off her wet underwear and walk home commando, but with him standing there like a brooding vampire, that wasn't an option. Instead, she tugged the dress over her head and, of course, the bloody thing got stuck on her damp skin and she struggled to pull it down. For a full thirty seconds her head was enveloped in fabric as she tried to extricate her elbows and work her way back into the dress like a snake trying to reclaim its discarded skin. She was horribly conscious that he could see her body and her wet, diaphanous underwear. Now she bitterly regretted her impulsiveness but she wasn't about to show it.

'There,' she said brightly. 'That's better.'

To her satisfaction, Dominic looked a little dazed and had the decency to suddenly avert his gaze.

'It really is beautiful in there.'

'Mm,' he said stiffly, and she realised that actually, although he'd seemed cross, he now seemed acutely uncomfortable and was eyeing the lake, rather than her, with dislike.

'Right, well, I'd best be off. I'll look forward to hearing from you,' she said, knowing full well she wouldn't.

'Wait a minute.' His face sharpened, as if shaking off a spell and coming back to the point. He frowned, almost as much at himself as her. 'Have you any idea how dangerous it is to swim on your own? In a lake that you don't know.' His words were edged with an undertone of firm authority.

'Oh, I've been swimming in there since I was a kid. I know it well,' she lied, with an airy smile. 'You don't need to worry about me.'

It was as if he hadn't heard a word she'd said.

'That's as may be, but you could have drowned, you know. What if you'd got into trouble? Cramp. Exhaustion. The shock of the cold can really affect your body. It can literally take your breath away. Even the strongest of swimmers can be affected. If you'd got into trouble, no one would have known. No one could have rescued you. You should never swim alone.'

Ettie bit her lip. As a trained lifeguard, she knew all of that and more. And clearly so did he.

'Well, I didn't. So you don't have to worry. All's well that ends well.' OK, so one of her less endearing traits was that she didn't like being in the wrong.

He gaped at her for a moment as if he couldn't quite believe what he was hearing. Despite knowing that she ought to apologise for her irresponsible behaviour, she couldn't quite bring herself to do so. Childish, she knew. Then he shook his head in obvious exasperation. 'It might have ended well this time, but what about the next?' he said. 'I have enough trouble with wild swimming enthusiasts without you joining in. Ever since some bloody blog-site posted what a great place this is to swim, I've had the world and his wife turning up at all times. That's why I put up these bloody great signs, which clearly are still not enough – even to people who can read.'

'Ah,' said Ettie, pretending to understand his irritation. She couldn't really see the problem. No one was doing any harm. The lady she'd seen earlier had swum and left, and no one would have known she was there. She brushed down her skirt, horribly aware of the damp patches showing through her dress in areas she'd rather not have drawn attention to.

Dominic looked down and had the grace to look embarrassed.

'If you don't mind, I ought be going.' She crossed her arms across her chest and gave him a hopeful smile.

'Yes. Yes. Of course,' he said, deliberately looking away from the damp-bra-and-knickers effect.

Barefoot, with her trainers in her hand, she picked up her bag and walked off towards the woods. She turned to find him watching her and gave him a cheery wave before waiting until she was hidden by the trees to put her shoes back on. *Nice going, Ettie.* Any chance of the job had been well and truly blown out of the water now.

Chapter Five

Feeling uncharacteristically dispirited, Ettie walked through the woods towards the main road that led back into Churchstone. She really didn't want to work at the mustard factory. Half the people there had been at school with her and most of those she'd be happy never to see again. Her phone buzzed as she approached the outskirts of the town.

'Hey, Grandad,' she said, trying to sound more like herself.

'Hey, Ettie. How did you get on? When do you start?'

'When hell freezes over.' She gave a little chuckle, her natural sense of humour starting to reassert itself.

'That bad, lass?'

'That bad, Grandad, but never mind. Onwards and upwards.' The cliché rattled off her tongue.

'Sounds like you could do with a drink. I'm in The Anchor. Come join me.'

Grandad always understood, even when she didn't say anything. Ettie might be sunshine on the surface but he had an uncanny ability to detect when there were clouds gathering on the horizon.

When she reached the wooden sign at the edge of the town, declaring *Churchstone, a market town since 1315 AD*, she turned left down towards the High Street, passing the station on her left and Victoria Park on her right. On the other side of the park were some lovely stone-built houses. Once upon a time, she'd hoped she might live in one of them one day. Fat chance now.

The pub loomed into view and she crossed the road and walked into the snug, which was one of Grandad's many regular haunts. He had the ability to make himself at home wherever he was, whether at the bowls club, down the allotment in his shed, in her mum's kitchen or here in the pub. Everywhere, it seemed, but his own home.

'Lemonade and orange juice for the lady.'

'Thanks, Grandad.' She smiled and sat down next to him.

'Give it a chance, love. Rome wasn't built and all that.'

'I know, but I don't want to be a burden.'

'You'll never be a burden and you shouldn't sell yourself short.'

'I'm not.' She patted his hand.

'I hate to say this, love—' he nodded to her chest '—but what have you been up to?'

She slapped a hand over her mouth and started to

snigger. 'I completely forgot. What must I look like? I went for a swim in the lake at the Hall.'

'Now I've heard it all. What made you do that?'

'I saw a lady swimming there before my interview. And I was so hot and sticky when I came out, I thought, why not? It was lovely. It's really not that deep, you know. Even out at the little island it's probably only six or seven feet.' She grinned to reassure him before adding, 'You know wild swimming is all the rage now.'

'Hmm, so I hear. In my day it were just swimming. I haven't been there in a long time. Me and your gran used to swim in that lake when we were courtin', dodging the estate manager. Your gran couldn't half run fast.' He paused, a wistful expression on his face, lost for a moment in memories, and then shook his head as if dislodging them. 'Got used to swimming pools. You know where you are with chlorine.'

'Especially the day after a mother-and-toddlers' session.'

'There is that,' said Grandad, taking a long sip of beer.

'You ought to try it, you know. It was great. Just me, the birds, the sky and the water. It was lovely once I was in.'

'You know it's not safe swimming on your own. Even if you are trained.' He scrunched his face up in disapproval.

'I know, I know, Grandad. It wasn't very sensible and I shouldn't have done it, but once I got in the water I couldn't resist having a little swim. I won't do it again.'

'Safety first,' he admonished and she nodded.

'I know.' He was right, as was Dominic, but she hadn't

wanted to give the latter the satisfaction. Sometimes she was too stubborn for her own good.

The barman handed over her drink and the two of them sat sipping in quiet accord. Her grandad had a wonderful ability to appreciate when nothing needed to be said. Since Granny Cynthia had died seven years before, as well as swimming, he'd filled his life with bowls, gardening at his allotment and coming to the pub every Friday, but she suspected that despite his conscious busyness, he still felt her absence keenly. He'd never said he was lonely, but it was the way that he made a deliberate effort to fill his hours, rather than be at home on his own, that said it all.

She studied the small bar that she'd been coming to since she was tiny. Despite the threadbare carpet, the stained upholstery on the bench seats lining the wall opposite and the scratched varnish on the tables, it was good to be back. In that moment she realised she liked the familiarity of being here, knowing that the third table on the right was wobbly, the second toilet in the ladies' didn't flush properly, and nowhere else did pork scratchings quite like here. With a small sigh of pleasure, she turned back to her drink.

'Want a packet of scratchings?' asked her grandad, after a while.

'Love some.'

They ambled back home from the pub in companionable silence, to find the smell of frozen burgers and oven chips coming from the kitchen.

Ettie's mum wasn't what you'd call an adventurous

cook. If you got a portion of frozen peas you were doing well. If it came out of a packet it was good enough for her, she was wont to say. And to be fair to her, given the hours she worked – going in to open up the school at seven, before cleaning the classrooms and then staying on to do the lunchtime duties, before popping into the mustard factory to do a couple of hours, and then back to school to clean again – who could blame her for wanting to cook something quickly and put her feet up in front of *Emmerdale* and her beloved *Coronation Street*?

'How did the job interview go?' asked Lindsey as she strapped a fretful Tiffany Eight into her high chair, while Mum served up dinner for them all.

'Rubbish. He didn't like my chequered CV.'

'Idiot,' said Lindsey. 'Some people call it experience.'

'Well, he didn't.' She shrugged, loving that her family were immediately on her side, even though they were the first to take the piss out of her for constantly changing jobs.

'Never mind. There's a supervisor job coming up at the factory, if you fancy it. Overtime is good.'

'Thanks, Linds.' Ettie's heart sank. Most of the people that worked there had been the people she'd wanted to escape from when she left school. The mean girls that picked on her because she was different, often because she was smarter than them.

Lindsey didn't care, she'd never been the least bit academic and had shown no interest in school. Ettie sighed and wondered if her life would have been any different if she hadn't left school at seventeen. Well, needs must. She'd have to go down there tomorrow and ask for a form. 'Please tell me Tracey Mears isn't still in HR.'

'Yup. Human Relations Assistant Executive, now.' Lindsey scowled. 'If she's told me once she's been promoted, she's told me a gazillion.'

'God, that girl always was desperate for a title.'

'Yup, thought she'd made it when they made her wing attack in the netball team. She's worked her way up from supervisor, so there's hope for you,' teased Lindsey.

Ettie grabbed a chip from her sister's plate and stabbed it into a puddle of tomato ketchup.

'Oy.' Lindsey slapped her hand, almost sending the plate flying.

'Girls, for God's sake, how old are you?' asked Mum.

'Twenty-five and thirty,' quipped Lindsey, snatching one of Ettie's chips.

'Going on five, the pair of you. What are you like?' Despite her words, her tone held warmth.

Lindsey and Ettie exchanged matching grins and looked at Grandad and waited.

'They're just like you and our Dawn were,' he said on cue.

Mum rolled her eyes and plonked herself down in her chair.

Ettie's phone began to ring and she turned it over. It was an unknown number and she ignored it, pushing it away from her plate, but Lindsey, incapable of ignoring a ringtone summons, snatched it up.

'What are you doing?' Ettie made a grab for the phone, almost knocking a cup of tea over.

'Girls!' said their mum, as Lindsey danced up out of her chair, waving the phone triumphantly in the air.

'Leave it, Linds, it'll be one of those tax people saying I'm off to prison because there's a problem with my National Insurance number, or asking if I've been involved in an accident.'

'I know, but I love winding them up,' said Lindsey with a gleam in her eye. 'It's the best fun.'

Ettie sank back in her seat as her sister swiped the screen and pressed speaker. 'Ettie Merman's personal assistant speaking, how may I help you?'

Ettie's mouth twitched. Sometimes her sister was as daft as a brush.

'Miss Merman? It's Dominic Villiers.'

Ettie's eyes widened in sudden alarm and she made a frantic *gimme, gimme* gesture with her hands.

Lindsey gave a gleeful, taunting grin. 'Miss Merman speaking. Can I help you?'

'Lindsey, hand over the phone!' snapped Ettie.

She heard an audible sigh from the other end of the phone. 'Miss Merman, I was ringing to offer you the job.'

Lindsey squealed. 'Hear that, Ettie? You got the job!'

Ettie groaned and took the phone from her sister.

'Hello, sorry about that, that was my sister, the other Miss Merman.'

'Right.' He didn't sound amused at all. 'I was ringing to

offer you the job of General Assistant at Hepplethwaite Hall.'

Mum and Grandad beamed at her, and she realised she was still on speaker-phone and hurried out into the narrow front passage.

'Seriously?' she asked.

'Seriously,' he replied, his voice as dry as dust.

'But…'

'Gracie really took a shine to you. She says she'd feel comfortable working with you.'

Ah, there it was. 'Not you.'

'It's a joint venture. We share the decision-making,' he replied, sounding so formal, she couldn't help smiling and wanting to wind him up just a bit more.

'That's great news. When does Gracie want me to start?'

He huffed out a sigh. 'Would Monday be convenient? Nine o'clock.'

'That would be great. I'll see you then.'

Chapter Six

'Hello, dear. Good morning.' Gracie greeted her on the doorstep of Hepplethwaite Hall, Dominic standing just behind. 'Would you like a cup of tea?'

'Yes, please,' said Ettie with enthusiasm, brushing her dishevelled hair back from her hot and flushed face. When she'd left home forty-five minutes ago, it had been brushed back and pinned into a neat, almost professional bun, but an unfortunate run-in with a holly bush en route while taking a short cut through the wood had put paid to that. So much for her determination to prove herself the perfect candidate for the job.

She followed Gracie into the black-and-white tiled entrance hall, her feet complaining because tromping through the woods in heels wasn't very comfortable. 'Sorry I'm late. The bus didn't go the way I hoped it might. I had to jump off and double back.' She rubbed at her legs and the nettle stings that mottled one calf. That had been an unpleasant shock when the 17A to Hepplethwaite had turned left instead of right and headed up the old Upper Hepplethwaite Road instead of the new Lower Hepplethwaite Road that passed the front gates of the Hall.

'Bus?' Dominic gave her an odd look. 'There's no bus route near here.'

'I know that now,' she said with a long-suffering sigh. 'I had to get off and cut through the woods, from the gate by the old lodge on the south side of the estate.' She'd had the mortifying moment of pressing the stop bell on the bus frantically to get the driver to stop before they'd gone too far down the road.

'You walked all the way from there?'

'Yes.'

'Why didn't you drive here?'

Ettie stared at him. 'In what?'

'A car?'

'I don't have a car,' she said with a frown.

'In the interview, you said you could drive. I assumed you had access to a car. It did say quite clearly in the job spec that you needed to be able to drive.'

She shrugged. 'And I can.'

'I meant in your own car. We're a couple of miles out of town here,' he waved a hand to indicate this fact. 'We're going to need you to run errands.'

She clamped her lips together in quick annoyance before saying, 'Why would you assume that? Not everyone can afford to buy a car, let alone pay for the insurance, the road tax, the MOT, the bills.' The only reason she'd passed her test was out of sheer bloody-mindedness because a boyfriend had told her she wouldn't pass a driving test the first time because she was a girl and everyone knew girls weren't as good as boys at driving. Scrimping and saving for those driving lessons had been hard work.

'Sorry, you're right, it was—' Dominic gave her an apologetic smile '—a stupid assumption.'

'Don't worry, dear.' Gracie patted her hand. 'I'm sure we can work something out. Now let's sort that tea out and I can show you around. I'm sure Dominic has important things to do.'

With that, Gracie rounded her up like an unassuming sheepdog, determined to avoid any conflict, and guided her down to the kitchen.

A dog of indeterminate breed came bounding towards them.

'Down, Scrapper,' said Gracie half-heartedly, which, of course, the dog ignored, jumping up and putting both paws on Ettie's stomach.

Gracie grabbed at his collar. 'Sorry. This is Scrapper. He belongs to Dominic and he's not very well behaved, are you, boy? Whatever you do, don't let him out, he'll make a beeline for the lake and it's impossible to get him out again. He's a merdog.'

'Hello, boy.' Ettie gave him a scratch behind the ears. 'I'm surprised Dominic would put up with a badly behaved dog.'

'He's a rescue. Dominic is trying to train him.' Gracie

gave her a conspiratorial smile. 'It's not going well. He's a terrible softie, really.'

'Ah, I see.' While not convinced, the thought amused Ettie. She had visions of Dominic being tugged along by the big dog.

Gracie pottered around the kitchen while making the tea.

Five minutes later Gracie was still chatting away to her but hadn't even managed to pour boiling water into the teapot she'd painstakingly warmed before putting tea bags into it.

'Can I help?' asked Ettie, itching to move things along. She was beginning to understand Dominic's impatience a bit better…

'No, no, dear. You just sit there. I won't be a minute. Aren't these pretty cups?' She lifted one of the bone-china tea cups up and Ettie could tell they were expensive because the cup was almost translucent. 'The previous owners of the Hall, Dominic's relatives umpteen times removed, spared no expense renovating the place. They were frightfully posh. Mind you, Dominic's quite well-to-do, you know. Such a shame they never got to enjoy it.' She fussed with the tea cups and saucers, sugar bowls and a milk jug.

'Yes, I heard they were killed in a car accident.' And Ettie knew that Dominic was quite well-to-do from the way he spoke and carried himself.

'Yes, although lucky for Dominic,' said Gracie with a blithe indifference which initially shocked Ettie. 'I mean, he didn't know them or anything. And it came at just the right time, just when he and my Bob were thinking about coming out of the Navy.'

'Did it?' Ettie realised that Gracie was actually completely unworldly and only focused on what was immediately in front of her. She seemed almost fey in her understanding of the world around her.

'Yes.' Gracie gave her a bright smile.

'So how did you and Dominic go into business together? Are you related?'

Gracie tittered. Ettie had never met anyone who tittered before, but the adjective suited Gracie down to the ground. 'Me and Dominic? Good lord, lovie, no. He's an Officer. Or rather he was. My Bob was just a Petty Officer. They were the ones that talked about going into business together when Dominic inherited this place out of the blue. They were both thinking of coming out of the Navy anyway, so it made sense. Unfortunately, my Bob died and Dominic … well, he had a few personal problems at the time, so it's taken a while for us to get here. Originally they were going to open some sort of outward-bound place, for people to learn orienteering, survival skills with team-building activities, while I did the cooking and looking after guests. But now with Bob not here to help, Dominic's not sure about the outdoor side of things. It would be too much for him on his own, especially after just having another operation on his leg. I used to do a bit of work in housekeeping at a big hotel in Harrogate, so Dominic thought between us we could turn this place into a hotel.'

She lowered her voice. 'I'm glad he's in charge, though. I mean, I know about linens and bed sheets and towels and the like, and I can cook, as long as it's nothing too fancy, but...' She pulled a slightly panicked face.

'I'm sure it will be fine,' said Ettie.

'Bless him, he's a good boy. He didn't have to look out for me, you know. I could have gone and lived with my sister, but her husband, he's got a nasty temper and I don't like a lot of shouting. My Bob, God rest his soul, never raised his voice, not all the time we were married.'

'How long were you married?' asked Ettie, guessing that Gracie had probably lived in her husband's shadow for most of her life.

'Since I were sixteen. This year would have been our Golden Wedding anniversary,' she sighed and pulled a mournful face. 'Even though he was away in the Navy a lot, I still miss him. Miss knowing he'll be back to sort everything out. He retired and had a heart attack within months.'

Ettie nodded in understanding even though she had never relied on anyone to sort anything out for her. She'd been sorting her mum and sister out for years. Even when she was in London, her mum would call her about the electricity bill or leaking toilets, and only a month ago Lindsey had called her to tell her she thought the chicken drumsticks she'd bought from Tesco were off and what should she do about it?

'Right, I'll show you around.'

Ettie followed Gracie out into the hallway and through

to a spacious lounge with dramatic duck-egg-blue wallpaper covered in peacocks and trailing flowers on three walls, while the fourth wall was painted in matching duck-egg-blue paint. The drapes and pelmets were in a dark teal that coordinated with the peacocks' tail feathers. The parquet floor shone and was covered by a variety of threadbare rugs. The room exuded retro grandeur, but it was all a bit dark and formal for Ettie's taste. She did, however, approve of the large fireplace dominating one wall, with log baskets on either side. It was easy to imagine sitting in front of a roaring fire.

From the lounge, Grace led her to a small drawing room with several sash windows looking out over the parkland. Decorated in pale green, it was a restful place with a matching sofa and a couple of armchairs. It was all very genteel and pretty and brought to mind Jane Austen heroines, in pastel muslins, embroidering and playing piano.

'I think this would be perfect for an early evening sherry, don't you?'

'Mm,' said Ettie, thinking it was a bit too twee and that sherry was definitely on the old-fashioned side. Without saying anything, she followed Grace to another, altogether more masculine room, with leather chesterfields, solid-looking coffee tables and brass lamps. This felt much more to Ettie's taste, although she wasn't a fan of leather upholstery – always too slippery.

The games room was more homely, with a well-used billiard table, several card tables and shelves of board games with everything from chess and backgammon through to boxes of playing cards, Cluedo, Monopoly and more recent innovations like Perudo and Articulate.

'The rooms were all done recently, so it seems a bit of a shame to change them. I'm not sure whether we should or not.' Gracie didn't quite wring her hands but it was a close-run thing. 'And Dominic thinks this room should stay as it is, but it does feel a little shabby. I mean, perhaps the walls should be painted, but then, what colour? He says it's up to me. But I don't know. What do you think?'

'Er … it looks … erm, welcoming, but it probably could do with a bit of a spruce-up,' said Ettie, hedging, not wanting to come between Ettie and Dominic.

Upstairs there were twenty-five bedrooms, all of which were empty of furniture and were essentially blank canvasses.

Ettie walked across to the window of the first bedroom and stared out over the parkland. Beyond the woodland surrounding the lake, the hills and dales in the distance blended into the sky. She'd forgotten how beautiful this part of Yorkshire could be. They were right on the very edge of the Dales here. She and Grandad used to go out walking when she was younger. She had a vivid memory of paddling in the frothing River Ure in Wensleydale as a child and jumping the stones in the River Wharfe at Bolton Abbey. Would coming back to live in Yorkshire be so bad? Or would it be an admission of failure? Wanting to live in London had been a purely arbitrary dream when she was seventeen. She'd only ever seen the city in films like *Notting*

Hill, *Bridget Jones's Diary* and *Love Actually*, where people led interesting, exciting lives. Since she'd been unable to go to university, like her friends, it had seemed like a way of proving that she'd made something of her life.

Could she stay? She really couldn't make up her mind.

She sat opposite Dominic in the study once again, clutching a second cup of tea.

'Gracie's given you the grand tour then.'

'Yes,' said Ettie, watching his face, trying to read the subtext there.

He waited for a moment as if he were hoping she might say more, and then sighed.

'There's still a lot to do and I'm managing the tech side, setting up the website, the online booking system, the marketing and advertising side of things. And also managing the build as well as the construction of the outdoor space. But I need some help…' He sighed again and she admired his loyalty.

'You need someone to project manage Gracie,' she said.

His head lifted in surprise, his eyes meeting hers. 'I hadn't meant to put it quite that bluntly, but to be honest, you've summed it up perfectly. I need her to get on with signing off things with the interior designer so that they can start ordering the bathroom fittings, the furniture, curtains, everything. Choose the paint colours. I need her to get on, otherwise I'll lose the builders, the plumbers and the decorators.' His jaw was tight. 'I don't know what the problem is. I just need her to get on with it. I don't understand what the hold-up is. This is supposed to be her baby. I thought she wanted to run a hotel.'

Ettie studied him for a moment, hiding a wry smile. Having worked in so many different environments with people at all levels, she knew exactly what Gracie's problem was.

'She's a people-pleaser. She's desperate to do a good job for you but she's terrified of getting things wrong. So, it's easier not to do anything than risk making a mistake. She's not very confident in her own judgement.'

'I don't care what the place looks like, I just want her to get on with it.'

Ettie refrained from rolling her eyes. They were both as bad as one another. It was a really good job they'd employed her. Neither of them seemed to be very invested in the place at all.

This was just the sort of work she enjoyed. Solving people's problems. Although on this occasion she really wasn't sure where to start. They needed their heads banging together but she could see it was important to both of them that this project worked. Bloody Bob was at the centre of it all; they both felt they owed it to him to make this happen.

By the end of her first morning, she'd got her bearings, set her own desk up in the study and had already created a to-do list. Top of which was *Buy decent coffee*. Gracie was a confirmed tea drinker and it showed.

When Dominic came in at lunchtime with Scrapper at his heels, she'd just got off the phone and was writing in pencil in the big desk diary.

'I'm going to pop down to the Marks and Spencer at the garage on the Upper Road, want anything?' he asked.

'Ooh, yes, please. I'm glad you're going. It's fatal me going in there – I end up getting far too much stuff.'

He laughed at her. 'I'd rather hoped to get you to go down there most days to pick up lunch. Save me some time. But as you haven't got a car, that's rather scuppered that idea, for today anyway.'

'Oh.' She flashed him a cheerful grin. 'Never mind.'

'Not to worry. I'll have to put you on the insurance on the Discovery.'

'Discovery?' Ettie gulped and looked out of the window at the beast of a machine parked on the other side of the gravel circle in front of the house.

'OK,' she said, brightly. He didn't need to know that she'd never driven anything bigger than a Toyota Aygo or that she hadn't been behind the wheel of a car since she passed her test.

'Can you dig out the insurance details? They'll be somewhere in the filing cabinet behind you. I can't remember quite where I put them.'

'Sure.' She wheeled her chair back and pulled open the top drawer, flicking through the files as if she knew what she was looking for, hoping that she looked efficient. Thankfully the tab marked *Car* made her life a lot easier, and Dominic gave her a slightly surprised and approving smile when she pulled out a plastic wallet containing an insurance policy and laid it on his desk. She would show him that he'd underestimated her.

'Anything else?' she asked with a deliberately sweet tone.

He burst out laughing. 'You're going to keep me on my toes, aren't you?'

'Yes,' she said with a demure smile.

'What can I get you?'

'Can I have one of those duck wraps with hoisin sauce? If they don't have that, then one of their egg-and-cress sandwiches. But it needs to have cress in it. And can I have some of those lentil curls. If they don't have the individual bags, then a pack of five is fine. And can I have a pack of their yum yums? Oh, and an orange juice.'

He stared at her for a moment before asking, 'Nothing else? We wouldn't want you to starve.'

'No, that'll be all.' She grinned at him as if she shopped at Marks and Spencer all the time. Tomorrow she'd be bringing a Tupperware box of Hovis-and-Marmite sandwiches.

'Don't suppose you could dock the cost out of my first pay packet?' she asked as he picked up the car keys, knowing that her purse was currently empty, drained by this morning's bus fare.

Now he rolled his eyes. 'As it's your first day, lunch is on me.'

'Great,' she said. 'In that case, could you throw in a pack of walnut whips as well, please?' She winked at him as she opened up the file on her desk and ran her finger through the papers inside. He attempted to give her a hard stare but she could see his mouth twitching as he turned on his heel and walked out of the room. Working with Dominic was going to be a lot of fun, she decided.

Chapter Seven

'Morning, Gracie.' Ettie rushed in and dropped her bag on the kitchen table. 'That bloody bus. Didn't turn up again today.' It was the fifth day out of eight that she'd arrived late, and it was only Wednesday in her second week.

'Hello, dear. Gosh, are you all right?'

Ettie nodded, wiping her hair from her sweaty forehead. 'I'm fine, just peed off that I have to walk so far every flipping day.' And equally peed off that she couldn't give in to the tantalising lure of the lake. Ignoring the siren call of the smooth water each morning was getting harder and harder, especially as she couldn't visit the local pool before work in the morning – there just wasn't time, and she hated that. The longing to swim was starting to feel like a physical ache.

'No harm done. Let me get you a cuppa, you look like you could do with one.'

'That would be lovely, thank you.'

'Take a seat. Let yourself catch your breath. You look a bit peaky. Have you had breakfast? I could make you a bacon butty if you fancy it.'

'Er...' Actually, she hadn't. 'I had a rough night. My sister's had a row with her boyfriend and so she's moved back home into my room, or rather it was *our* room when we were kids. Lucky me, I got to share a bed with her and my niece.'

'Oh, you poor thing.' Gracie paused as she busied herself getting several rashers of bacon out of the fridge and gave Ettie a sympathetic study. 'You must be exhausted.'

'Mm, shattered.' Ettie thought of Tiffany Eight's two and four o'clock wake-up calls and wanted to lay her head on the table. Instead, she sighed. 'I really ought to get to work.'

'Go on. It'll only take me a minute. I can make it while you drink your tea.'

'Do you know what? That would be lovely.'

Gracie was serving up Ettie's bacon butty when Dominic walked in somewhat stiffly with a perplexed frown on his face, his injured leg clearly giving him more trouble this morning than usual. 'Good morning, Ettie. Nice of you to join us.'

'Don't worry,' she said, completely ignoring his sarcasm as she added with a confident expression, her eyes shining with a reassuring smile, 'I'll catch up and get everything done.'

Dominic nodded. 'Right,' he said faintly before frowning again, patting his pockets and turning to Gracie.

'Have you seen my car keys anywhere? I'm going to be late.'

'Oh, you're as bad as Bob. He was always losing his car keys. I even got him to put a hook by the front door, but did he remember to use it? Where did you last have them, love?'

Ettie watched, amused, as he gritted his teeth. Gracie slid a plate in front of her and began sorting through papers on the other end of the big pine table, lifting folders and books up.

'If I knew that, I wouldn't be looking for them,' he said in a mild voice which belied his obvious impatience.

Ettie took a bite of her sandwich and kept quiet.

'I know that, dear,' said Gracie calmly, as if placating a ten-year-old boy instead of a grumpy, irritated, grown man.

'They were in the office,' he said finally. 'But I looked there.'

Gracie gave him a gentle, not quite but very nearly patronising smile and bustled off out of the kitchen.

He turned to Ettie. 'When you've finished having your breakfast, perhaps you could see your way to reaching your desk. I've left a list of things that need doing. When you have time, of course.'

Ettie grinned at him, ignoring the sarcasm. 'Great. Thank you.'

He stared at her for a moment and then gave an unexpected smile and laughed to himself. 'You don't give a damn, do you?'

'I do, but you were predisposed to be in a bad mood,

whatever I did, so there didn't seem much point in being contrite.'

'Predisposed?'

'Yes, you stomped in here like an angry giant. I was just waiting for a fee fi fo fum.'

'I've got physiotherapy this morning.'

'Not nice?' asked Ettie.

'My physio makes Attila the Hun look like Mother Theresa.'

'Ouch.' Ettie gave him a sympathetic smile. 'But I'm sure it will help. Eventually. What happened?' She nodded towards his leg.

He grimaced. 'I had an accident. Bad break. Femur, tibia and fibula. I'd planned to leave the Navy, this just precipitated things. It happened a couple of years ago but I've just had another operation on it, hence the current round of physiotherapy.'

'Wow. All three bones in your leg. How on earth did you do that?'

'It's a long story,' he said, his voice suddenly clipped. 'How come you were so late? Again.'

'Some of us rely on public transport and unfortunately, the bus is very unreliable. It didn't turn up *again*, so I had to … make alternative arrangements.'

He raised a curious eyebrow.

She huffed out a sigh. 'I walked here.'

'Why didn't you get a taxi?'

'Because I'm skint until I get paid. I've had to borrow money from my mum for the bus fare here.'

'Where do you live?'

Hadn't he looked at her application?

'On the outskirts of Churchstone.'

'And you walked.'

'It's only three miles … ish.'

'That's mad.' Despite his words she could tell he was impressed.

She shrugged. 'Needs must.'

'Well, that's ridiculous, especially when we've got umpteen bedrooms here. Why don't you move into one of the rooms here during the week, while we're setting up? I could run you home on a Friday and pick you up on a Monday, if that makes things easier.'

The offer took her by surprise. 'That's … that would be great! Especially as my sister isn't planning on speaking to her boyfriend until he proposes. Sharing a bed with her and my niece indefinitely is not my idea of fun.'

'There are so many questions that raises, but I haven't got time. I really need to get to the physio, if I can find my sodding keys.'

'I've found them,' said Gracie, walking back into the kitchen with them dangling from her fingers.

'Where were they?'

'On your desk. I remembered you putting them there yesterday when you came back from the supermarket.'

'I looked there.'

'Yes, dear.' Gracie exchanged a quick smile with Ettie.

'Would you mind doing something for me, while I'm out? Ettie's going to come and stay, to solve her transport issues. Would you mind making up a bed for her in one of the rooms in the East Wing?'

'Oh, what a good idea. It'll be nice to have some female company in the evenings,' said Gracie, clapping her hands, already halfway to the door.

'I can do…'

'I'll do it,' said Gracie with surprising steel in her voice.

'Yes, Mum,' said Ettie, straightening in her seat and pretending to be put in her place.

'It's no trouble and it'll make me feel useful for a change.'

Ettie shot Dominic a quick glance and noticed he looked a little confused.

'Gracie, you're always useful,' he said. 'I couldn't do, or want to do, this without you.'

'Hmm.' Gracie's eyes shone and she made a hasty retreat, muttering about sheets and blankets as she went.

They both stared after her but neither commented. Ettie wasn't sure what to say, but she was saddened by the knowledge that the other woman felt that way.

Dominic turned his wrist to check the time on his watch. 'I need to go, but I'll run you home this evening to collect your things, if you'd like. I'll leave Scrapper here. I'll be gone for at least two hours. Can you take him out to stretch his legs if I'm any longer, and can you have a look at the builders' estimates that have come in and put them in a spreadsheet to compare how they've costed things? And can you call this guy back? I think he's from the local paper. Find out what he wants.'

He handed her a Post-it note with a name and number on it.

'Mark. Mark Armstrong.'

'Do you know him?'

Ettie laughed. 'Yes, I was at school with him, he used to go out with one of my friends. We were great mates.'

'Excellent! If you can get some good publicity for the hotel, that would be brilliant.'

'No problem. Perhaps we can invite him round for the grand tour once we're ready to open.'

———

Ettie worked steadily through Dominic's list, with Scrapper curled up by her feet snoring gently, and when he woke up and whined at the French doors to go out, she realised the morning had flown by. She picked up the phone and dialled the number for the *Evening Courier*.

'Mark Armstrong,' a voice snapped in her ear.

'Ettie Merman,' she snapped back with a grin. 'How are you, Mark?'

'Ettie! I'm great, working here, obviously. How did you get my number?'

'I was asked to give you a call; you called my boss. I'm working at Hepplethwaite Hall.'

'You're back from the big smoke, then? What are you doing there?'

'I am. I'm working for the owner and his business partner.'

'I've been trying to speak to the owner for a couple of weeks. Elusive so-and-so.'

'He's busy.'

'Yeah, right. So, what's the story? And what are you doing at Hepplethwaite Hall?' There was sharp eagerness in his voice.

'At the moment I'm sitting at a desk talking to you.' Scrapper, having taken a quick wee, now returned and came to sit back under the desk, leaning his wiry body against her leg.

'So, you're not going to tell me what's really going on?'

'What do you mean? There's not much to tell yet.' She reached down to give Scrapper a rub behind his ears, her fingers stroking through the wiry blond fur. 'At the moment the rooms are being decorated and altered, and the hotel is due to open in early September.'

'Hotel? Come on, Ettie,' he scoffed in her ear, clear disbelief echoing in his words. 'Is that the line you're giving me?'

She frowned. 'What do you mean?'

'Well, according to my sources…'

'Sources?' she laughed. 'You're writing for the *Evening Courier*, not the *New York Post*.'

'Come on, the rumours are flying. Why is the owner chasing people off the site? It doesn't look good. It's obvious he doesn't want anyone to know what's really going on.'

'What do you mean, really going on?'

'You mean you don't know? Is it going to be a retreat of some sort?'

'A retreat?'

'Yes, for Buddhist monks, delinquent tearaways, or the latest theory is that it's going to be the headquarters of a cult.'

'Are you getting your information from the old boys down The Dog and Duck? That's all nonsense.'

'Well, Ted down there swore blind that it's that cult that believe the royal family are all alien lizards.'

Ettie laughed. 'You've got it completely wrong, Mark. Hepplethwaite Hall is going to be a hotel.'

'Yes, but what kind of hotel? Apparently that's just a cover story.'

That was a good question, she thought. Neither Dominic nor Gracie knew what kind of hotel they wanted it to be, but despite that she managed to spit out another laugh. Mark really was desperate for a good story. He'd always been the ambitious type. He was focused, knew what he wanted. She envied him that. He'd always been sure of himself too, but on this occasion he'd got his facts wrong.

'Well, I'm pretty confident that I know what I'm talking about, as I'm helping the business partners with organising the building and decoration work.' That sounded a lot grander than 'I'm the assistant at everyone's beck and call.'

'Are you sure?'

'Absolutely. I promise you. I've not heard the word "retreat" used and Dominic Villiers and Gracie, the business partners, are the least cult-like people I've ever met. Gracie probably doesn't even know what a Buddhist is, and Dominic – well, he was in the Navy, and I'm pretty sure being in the armed services and prepared to kill for your country goes against the basic beliefs of being a Buddhist.'

'Oh. No chance you're wrong?'

'Sorry to disappoint you.'

Now it was his turn to laugh. 'Back to "Local woman runs marathon for charity", then.'

''Fraid so. But how about, when we're ready, I'll invite you over to have a look around. It would be great if you would do a story about the hotel launch.'

'For you, Ettie, I will. How long are you back for? Fancy meeting up for a drink sometime?'

'That would be lovely. I'll be here for the foreseeable future.'

'What happened to your high-flying London life?'

'It crash-landed.'

'I'm sure there's a story there.'

'Not a particularly interesting one. I'm stuck back here for a while.'

'It's not that bad. There are worse places to live.'

He was right, there were, and she'd lived in a few of them in London. It was more the idea of being back. Coming home felt like failure. She'd been, gone and not conquered.

'Perhaps I can persuade you to stay?'

She paused for a moment. 'Perhaps you can,' she replied, a smile touching her lips. He'd always been a decent guy, much more reliable than a lot of men she'd met.

He made her laugh; he was a good friend and ... maybe going out for a drink with him was a good idea.

'Cup of tea?' asked Gracie, appearing with a tray in her hand as soon as Ettie put down the phone. 'And I've made some shortbread biscuits.'

Ettie beamed at her. 'Mmm, that smell.' The room was filled with the scent of buttery goodness.

'My Bob used to love these.' Gracie presented her with a plate of still-warm, pale biscuits and a mug of tea.

'They smell amazing. Thank you.'

'Don't thank me. It gave me something to do this morning. I thought I might make them for the guests each morning. An eleven o'clock snack served in the drawing room – what do you think?'

'I think that if they taste as good as they smell, guests will love them.' Ettie took a bite and moaned with pleasure as the shortbread dissolved on her tongue. 'Oh my, they're delicious. So light.'

'Secret ingredient. I use a touch of cornflour.' Gracie beamed with pride and sat down opposite Ettie. 'How are you getting on?'

'Good. Dominic should be back soon. He told me how badly he'd broken his leg, but didn't say how.'

'He doesn't like to talk about it. There was an accident at sea, during a rescue operation. I'm not sure of all the details. Bob didn't tell me much; it was just before he died. A young sailor died. I know it was all very traumatic.' Gracie's mouth pursed. 'And his wife wasn't the most supportive.'

'Wife?'

Guilt rippled across Gracie's face. 'I probably shouldn't have mentioned that, either. He definitely doesn't like talking about Paula. Not that I blame him. Led him a merry dance, that one. He's well shot of her.'

Ettie was dying to ask more questions. Was he still married? How long ago had he split up or separated from her? Where was she now? And why was he well shot of her? One look at Gracie's mouth, which had pursed up as tight as a cat's bum, told her she wouldn't get any more information out of her today. She changed tack.

'So have you had any thoughts about decorating the bedrooms?'

Gracie huffed out a sigh. 'Can we talk about it later? I'm a bit busy this morning. I've got some bread in the oven.' With that she stood up and hurried out of the room, leaving Ettie staring thoughtfully after her. Not too busy to make bacon butties and knock up home-made shortbread.

When Dominic came back, Ettie had only just started looking at the builders' quotes, as he'd requested, because her curiosity about his wife had run rampant. Instead, she'd been Googling Paula Villiers to no avail – she doubted Dominic's ex-wife ran a care home in Sydney or was the current wife of an American senator in Kentucky.

'How've you got on this morning?' he asked, as Scrapper danced around his feet, his tail wagging with as much gusto as if Dominic had just returned from a six-month polar exploration.

'Good,' she said. 'But these quotes—' or at least the ones she'd briefly run an eye over '—they're taking the piss.

These are London prices.' Or at least she was pretty sure they were. She was going to have to bluff it in front of him.

She picked up the phone and put it on speaker-phone as she dialled the number.

Dominic sank into one of the leather chesterfields, the dog's head resting on his knee.

'Hello, Reckitt Builders.'

'Hello, can I speak to Jonas Reckitt.'

'I'll put you through to his secretary.'

Ettie put a hand over the mouthpiece and rolled her eyes at Dominic. 'Secretary, my arse. That's his mum.'

'Hello, Reckitt Builders. How may I help you?'

'Hello, Mrs Reckitt, it's Ettie Merman. Can I speak to Jonas, please?'

'Ettie, love! How are you? I heard you were back. I bet your mum's glad to see you. And your Lindsey. She still with that Darren Scott? He's a waste of space, I tell you.'

'You don't need to tell me, Mrs R. Is Jonas there?'

''Course he is, love. Let me put you through.'

Elton John's 'Goodbye Yellow Brick Road' came blasting out of the speaker as she was put on hold and she hummed along for a few bars.

'You know Jonas Reckitt?'

'I was at school with him. And John Timms, the other builder who's trying to rip you—'

'Ettie. Is that you?'

'It is, Jonas. I'm working at Hepplethwaite Hall.'

'Are you now? We've been asked to quote for a couple of jobs up there.'

'I know you have, because I'm looking at your ridiculously overpriced quote at this very minute.' She paused, shaking her head, even though he couldn't see her, but she was confident her voice rang with that 'I'm seriously disappointed' tone. 'Is this some sort of fairy-tale, Jonas?'

'Well … it's a fair price.'

'Only if you're daft.' She picked up several sheets of paper and picked out a line at random. 'Five hundred quid to hang a couple of doors. Never mind your building costs. Come on, it's a small job, putting up dividing walls, plumbing and electrics. You're not rebuilding the Taj Mahal. It's only bedrooms and bathrooms. Do me a favour. If you want the work, you're going to have to come back with a competitive price. You know John Timms is quoting as well, and I'm not paying silly prices.'

'Timms has quoted?' Ettie grinned to herself at the sudden sharpness in Jonas's voice. *Gotcha*, she thought.

''Course he has. And he might not be as good as you, but it all mounts up. We've got a budget and my boss is going to want a better price.'

'Let me see what I can do.'

'You do that, Jonas. You do that.'

With that, she put the phone down, crossed her arms and looked up at Dominic.

'Is Timms much cheaper?'

Ettie shook her head. 'Nope, he's even more expensive.' She gave a naughty chuckle. 'The two of them have been fighting since school. This way they'll both sort out a decent price at a fair market rate.'

Dominic laughed. 'I'm not sure about your methods, but I like the results.'

Ettie shrugged with a light-hearted smile, enjoying the amusement in his eyes. 'You think they were being honest with you? They were both trying it on.'

'I guess so. Although I think in life transparency is always better. Everyone knows where they are then.'

'All well and good, if people are being transparent with you. As my grandad says, you have to fight fire with fire. Like with like.'

'If that translates into lies with lies, that's never going to end well.'

'I guess not,' said Ettie, although she was a great believer in white lies. Why tell the truth when it was going to hurt someone? Feeling very slightly uncomfortable about the turn the conversation was taking, she changed the subject.

'So, earlier, you said something about seeing the grounds.'

'Yes. Do you want to go now?'

'Yes.' She jumped up without a second thought and Scrapper gave a happy little yip. It was far too nice a day to be indoors. This June was turning out to be the end of the most glorious spring. The bluebells in the woods were starting to bloom, tinting the spring green of the undergrowth with that magical sheen of deep purple-blue, and the buds had burst into young leaves, which dappled the paths with delicate shadows. On her walk to work, the colours and shapes of the countryside each day made her spirits soar. Maybe it wasn't so bad being exiled from London for the time being. There was something about being outside bathed in nature that spoke to her. She hadn't even realised until now how much she missed it.

Chapter Eight

Dominic, with the dog at his heels, led the way through the house and out of a set of French doors from the drawing room onto a beautiful veranda with wrought-iron tracery columns holding up the fluted roof.

Ettie stopped and spread her hands out, looking up. 'Well, isn't this just lovely? How gorgeous, and what a suntrap! You can smell the roses, proper roses. This would be a perfect spot for afternoon tea overlooking the flowers.' She gestured to the cloud-shaped beds dotting a neat green lawn that extended a good way back to a brick wall that enclosed the garden. She did a little twirl. 'I can imagine it. Little plates of smoked salmon sandwiches decorated with curls of cucumber, and mini chocolate eclairs and china tea cups and saucers. And ladies in pretty summer dresses. Mums and daughters. Grannies for their eightieth birthdays.'

Dominic studied her, a faint smile on his lips. 'You have a very active imagination.'

'It's called marketing,' she said with mock reproof.

'You're definitely on the same page as Gracie there,' said Dominic, with a quick sigh of obvious frustration. 'The only thing she's showed any interest in is tiered cake plates.'

'I'm sure you're exaggerating.' Ettie wagged a finger at him.

'Possibly. It's just, I want her to think of this place as hers too. You know she's invested in the business with the proceeds of the sale of her and Bob's house?'

'Really? I didn't know that.'

'I didn't want her to, but that was what Bob had planned and she wouldn't have it any other way.' He glanced over his shoulder, checking no one was about, and lowered his voice. 'I've kept the money separate, so it will always be there for her. If anything went wrong, I would hate her to end up with nothing.'

'But what about you?'

He lifted his shoulders and squinted up at the sky. Ettie looked up into his face, his expression suddenly without its usual confidence, and her heart burst with warmth. Then she stood up on tiptoes and kissed his cheek because she couldn't help herself.

He smiled down at her, a quizzical gleam in his eyes. 'What was that for?'

Her heart fluttered just a little at the thought of kissing him again and wondered what he'd say. Instead, she tucked an arm through his and said, 'Because you, Dominic

Villiers, are a very nice man. Come on, Mr Caped Crusader, show me the rest of the grounds.'

It was rather cute when a slight blush tinted his cheekbones.

They left the veranda via a set of shallow steps that led onto a crazy-paved path, velvety moss outlining the stones in a tracery of vivid emerald, and followed it to a gate in the wall.

'This is exciting,' said Ettie as Dominic unlocked the gate with a big wrought-iron key.

'Is it?' he asked.

'Yes, I have no idea what is through here.'

He rolled his eyes but they crinkled in amusement at the same time.

On the other side of the gate was a large, cobbled courtyard with buildings on three sides.

'This is the old stable block. I'm going to convert some of it to offices and the rest at the moment is storage, which will be handy.'

'You're not going to make me ride a horse, are you?' asked Ettie with wide eyes, when he led her towards one of the stables. 'I don't do horses. They're big scary things.'

'Ettie, you amaze me. I thought you weren't scared of anything.'

'Horses are different. Cows too. They have four legs and they can move very fast indeed. I like to make sure there's always a fence or a wall between me and them.'

'Bang goes putting you in charge of the cow wrangling,' said Dominic, his heavy sigh just a bit too much.

'Oh, you.' She nudged him in the ribs. 'Very funny.'

He disappeared inside and seconds later re-emerged, backing out a red quad bike with a helmet hanging from each handle. 'We'll take this.'

'Ha!' Ettie straightened up. 'Now you're talking. That looks fun. I've never been on one before. What about Scrapper?'

'He'll be fine. He's got a touch of lurcher in him, he can shift when he wants to. Hop on,' he said, straddling the bike, once she'd finally managed to do up the chin strap without garrotting herself. In her eagerness to get on board, it didn't occur to her until too late that, sitting behind, she was very up close and personal with him. Those shoulders under the tight-fitting T-shirt were extremely broad and she could smell the light citrus of his aftershave. What to do with her hands? Tentatively, she put them on his waist as he turned the ignition. He turned his head and gave her a big grin, and her heart did a funny little flip as his deep-blue eyes sparkled at her, as if he knew something she didn't.

'What?' she asked suspiciously.

'Nothing,' he said, all innocence, which made her senses prickle. 'All set?'

She nodded, the helmet feeling heavy on her head. He pulled off suddenly, and she looped her arms around his waist as they bounced rapidly over the cobbles. She could smell washing powder on the soft cotton of his T-shirt and feel the heat of his body through the thin fabric. It had been a while since she'd been this close to a male body, let alone one as well toned and delicious as this one. She took in a deep breath, a little light-headed. The sensation of being tucked behind him was rather intoxicating.

They drove through an archway and she instinctively ducked even though it was way above her, and then Dominic opened up the throttle as they sped down the long tarmac drive bordered by trees on either side.

'That takes you down to the North Gate on the main road,' he shouted over his shoulder, 'but we'll go across the field to the woods on the far side.' With a sudden turn, they veered off the track onto the grass, and still careering along at speed, they bumped along towards several stands of copper beeches and limes, Scrapper keeping up easily with a long-legged lope. Ettie clung on tight to Dominic, her thighs tucked behind his, feeling his flat stomach and lean, hard muscles beneath her hands. She would not give in to the temptation to run her fingers over them, she told herself sternly, and instead focused on peering over his shoulder and enjoying the sensation of the wind whipping at her face. At the edge of the wooded area, Dominic slowed the bike and they gradually came to a stop beneath a broad-trunked tree. He pointed upwards into the leafy canopy.

'Oh!' said Ettie, immediately spotting what he was pointing to. 'A tree house!'

'Yes. I've no idea why it was built, but I'm thinking we must be able to use it in some way.'

Ettie jumped off the bike and tried to yank her helmet off, almost choking herself on the strap in her haste. 'How wonderful! I've always wanted a tree house. It must be like being a bird or a squirrel.'

'Here, let me,' said Dominic, reaching his hands out towards her. She stepped closer and waited as his fingers brushed the soft skin under her chin. She looked up at him, his head tilted in concentration as he gently tugged at the plastic clasp. He was so close, she could see the glossy bristles breaking out through his skin, the white of the scar bisecting the end of his right eyebrow, and the determined set of his lips as he applied himself to the task.

With sudden awareness of how close he was, she swallowed, feeling a tug in her chest. He glanced up at her, his fingers stilling on the chin strap, and their eyes met. Awareness hummed between them and she couldn't look away. The sounds of the birds in the trees around receded for a moment, and her head filled with a background buzz of electricity. She opened her mouth; she had no idea what to say. The thought of kissing him consumed her. The audible click of the plastic clip and the release of the strap brought her back to earth as Dominic lifted her helmet off.

'There you go.'

She dropped her eyes, almost but not quite wincing at the matter-of-fact tone in his voice.

'Thank you,' she mumbled, feeling she might just have made a bit of a fool of herself.

'Let's see this tree house, then,' she said, in an overly bright voice, and she had already got one foot on the bottom rung of a sturdy wooden ladder before she turned back to him and asked, 'May I?'

'Sure,' he laughed. 'I think I'd have a hard time stopping you.'

With quick agile steps she began to climb, cursing herself for being such an idiot. He had an effect on her, that was for sure. Had she given herself away, just then? That would be embarrassing, having a crush on your boss, especially if he guessed.

Scrapper, at the bottom of the ladder, whined for a moment as Dominic began to climb up, and then wandered off, enticed by the smells among the damp leaf mulch.

Reaching the top, she tried to compose herself as she took in the wide fenced platform and the central structure with three sides. Above her leaves rustled, casting dancing shadows on the surface of the floor, and birdsong echoed around them. Hidden in the leaves, this place was a secret eyrie, and she liked the sense of being tucked away from the rest of the world. She could already picture it filled with a wicker sofa and cushions that would make the most of the gorgeous view, which was quite simply breath-taking.

Leaning on the top rail of the fence, she surveyed the scene. On the horizon a rolling rise of trees, in their summer finery of bright green, carpeted the small incline that encircled the lake, which glittered in the day's bright sunshine.

Dominic came to stand beside her, his forearms resting on the top bar of the balustrade next to hers. She tried to ignore the way her skin tingled at the very slight touch.

'Great, isn't it?' he said, nodding out towards the panoramic view.

'Yes,' she said, surprised to find her voice a little husky. Disappointment could do that to a girl.

'Ettie?' She could feel him studying her as she stared determinedly straight forward.

'Mm,' she replied, deliberately not looking at him.

A gentle hand cupped her chin and instinctively she turned to face him, her back to the balustrade. His thumb skimmed her jaw and she felt her heart clench in sudden anticipation. It fluttered in her chest as he lowered his mouth to hers…

'Bloody hell!' He moved away from her and leaned out over the balcony of the tree house. 'They're back again.'

'Who?' Dazed, she stared at him.

'Bloody wild swimmers.' He was already at the top of the ladder. 'Come on.'

'Where?' What was going on? And seriously? Hadn't he been about to kiss her?

'To the lake, to get rid of them.' His head had already disappeared from sight. Ruefully she followed, wondering if she'd imagined him almost kissing her. By the time she'd reached the bottom of the ladder he was revving the engine impatiently. As soon as she got on, still fastening her helmet, he took off and she had to grab a handful of his T-shirt to stay on before she wrapped her arms around his waist. They raced over the field at quite a lick, bumping and twisting over the uneven ground, Scrapper racing alongside, his tongue hanging out, and barking every now and then.

'What's the problem?' asked Ettie as they reached the lake and began to run parallel to its edge down towards the beach area.

'They shouldn't be there.'

She kept her counsel but she couldn't help thinking they weren't doing any harm. And what was the urgency? There weren't any lone swimmers this time.

When they crested the slope down to the beach, she could see that there were three people in the water, two wearing bright swimming caps and the other, a man, with long straggly grey hair fanning out behind him.

Dominic slammed on the brakes and she bumped her nose into his back with an 'Oof!' But he didn't stop, he hurled himself off the bike and went running down to the shoreline, fingers at his chin strap and Scrapper hot on his heels.

'Oi, you lot! This is private property!' he yelled, the helmet dangling in his hand as he stopped at the lake's edge. The dog charged past him with a joyful yip, splashing into the water and launching himself forward until he was swimming.

'Hey!' he shouted again. One of the two swimmers in hats, doing a steady breast stroke, paused and looked up. 'Yes, you!' he yelled. 'This is private property.'

Ettie winced, recognising her immediately. It was Hazel. Ettie would have done anything to spare her this embarrassment and wondered if she could drag Dominic away.

Guilt filled Hazel's face as she began swimming reluctantly back to the shore. The other hat-wearing swimmer, who was doing a languid crawl, was oblivious and carried on, as did the third swimmer, the man, currently powering through the water with precise, powerful strokes out towards the little island.

Dominic shouted again but neither showed any sign of hearing him. In the foreground, the dog was swimming in circles with joyful barks.

'Scrapper, come here!' yelled Dominic but the dog took no notice, splashing about, his tail sluicing through the water, sending droplets flying.

Ettie bit back a small giggle. Scrapper had absolutely no intention of leaving the water – he was in his element.

Hazel reached the sandy cove, doing her best to appear dignified in the face of being completely in the wrong and only wearing a swimming costume, which Ettie felt put her at a distinct disadvantage. Without a second thought, she crossed to the bush and grabbed the towel hanging there and handed it to the other woman. 'Sorry about him.'

'Thanks,' Hazel said, wrapping it around her before muttering, 'Oh God, he's on the warpath again.'

'Sorry, but he's the boss.'

'Poor you.'

Ettie was about to defend him and explain that he really wasn't that bad, when Dominic marched over.

'I've told you before,' he said, with exasperation in his words and a heavy, impatient sigh. 'This is private property. I don't want to see you here again.'

'But,' said Hazel, lifting her chin, ready to brazen things out, 'what if we paid you? I'm not the only one who wants to swim here.' She indicated the two other swimmers who had now rounded the island and were swimming towards them. 'It's such a perfect place to swim and there's no other water like it for miles.'

'I don't give a damn. This is private property and I don't want you swimming here.'

'Don't you think you're being a tad unreasonable?' Hazel folded her arms over the top of the towel. 'We're not doing any harm and we're not causing any trouble. It's not like we're kids larking about. We know what we're doing. What's your objection?'

Dominic's attention was diverted by the other swimmers coming closer.

'Hey!' he bellowed as the man came close. 'Hey, you!'

The man lifted his head and slowed before giving a cheery wave and continuing his powerful strokes towards them.

'I don't have time for this. Like I've told you before, this is private property.'

The man had reached the shore just ahead of the other swimmer, a woman in a dark-blue swimsuit. He rose up out of the water, shaking his long straggly hair. Daniel Craig he was not. In fact, he reminded Ettie of a pale-skinned Iggy Pop with long lean limbs, firm muscles and taut tendons and lots of saggy skin. For a man in his early seventies, he was in excellent shape. Probably because of all the swimming he did. He was the one who'd taught her to swim all those years ago and encouraged her to do her lifeguard training. Yes, it was Grandad.

'Hello,' he said, with a grin at Dominic. 'You must be the new lord of the manor. The great-great-second-cousin, twice or is it thrice removed.' He strode over, nonchalantly picking up an ancient stripy towel which Ettie recognised only too well, and wrapped it around his skinny waist and marched up to Dominic with an outstretched hand. 'Nice to meet you.'

Ettie pinched her lips together, not sure whether to laugh or groan. Typical Grandad, he wasn't the least bit fazed.

'You do know you're trespassing,' said Dominic, slightly nonplussed.

The third swimmer had slunk out of the water behind Grandad and was pulling off her swimming cap. A cloud of dark-red hair spilled out over her pale bony shoulders. Her mouth was set in a mutinous line but her eyes were blank as she stared at Dominic from a sunken face. She was all arms and legs, her knees huge compared to the bones above and below.

The three swimmers, now lined up in a row, almost as if they were facing a firing squad, glanced at each other, as if trying to silently nominate a spokesperson.

'And I'm sure they won't do it again,' said Ettie in what she hoped was a placating way, shooting the old man a behave-yourself look, knowing full well that he was a law unto himself.

It was all a bit awkward because they couldn't leave gracefully without getting dressed and Ettie certainly didn't want to stand there watching them. It was too much like public humiliation.

'Maybe we should leave them to sort themselves out,'

she suggested, putting a gentle hand on Dominic's arm. 'I think they've got the message.'

'Hmm,' said Dominic, shaking his head. 'Make sure I don't see you again. Otherwise, I'll be calling the police and I really don't want to have to do that. You do know you're trespassing, don't you?' he said again.

Ettie had a feeling that might be quite tricky once the place was a hotel; she wasn't sure that Dominic had thought that one through.

Hazel shuffled towards her backpack lying on the ground just to the right, as if keen to get away. The redhead stalked to a duffle bag, her mouth twisted in an expression of resentment, while Grandad, unabashed, turned cheerfully back to Dominic. 'I hear you're turning the place into a hotel. I remember when the original old fella lived here. In them days, the old boat house was full of boats. He was a great rower. He'd been to the regatta down in Henley. Him and his pals used to have races here every summer. Quite an occasion, it was. All the posh nobs wore boaters and blazers, and we'd put up a big marquee and the ladies would come down for tea.'

Dominic stared at him, the wind clearly taken out of his sails, while Hazel and the other woman took this as a suitable distraction for them to scramble into their clothes.

'Nice to meet you, Cyril,' muttered Hazel, walking stiffly past them towards the path to the woods. Ettie gave her a small smile, trying to reassure her. Hazel rolled her eyes and returned the smile behind Dominic's back. The other woman just glared at Ettie and marched past Hazel, tossing her hair over her shoulder. Ettie guessed they had walked through the woods from the back of the estate and left a car in the layby just by the gates.

'You too, ladies.' Grandad began to dry himself off with his towel. 'Grand day, isn't it? Have you been in the water?'

Dominic shook his head, clearly nonplussed by Grandad's chatty indifference to his authority.

'You ought to try it. Very relaxing. Swimming's good for the spirit. Might reduce a bit of that there tension you're carrying.' He nodded towards the Hall in the distance. 'I bet fixing that place up is giving you a fair few headaches. I've always found a good swim clears the head.' He nodded at Ettie.

And she found herself nodding back at the same time, praying that he wasn't going to acknowledge their familial relationship even though she was dying to hiss at him, *What are you doing here?*

'Right, I'd best be off. Nice to meet you.' He pulled a pair of jeans over his wet swimming shorts and yanked a faded red sweatshirt over his head before squeezing water out of his thinning hair and snapping a band from his wrist to pop it in a ponytail.

Ettie wanted to laugh. Grandad was completely at ease and now Dominic was left looking awkward.

'Now, look here…' Ettie did snigger at that. She couldn't help herself. He sounded just like a blustering Captain Mainwaring. Grandad often had that effect on people. 'This is private property.'

'Aye, lad. So you said.'

'I don't want to see you here again.'

Grandad shrugged. 'Water's grand. Dog's enjoying it,' he said, slinging the towel around his neck.

They all turned to watch the dog, who was yipping with ecstatic little barks, shaking his head, flinging water from his whiskers. Scrapper was one happy dog. The sheer joy he exuded brought yet another smile to Ettie's face, even though she realised she ought to show some gravitas while at Dominic's side. He wasn't the least bit amused or entertained by the dog's antics.

'Scrapper! Come out!' The dog raised his head, looked over and promptly turned to swim off in the other direction.

'Now!' bellowed Dominic, to absolutely no avail.

'I'd offer to go get him,' said Grandad, 'but you've made it quite clear that I'm not to go in t' lake again.' Grandad's Yorkshire accent had deepened and he was giving Dominic a raffish smile.

Ettie wanted to kill him. He was deliberately winding Dominic up. God forbid Dominic ever found out they were related. He'd probably sack her on the spot.

They all stood and watched Scrapper. A pulse jumped in Dominic's neck and he glared at Grandad. 'You should be leaving.'

'What, and miss the entertainment?'

Ettie glared at her grandad. Dominic's jaw tightened and he turned and stalked to the water's edge, bellowing again in a loud alpha yell, 'Scrapper! Here! Now!'

Despite his imperative summons – which, to be fair, made Ettie want to obey – the dog blithely ignored him, splashing about with complete abandon, and whining squeals of pure pleasure.

Grandad sauntered up the beach and gave Ettie a devilish wink. 'See you later,' he mouthed and walked away up the same path as the two women. No doubt his ancient motorbike was parked in the layby as well.

'Bloody dog,' said Dominic grimly, after another fruitless shout. He looked at his watch. 'Hell. I've got the building regs man coming in half an hour. I can't wait here all day for him.'

'He's having a lovely time,' said Ettie. 'I'm sure he'll come out when he's had enough.'

'Yes, knowing him, that'll be about midnight. I can't leave him. What if he got into real trouble? I don't know. Do dogs get cramp?'

Ettie lifted her shoulders. 'I've no idea.'

'Buggering hell. Scrapper, come here, now!' The dog lifted his head and then with a happy, playful bark, began to swim further out.

Dominic crossed his arms over his chest and picked up the hem of his T-shirt and, for a moment, Ettie thought he was going to pull it off. Then he stopped, his face turning pale. His mouth twisted and he squinted out over the lake, taking a few careful, even breaths.

Then he hissed out a sigh, followed by 'Bloody dog.' To Ettie's surprise, with a quick turn he stomped back across the sand to the grassy bank and sat down, his elbows propped on his knees, his face wiped of all emotion. 'We'll just have to wait for him.'

With a frown, she looked from him to the dog and back again, confused by Dominic's about-turn and his odd acceptance of the situation.

'Do you want me to go in and get him?' she asked, worried and uncertain.

'No!' He almost shouted the words. 'Thank you. He'll come out when he's ready. If we go in after him, he'll … he'll think it's a game.'

Ettie stared at Dominic. One minute he'd been alpha male, tearing across the field, shouting and giving orders, and the next he was almost docile, sitting waiting for the dog. The only thing that suggested something wasn't quite right was the way that he kept tugging at the fabric of his socks just at the ankle. A nervous, un-Dominic-like tic. He always seemed so in control and in command of himself.

'Are you all right?' she asked, sinking down next to him, watching the dog, who was completely oblivious to them. His sheer joy, as he circled and splashed, was rather wonderful and highly entertaining – well, at least to her. She wanted to laugh but with Dominic's strange mood, she didn't dare.

'I'm fine,' said Dominic in the clipped way that suggested he was anything but.

'Sure?'

'Didn't I just say I was? I'm irritated by the dog. I'll be late for my meeting.'

'Do you want me to wait for Scrapper? Maybe if he sees you go, he'll come out?'

'No, we'll give it a few more minutes.' Dominic stiffened. 'He's not too far out.'

After a couple more minutes of deliriously joyful swimming, Scrapper began to swim out of the water towards them and then came racing up the beach.

'Good dog,' said Dominic begrudgingly and rose to his feet. He held out a hand and helped Ettie up. 'Time to go home.'

They'd barely taken a step when Scrapper, nosing around Dominic's feet, stopped and looked guilelessly up at Dominic before giving himself a thorough shake, sending a spray of lake water everywhere.

All the laughter that Ettie had been holding in for the last half hour came bubbling out. Scrapper had definitely had the last word.

Chapter Nine

'Are you sure you want to come in?' asked Ettie for the second time, crossing her fingers in her pocket, as the Land Rover drew up to the kerb outside the house. *Please, please, please, let Grandad be out.*

Once they'd returned to the house from the lake earlier in the afternoon, Dominic had been immersed in meetings. After the almost kiss, she'd wondered if he might change his mind about her moving in, but at the end of the day he found her at her desk and offered to run her home to collect her things.

'Yes, it's not a problem. It won't take long for you to pack, will it?'

That wasn't what was worrying her. Packing was her superpower – she'd moved so many times. She should have told Dominic earlier that Cyril was her grandad, but she'd let the moment pass and now it was too late. If Grandad was in, it was going to be mortifying.

Dominic followed her round to the back door. 'Hi, Mum, I'm home,' called Ettie as she stepped into the kitchen, scanning the room quickly to make sure Grandad wasn't in his usual spot at the table, squished in beside the fridge. Easy access to the beer, apparently.

'Make sure you didn't walk in the dog shit, down the alley,' said her mum, without turning around from her position in front of the oven. 'Little terror next door left his pile of doings right in the middle of the path.'

'I'm all for posting it through the letterbox, but Mum won't let me,' added Lindsey, from where she was feeding her daughter at the table.

Ettie grimaced. 'Mum, Linds, this is my boss, Dominic.'

They both looked up with identical expressions of horror.

'Hello,' said Lindsey, shovelling a forkful of something into Tiffany Eight's mouth.

'Oh, 'ello, love.' Sandra Merman gave Dominic a quick appraising look and grinned tactlessly at Ettie. It was pretty obvious she approved. 'Come on in. You want a cuppa?'

'No, Mum. I'm not stopping long.' Ettie could tell exactly which lines her mum's thoughts were running down. *Handsome man. Two arms. Two legs. Ettie's single. He'll do.*

'Mr Villiers has invited me to stay up at the hotel. Bus didn't turn up again this morning and I had to walk.'

Dominic shot her a startled look at the formality.

'Since that new lot took over the bus company, they can't

get the drivers. Useless. Are you not stopping for your tea? Your friend can stop too. Fish fingers.'

'He's my boss,' she hissed, giving Dominic an apologetic strained smile.

'I love fish fingers,' said Dominic unexpectedly, winking at Ettie.

Ettie's mum didn't quite squeal in delight but it was a close-run thing. 'So does Ettie.'

Ettie rolled her eyes. A mutual love of fish fingers was not the basis for a lifelong relationship.

'Have a seat, love. Want white or brown bread?'

'White would be great, thanks.'

Tiffany Eight pointed at Dominic. 'This is Tiffany Eight,' said Lindsey.

A quick look of alarm crossed Dominic's face before he said, 'I'm guessing there aren't Tiffanys One, Two, Three, Four, Five, Six and Seven.'

Lindsey squawked with laughter. 'That's hilarious. Mum, did you hear that? Heck, can you imagine having octopuslets.' She gave a theatrical shudder. 'Oh my God. My poor fanny would be a mess.'

'Ahem,' said Ettie, widening her eyes and motioning towards Dominic.

'Don't mind me,' he said, his eyes twinkling in amusement.

'See, he doesn't mind.' Lindsey turned to him. 'It's Tiffany Eight, like the Beckhams – you know, they had Harper Seven, except I thought I'd be original.'

'It's certainly original,' said Dominic with a straight face. 'It's a lovely name.'

Ettie wrinkled her face at him behind her sister's back. It was a perfectly ridiculous name but she was the only one in the family that seemed to think so, although Grandad was convinced Eight was his great-granddaughter's middle name and not actually part of her first name.

'How many fish fingers, Dominic?'

'Er, three.'

'Three! I'd have had you down as at least a six-finger lad.' Ettie's mum shook her head. 'Big strapping fella like you. I bet you can manage more than that, can't you? It's all right – I got a couple of twenty-eight packs from Iceland on a multi-buy offer.'

'I'll just go up and pack some stuff,' said Ettie, wondering if she dare leave Dominic with her mother. As she climbed the first step, she heard her say. 'So, are you married?'

———

As soon as Ettie reached her bedroom, she peered out of the back window down at the shed. Phew, no sign of Grandad. That meant he probably was at bowls. Wasn't that Wednesday nights? She packed in record time, even for her. The sooner they could leave, the less chance they had of running into him. Besides, she didn't want her mum revealing too much about her. Her latest CV had been carefully curated, and while every job she'd listed had been genuine, there were a couple of gaps in her employment history she'd really rather no one revisited. The two-day job as a pest exterminator, chased off by the first rat she saw; the four hours she managed dressed as a dinosaur before a five-year-old threw up all over her; and the single day as an admin assistant in a colonic irrigation clinic, which included cleaning duties – all of which were subjects of great hilarity among her family. It appeared she could put up with most things, but she wasn't very good with sick or poo.

Quickly stuffing in enough underwear for the next two days, a change of jeans, several T-shirts and her make-up and toiletries, she hurtled back downstairs.

To her absolute amazement, Dominic was standing by the back door with Tiffany Eight on his hip, chatting away to Sandra as she deep-fried some chips (a special treat for guests), seemingly completely unconcerned by the baby tugging at his dark hair and gurgling up at him.

'He's a keeper,' said Lindsey in more of a stadium whisper than a stage one. 'A natural with kids.'

Dominic's mouth twitched behind Lindsey's back, but apart from that he gave no sign he'd heard her.

'I don't know where your grandad's got to,' said Mum, dishing up a fifth plate, covering it with another plate and shoving it into the oven.

Ettie sucked in a breath. 'Thought he was at bowls tonight.'

'No, he's gone to see Josh, the lad with the leg.'

'Or without the leg,' quipped Lindsey, holding up both hands in apology when Mum and Ettie rounded on her.

'I thought he'd be back by now. Come sit down, lad.'

Ettie looked towards the door and wondered how quickly she could inhale her fish fingers and leave. Dominic looked quite comfortable, even more so when her mum offered him one of Grandad's precious Boddies from the fridge.

'You all right, Ettie?' asked her mum halfway through tea. 'Do you need a wee or something?'

'No. I'm fine.'

'You keep looking at that door like you're expecting Superman to come bursting through.'

Ettie gave the door one last look and focused on her fish fingers, which tonight tasted like sawdust.

———

Tea was excruciating, with her mum and sister blatantly quizzing Dominic about his plans, his prospects and how long he'd be staying in Churchstone. With each of the answers, which they deemed positive signs of a man planning to settle down, they'd turn to Ettie with eye-wateringly obvious signals. Thank goodness for Tiffany Eight, who decided to throw a tantrum at the end of the meal, which allowed their attention to be diverted, and Ettie to dump their plates in the sink and make a hasty retreat. She almost wished Grandad had turned up, it would have been light relief.

'Sorry about that,' she said as Dominic started up the engine.

'About what?'

'My mum and sister.'

He laughed. 'They were great. Funny and kind. They were so obvious, it was entertaining, and it was all well meant.'

'Hmm,' muttered Ettie.

'So, you know all about me after that, but what about you? What are your plans?'

'As soon as I get my bookkeeping qualification, I'll head back to London.'

'Why London?'

'Because ... it's away from here.'

'Is away from here better? You seem quite close to your family.'

Her heavy sigh was as much a delaying tactic as an admission that she missed them terribly when she was away, but at the same time was glad of the distance. She wanted something different for herself, she just didn't know what it was yet.

'I am, but they drive me mad too. It's too late for Mum, but I just want to give our Lindsey a good shake. She'll end up with Darren – he's Tiffany Eight's dad, a feckless loser who spends all his time out with the lads and down the pub. He never has the rent money and Lindsey can't afford to work full-time, as she'd never cover the childcare. Mum helps out a lot so she can work part-time. But it's just an endless cycle of living from one pay packet to the next and never having any security – one that I want to break. I want to earn a decent wage, take them on holiday for a change, know that the lecky bill will get paid and not have to worry about putting the heating on. I'd quite like a car. And I always said I'd go to London.' And because she'd been so vocal about it, she'd had to stick to it, even when she found it tough going. Swimming had helped her settle, especially when the loneliness hit her and almost consumed her.

'It's good to have ambition.'

'It is, if you know what you want to do. Thing is, I get bored easily if the work isn't interesting and then,' she paused and shot him a mischievous grin, 'I get into trouble.'

'Lucky for me, then, that you still seem interested.'

'Oh, I'm very interested,' she replied, placing her hands demurely on her lap.

He shot her a suspicious glance as her mouth twitched, and she noticed his grip tighten on the steering wheel. He didn't say anything for a moment until he turned and said, shaking his head with a laugh, 'Ettie, you're a menace.'

She sat back in her seat, relishing the tension between them. So she hadn't imagined that near-kiss earlier. The big question was, whether he'd act upon it.

When they returned to the house, Gracie must have been waiting for them because she appeared on the top step as soon as Dominic switched off the engine.

He and Ettie exchanged a quick look, silently acknowledging the rain check.

'You're back!' Gracie squealed, clapping her hands together. 'I've made up your room for you. Do you want me to show you?' She'd already darted to the staircase. 'Come on.'

'I'll bring your bag up,' said Dominic dryly, as Gracie took Ettie's arm, chattering away as she led the way.

'It's going to be so nice to have some female company in the evenings. And I've got some lovely recipes lined up for dinner. We're going to have so much fun.'

Ettie didn't dare look back at Dominic's face.

A few minutes later, Gracie threw open a bedroom door. 'Here you go.' Ettie walked in and stopped dead, her heart quickening.

'Oh, Gracie!' She stared around the room. 'It's beautiful. You did all this today?'

'Click and collect. Dunelm Mill. I got Dominic to pick it all up on his way back from Harrogate at lunchtime. Do you like it?' Gracie hopped from foot to foot like an eager sparrow.

The double bed was covered in a pretty pale-blue duvet cover patterned with birds and butterflies, with several plump pillows in different shapes along with some co-ordinating plain cushions. On either side of the bed were little white chests, topped with elegant lampstands with blue shades, and there was even a little glass carafe with a water glass, etched with white flowers. On the dressing table, which had been brought in from another room, sat a blue vase filled with a glorious cloud of fresh flowers which must have been cut from the garden. Ettie could smell the scent of rose and lavender.

'It's lovely. The nicest room I've ever had.'

Gracie preened. 'Really?'

'Yes.' Ettie threw her arms around the other woman.

'Thank you so much, it's really sweet of you. It's gorgeous.' And it was. She felt a little teary and a bit overcome that Gracie had gone to so much trouble.

'I think perhaps we should leave you to settle in,' said Dominic. 'Perhaps this calls for a glass of wine in celebration.'

'Prosecco,' said Gracie. 'I know Ettie likes it and I put a bottle in the fridge. You can go and open it.' She dismissed him with a wave of her hand before turning back to Ettie. 'But first, you need to see the bathroom.'

She dragged Ettie to the en suite room as Dominic gave her a grin and left the room. 'What do you think?'

'I think you've got excellent taste, Gracie,' said Ettie, looking at the plush white towels and the collection of toiletries on the side of the sink, along with the pretty china soap dish, matching toothbrush mug and soap dispenser. It was rather humbling that someone had gone to so much trouble to make her feel at home.

'Thank you.' Gracie patted her on the arm. 'It's so lovely to have you here. You're a positive breath of fresh air. I mean, Dominic is wonderful, but he's a man's man, if you know what I mean. I'm sure I get on his nerves terribly because I'm so twittery and silly.'

Ettie shook her head. 'Don't say that. I'm sure Dominic doesn't think anything of the sort. He's very fond of you.'

'Ugh,' said Gracie. 'Fond, that makes me sound like some maiden aunt. I want him to like me and for me to be a bit more likeable. I wish I was a bit more like you.'

'Me?' Ettie was surprised. She hadn't exactly achieved much in her life.

'Yes, you're confident and sure of yourself. I spent so long doing as Bob told me, I find it a bit difficult to think for myself or to have the confidence to say out loud what I think. I tend to let everyone else do the thinking. You're a very good influence. And you won't take any nonsense from Dominic. I think I need to take a leaf out of your book.'

Ettie gave her another hug. 'Poor guy, he's not going to know what hit him.'

Chapter Ten

Ettie was a morning person, Dominic was more of an I'm-not-really-human-until-I've-had-at-least-two-cups-of-coffee sort of person, whereas Gracie maintained an even keel at all times, fuelled by an ever-full teapot. After three weeks of living together in the house, they'd settled into an amicable routine that suited all of them, although Ettie felt a little frustrated. They still didn't seem to have made much headway. Dominic was in incessant meetings and discussions about websites and software, whereas all Gracie wanted to do was bake. She felt she was bouncing back and forth between the two of them, trying to get decisions made.

Her big mistake that morning was marching into the study when Dominic had only had half of his essential caffeine fix.

'What am I supposed to tell the builders?' she said. 'You've changed the spec of the brief again.'

He scowled at her and picked up his mug, taking a slug before answering.

'I'm waiting,' he snapped, 'for Gracie to decide on the style of the bedrooms, which will inform the bathroom choices – whether we have walk-in showers or cubicles.'

Ettie threw her hands up in the air and marched over to his desk, putting her hands on the surface, prepared to remonstrate with him. As soon as she did, she realised her second big mistake. Dominic rose to his feet and planted his hands on the desk too. The two of them stood almost nose to nose, the air bristling with their equal frustration.

They stared at one another, in a Mexican stand-off for a few long seconds, eyes studying each other's faces. Ettie swallowed; she was so close, she could see the tiny darker flecks of blue in his eyes and the faint pinpricks of dark bristle where he'd shaved this morning. He smelled delicious, a combination of freshly washed hair and some smoky aftershave. For some ridiculous reason, her breath hitched and his eyes immediately dropped to her mouth. A coil of warmth unfurled in her belly as she saw him swallow too. Despite telling herself not to do it, because it was a massive cliché, she couldn't help herself when she moistened her lips. His eyes tracked the movement before rising back to hers. The moment between them was caught in electrified silence.

For once in her life, Ettie was completely tongue-tied. Words in her head batted about like a moth against a light. She was trying to find the right ones, but she was pretty sure *I'd really like to kiss you right now and I think you might want to kiss me back* weren't quite right.

Luckily, of the two of them, Dominic proved marginally more articulate. 'I need another cup of coffee,' he rasped and turned on his heel to walk out of the room.

Ettie stared after him, catching her lip between her teeth. Since that almost-kiss in the tree house he'd been very professional and kept his distance, to such an extent that she thought she'd imagined it, but this morning proved she hadn't made up the attraction between them.

She sat back at her desk and an hour later, Gracie came in bearing a cup of tea and some freshly made butterfly buns.

'Ooh, I love these, I've not had one in years,' Ettie said, snaffling a cake. 'Do you know what's happened to Dominic?'

'Yes, he's gone into Leeds to meet his solicitor. He seemed to be in a bit of a tizz.'

Ettie smiled to herself, glad to know she wasn't the only one affected.

Gracie shook her head. 'That bloody woman.'

'Who?' asked Ettie, a little deflated that it wasn't her that had put him off-balance.

'Ex-wife. She never gives up. Always wants more.'

'He's divorced?'

'Oh yes, didn't I tell you that? Bless him, he did try to keep things going, but … well, the baby … which was the last straw.'

'Dominic's got a baby?'

'Well, not exactly,' said Gracie, suddenly looking guilty. 'Probably best you hear it all from him.' Her mouth closed in a firm, straight line like a razor shell and Ettie had the feeling that it would take a lot to prise it open again.

Now she was really intrigued. How did one 'not exactly' have a baby? Despite her raging curiosity, all she said was, 'Yes, of course.'

'It's hot today. I'm going to make some lemonade. Do you want some?'

'In a while, I could do with a shower,' said Ettie. 'I need to cool down.'

With sudden longing she thought of the cool, clear lake. She hadn't been swimming for over three weeks now and she felt antsy, with that awful wanting-to-scratch-her-skin-off-for-no-reason feeling. Or maybe it was down to good old-fashioned sexual frustration. There was no denying she was attracted to Dominic, even though she didn't want to be. He was her boss, and not her type, and furthermore... Oh, hang it, she fancied the pants off him.

She was just crossing the marble floor to the front door when Gracie's voice interrupted her.

'Are you going out?' Gracie asked with a puzzled frown.

'Er, yes,' Ettie said brightly. 'Thought I'd get some fresh air before I shower.'

'In your dressing gown?'

'Yes, it's a new ... er ... new trend. I'm researching it as an idea for the hotel. Going out before you get into the minutiae of the day – you know, cleaning your teeth, showering. It's … erm, supposed to get your body in tune with nature.' She lowered her voice. 'You're supposed to go and roll in the morning dew. A bit late this morning, but you know… Apparently it's really good for your skin.'

'Oh,' said Gracie in surprise, her eyes wide with interest. 'It takes all sorts, I suppose. Good for you. I suppose you don't want Dominic catching you in the altogether.'

'Exactly.' Ettie pulled the collar of her dressing gown together. 'Won't be long.'

'You take your time, lovie. I'm going to get cracking in the kitchen. I've a mind to make a nice salmon en croute for dinner this evening.'

With that she bustled off, leaving Ettie feeling just a touch guilty at taking advantage of her good-natured naivety.

The cold of the water was a welcome hit, instantly cooling her heated skin and the helter-skelter thoughts which had been crashing about in her head ever since Gracie's inadvertent revelations. In that electric moment this morning, she'd hoped that Dominic might be as attracted to her as she was to him. Now she realised he was probably just anxious about his meeting, which was a bit of a depressing thought. Had she made a bit of a tit of herself?

Ever since she'd seen the others swimming a few weeks back, she'd been dying for a swim. She slid into a smooth breast stroke, feeling the familiar pull of the muscles in her shoulders as they flexed and stretched. Something pinged in her brain, the familiar Pavlovian response to being immersed and weightless. Every time, it was as if a switch had been flicked, allowing her to shift into being someone else. If she tried, she couldn't have explained it to someone else without sounding a bit kooky, but being in the water immediately made her feel limitless, that nothing could contain her or box her in. She could just be herself, alone with her own thoughts with no one to tell her what to do or how to do it. It was empowering and also grounding. Maybe she'd been a mermaid in a former life. Reaching forward and kicking out, she swam a few strokes before rolling over onto her back and gazing up at the blue sky above her. Her hair spilled around her as she floated, just kicking her feet occasionally to move. Across the sky a couple of swifts soared above, before skimming the surface of the lake to take a quick drink.

She let her thoughts settle, enjoying the beautiful morning and how happy she was. The job at the hotel was turning out to be much better than she could have hoped. Gracie was a sweetheart, although patently not suited to be a manager or project manager in any shape or form, and Dominic, while organised, didn't really seem to know what he wanted. His heart wasn't in it. It felt as if he were compromising to please Gracie, to give her what she wanted, but at the same time she was wanting to please him. To be honest, it was a recipe for disaster.

As Ettie drifted in the water, ideas came and went, and she was just beginning to move towards an idea, when the sound of splashing startled her. She flipped onto her front to see Hazel pulling down her goggles and the ear-flaps on her swimming hat as she waded into the water. Almost immediately she set off doing a busy breast stroke, with short fast strokes, bobbing up and down with neat rhythmic precision. There was an almost frantic hunger to her busyness, as if she needed to eat up the distance.

Hazel stopped just in front of Ettie. 'Hi, again! Fancy seeing you here.'

Ettie laughed. 'You don't give up, do you?'

Hazel said with a sad smile, 'Would you? It's so beautiful and so special. There's just something about swimming out in the open air. You clearly couldn't resist either. Has old grumpy guts given you permission? You know, you really shouldn't be swimming out here on your own. It's not safe.'

'You were, the first day I saw you.'

'I know, but Rachel, the other woman, often comes too. She lives round the corner from me. She toots on her horn when she's coming up. But it's not safe to come on your own.'

'I know.' Ettie bit her lip, treading water. It broke all the swimming rules. 'But it's such a beautiful morning and the water is so lovely. I'm an experienced swimmer and I should know better, but I couldn't resist. And he's out. He doesn't know I'm here. There's no way he would give me permission.' She ought to have felt guilty, but now that the delicious water was lapping at her body and her muscles felt sleek and relaxed, it was very hard to feel that she was doing anything wrong.

'It's such a shame he doesn't want us here,' said Hazel, with a mournful sigh, looking up at the sky. She looked troubled and a little sad. 'It's the only place for miles with decent wild water. There are no weeds, the water is lovely and clear and you've got a good shallow to get in and out.'

Ettie got the impression she was saying a lot but not saying anything of what she really wanted to talk about at all.

'I know it sounds daft but I really need this,' said Hazel, casting her a pleading look. 'Somewhere to escape the pressures of the outside world.'

'I understand that,' said Ettie. She'd always swum for escape.

'Why do people make life so difficult?' Hazel sighed.

Ettie shook her head. 'I don't know.' She began to swim alongside Hazel, somehow feeling it was the right thing to do.

'All we want to do is get married,' Hazel's face crumpled. Ettie nodded. That didn't sound so bad.

'What's wrong with that? Who's stopping you?' Ettie kept her questions gentle. She didn't want to be intrusive but instinctively she knew that Hazel wanted to talk about whatever was troubling her.

'Jane's parents are being absolutely vile.'

'Ah—' understanding bloomed '—I'm sorry, that's rough.' Ettie wondered what her own mum would say if she went back and announced she wanted to marry another woman. Knowing her mum, she would take it in her stride. 'As long as you're happy' had been her mantra for as long as Ettie could remember. Perhaps that was why Ettie had never felt under any pressure to stay put in a job or to pursue a career before.

'We just never imagined they'd be like that. They always seemed fine with us living together. In fact, it never occurred to me that there was a problem. But when we said we were getting married, oh my God, it was awful! Jane's mum started crying.' A bleak expression filled Hazel's eyes.

'That's sad,' said Ettie. It sounded as if everyone involved was hurting.

'My parents are a little more open-minded. With the stress on the *little*. They're more worried about how other people will treat us. As my mother says, "It's a hard road you've chosen." Like it's a choice. Sorry, don't get me started.'

'Don't worry. It's often easier to talk to people who don't know you in your real life, don't you find?'

'Yes. That's it. When you come to swim, you're just you.'

Ettie nodded. That was exactly it. How she felt about swimming. Her heart went out to the woman. If swimming here helped her, who was she to stop her? In fact, it was in Ettie's power to facilitate it.

'Look, I probably shouldn't say this, but … Dominic goes to physiotherapy on Wednesday mornings. He goes to some special place that's an hour's drive away. He leaves at half seven and he's back at about half past ten. But you can't swim on your own. Do you think you could ask the other lady to come with you?'

Hazel jerked her head up sharply, hope chasing the

bleakness out of her eyes. 'Really? If we came, you wouldn't say anything?'

Ettie shook her head. 'Just don't tell anyone else or broadcast it.'

'I promise. That's really good of you.'

Ettie smiled. 'Well, I also have an ulterior motive. If you're swimming here at the same time, then I can come too.'

'We should set a regular time then,' suggested Hazel.

'That would be brilliant. What about eight o'clock? Then I can come, swim and get showered and dressed in time to start work.'

'Sounds perfect. I'm self-employed, so my time is flexible. I'll knock on Rachel's door, see if she can make it then. Wednesdays at eight.'

'The Wednesday Wild Swim Club,' said Ettie, beaming.

'Brilliant.'

They swam side by side for the next ten minutes, both of them quiet as they absorbed the sights and smells of the fresh morning.

'This is just wonderful. Thanks so much for letting me swim here,' said Hazel, with a sudden warm smile that dissolved the strain around her eyes.

Ettie immediately felt she'd done the right thing. 'Well, to be honest, it's not up to me. But … well, what Dominic doesn't know won't harm him. Just make sure you're away by ten-fifteen.'

'Not a problem,' said Hazel. 'Perhaps we should set up a WhatsApp group. Just in case things change. I can add

Rachel if she's interested. Say we can't make it, so you don't end up swimming on your own, or say he has a change of plan. I don't want to get you into trouble.'

'That's a good idea.'

'And perhaps we ought to give ourselves a name.'

'Splashing Around,' said Ettie, the name just appearing in her head.

'Perfect.' They exchanged smiles as if both of them thought this might be a momentous occasion.

'So, what is it you do?'

'A bit of everything, although it's a bit crazy, as neither Dominic nor Gracie know what they want.'

'Sounds tricky.'

'It is. Very. It was going to be some sort of outdoor activity centre but Bob, who was Gracie's husband, died, and Dominic is injured, so is a bit restricted, and as Gracie worked in a hotel and without Bob was a bit lost, he's given her the chance to be involved in the hotel.'

'So, it'll be another hotel.' Hazel's mouth curled. 'Because we need another one round here.' She shook her head. 'What a waste.'

'What do you mean?'

'Well, he's got all this land. This lake. He could capitalise on this. Wild swimming is getting more and more popular. Hotels are ten a penny. He needs something to differentiate it from all the others. Something unique, and offering the swimming would definitely make it that.'

Ettie scrunched up her face. 'For some reason he's dead

set against swimming. Which is odd, because he was in the Navy. You'd have thought he liked water.'

'Some skeletons in his water closet?' asked Hazel, her eyes twinkling at the ridiculous pun.

'Maybe,' mused Ettie. That hadn't occurred to her before.

'Even so, with all this, he could do something amazing. The outdoor activity idea is a start, but he should capitalise on that and develop it further. There's a real appetite in people wanting to get back to nature. Escape from technology. I'd have thought he could have come up with something a bit more imaginative.'

Ettie frowned. 'You know, I think you might have something there.'

Hazel paused, treading water, and pushed up her goggles. 'Hmm, I'm afraid I need to get home and start work.'

'I'm going to swim for another ten minutes, but I'll be fine,' Ettie assured her before Hazel could object. 'I know what I'm doing.'

'OK, but be careful, and I'll see you next Wednesday. I'll leave my number by your shoes.'

'That's great, and then if there's a problem, I'll message you.'

Ettie watched Hazel swim off in the opposite direction and then altered her stroke from the lazy breast stroke to a fierce crawl, ploughing through the water, watching the shadows and light rippling on the bed of the lake beneath her. Her body tingled with cold but also that glorious blood-pumping-around-the-body sensation. As she neared the island she slowed and flipped onto her back, looking up at the sky and the puffs of cloud drifting overhead. Lifting her head out of the water, she listened to the chorus of the birds, from the high piercing song of a blackbird to the strident quacks of a paddling of mallards over to her left. She bobbed on the surface of the lake, letting the water hold her up, relishing the sensation of being at peace with nature. No phones, no noise, just the birdsong and the wind whispering through the trees. People needed to do more of this, she thought. And then it came to her. A hotel with a difference. A place where people left their mobiles behind and switched off the WiFi. A place which espoused greener values and looked at sustainable practices.

A lot of regulars at the vintage shop were keen to reuse, recycle and upcycle. The more she thought about it, the more she realised that there was a real appetite for people going back to basics, trying to make a difference and increase sustainability. There was a lot of talk about people being on their phones too much, but hardly anyone ever did anything about it. What if you offered a mobile detox as part of a hotel break, plus outdoor activities to reconnect with nature?

It was perfect, and the more she pondered it, the more enthused she was, so by the time she was nearly back at the house, she was practically skipping. She laughed out loud as a thought struck her: people should do more skipping!

She needed to do some research, but she was confident that she might just have come up with something that would enthuse both Dominic and Gracie a bit more. You never knew, it might get *them* skipping.

Chapter Eleven

There was a delicious smell of chocolate when Ettie came downstairs after her shower. Thankfully, Gracie didn't seem to have noticed how long she'd been. She'd been ruminating over her idea ,which had been growing and growing in her head until it was fairly bursting with beanstalk proportions. A quick Google search had cemented her confidence and she was dying to share it with Dominic. She'd also decided to pretend that this morning hadn't happened.

'When's Dominic back?' she asked Gracie, who was busy slicing sandwiches in the kitchen.

'He phoned five minutes ago and said he'd be back in twenty minutes. I've made some sandwiches. Do you want one now or do you want to wait for him?'

Ettie's stomach rumbled; after her swim she was starving. 'I thought I could smell chocolate cake.'

'You can – that's for afters.' Gracie wrinkled her nose in

sudden mischief. 'Tell you what, why don't we have dessert first and sandwiches when he gets here?'

'Perfect,' said Ettie, crossing to put the kettle on. Despite the heat of another beautiful summer's day, after a swim she always wanted something hot, as if she needed to warm up her core temperature.

When Dominic walked in, both of them were sitting at the table with nothing but cake crumbs on the plates in front of them.

'Nice to see you're not working too hard,' he said with a wry smile. Ettie relaxed. It looked as if he was also going to pretend nothing had happened this morning.

'We've worked very hard this morning. And I've made lunch and a cake.' Gracie puffed up like an indignant hen, jumping to her feet and rescuing the plate of sandwiches from the fridge and bringing them to the table.

'Ignore him, he's teasing,' said Ettie, putting a placating hand on the other woman's arm.

'These look wonderful,' said Dominic. 'You didn't need to go to so much trouble.'

The words and his grateful smile pacified Gracie and she sat down again. 'Help yourself. I'm afraid we started the cake. I need to go hang out some washing, I'll leave you two to it.' She bustled out, with a slightly pleased air about her. Ettie could have done without being left on her own with him. She focused on eating and framing in her head what she'd say about her suggestion for the hotel.

Ettie waited until he'd downed two sandwiches before she spoke. 'I've had an idea.'

When Dominic turned her way, she realised that perhaps she'd made it sound a bit too much like an announcement, but she was too revved about it to back down.

'Have you thought perhaps of doing things differently?' She spread her hands out on the kitchen table.

'Like what?' asked Dominic.

It was a good start, he sounded interested, although she paused for a moment. She was hardly qualified to be suggesting anything. It wasn't as if she'd ever stuck at anything in her life. 'Originally you wanted to open an outdoor activity centre here, didn't you?'

'Yes.' Impatience and a touch of frustration tinged his voice. She could imagine him running outdoor activities a lot more than running a hotel. He had an air of command about him, he was used to giving orders and doing practical things.

'But,' he continued, 'with this leg and no second in command, it was a non-starter.'

'Do you know what I think?'

'I'm sure you're about to tell me.'

'Your heart isn't really in it.' She held his slightly shocked gaze.

'I'm sorry.' He glared at her. 'I think you mean Gracie, rather than me.'

'No, I don't. Gracie will follow your lead. So, you need to lead by example.'

'Which management training course did you pick that up on?'

137

'Very funny.' She gave him a snide smile, aware that her CV was obviously blank of any sort of training. 'It's common sense. You're not really that enthusiastic, are you?'

'Thanks. That's really helpful.' He snatched up another sandwich.

'It's supposed to be. Sort of.'

'Well, it isn't.' He huffed out a sigh.

'Seriously, Dominic. You say you want to open a hotel but your heart isn't in it.'

He stared at her and snorted. 'And what makes you so sure about that? At the end of the day, it's an investment. A business for me and Gracie, and a good use of an asset I happen to own.'

'But surely you should enjoy running it. Wouldn't it be better if it was something you felt passionate about?'

'It's a hotel. It has guest rooms, provides beds and food. What's to get passionate about?'

'Well, if your hotel was going to have a chef that was going to put it on the map, you'd be passionate about the food.'

'Sorry, but I can't get passionate about beds or furniture.'

'But you could if the ethos of the place was right.'

'What do you mean?'

'What if you created a different sort of hotel? Forget the idea of a standard hotel. There are loads of them. Offer something completely different. A haven for stressed-out, burned-out people, or just people who want to get away from it all. Kind of a back-to-nature hotel, where there are no phones, no televisions, no WiFi. Outdoor barbeques.

Nature walks. Meditation in the tree houses. Yoga on the lawn. Baking classes. You could do some outdoor activities, like you'd planned with Bob. A complete break. Make it luxury rustic. You'd have all mod cons, but it's comfortable and eclectic rather than super-posh.'

Ettie stopped, realising she'd got a bit carried away. Dominic stared at her and she was starting to feel a little awkward, when he said, 'Carry on.'

'Well, I've been doing a little research, and current consumer trends are looking towards being more in tune with nature, enjoying the outdoors and being more spiritual.'

'OK.' Dominic nodded, his expression a little dazed but also intrigued. He sank his chin on his hands and closed his eyes for a moment. Ettie crossed her fingers – that was definitely a thinking face. Now she'd spoken to him, enthusiasm for the idea throbbed through her veins. They could make this place something really special.

Frowning heavily, he opened his eyes. 'But what about...' He waved a hand around the room. 'And Gracie.'

'Do you like the idea?'

There was a pause and his face blossomed with a slow smile. 'I love the idea,' he said, and slammed his palm down on the table. 'You're a bloody genius, Ettie! I'm already thinking firepits for the woods. People could cook their own breakfasts. But what about Gracie?'

'I think Gracie will be happy looking after people. In fact, with this idea, I think she'll be happier. She's not materialistic or fancy herself. And she could run cooking classes, like breadmaking and things. I bet she'd love that. In fact, you could have a whole schedule of lots of different activities for guests to do while they're staying. I think if you changed your approach and you were more enthusiastic, she'd be more interested and would get more involved.' Ettie winced. 'Not that I'm criticising you or anything. It's just my take on it.'

Dominic shook his head and gave her an admiring nod. 'I think … I think you are a very smart cookie. There are lots of people who want to get back to a simpler life. Take a proper break from work and the digital world. It's perfect, and you're right about Gracie. I've been feeling bad about trying to force her into a role she's really not comfortable with.'

'Seriously?'

'Yes. As I said, it's perfect. You're right. We need to be different. Hotels are ten a penny. We need to offer something unique. Where did you get this idea?'

'Er…' She smiled at him brightly. 'Well … it just came to me, I suppose,' she lied glibly. She could hardly tell him the idea had come to her while she was swimming in the lake.

'Ettie, you really are a marvel – which reminds me, I need to talk to you about builders' quotes.'

'Well, of course I am,' said Ettie, preening, taking a slug of Gracie's latest cup of tea. 'What about them?'

'They're so much cheaper. Both of them.'

'Good.'

'So, which one should I go with?'

'Jonas, definitely. He's reliable. Nice guy.'

'Why not Timms? His quote is cheaper. Is he no good?'

Ettie lifted her shoulders, her mouth quirking in mischief. 'No idea.'

'So why not?'

'One, because he was a dick at school; and two, because he was a dick at school. Once a dick, always a dick.'

Dominic let out a bark of laughter. 'Well, that's told me!'

'You asked.' She gave him a gleeful smile. 'And I'll have great pleasure in telling him he didn't get the job.'

'Ouch.'

'Oh yes, I'm a bitch and revenge is sweet. He did the dirty on my sister at secondary school. We Mermans have very long memories.'

'I'll remember that.' He paused. 'I was going to ask if you fancied a drink on the terrace when we finish this evening, a toast to your rather brilliant plan – but after that story, I'm not so sure a drink would be a good idea.' He quirked one eyebrow at her in question. 'Will it be safe?'

'If you behave yourself,' she said primly.

'I'll do my best.' Despite his grave tone, his eyes were full of flirtation and Ettie couldn't resist.

'See that you do,' she replied with an equally flirtatious smile.

'Do you have any preferences?'

'Preferences?' Now it was her turn to raise an eyebrow.

He laughed. 'Wine. I've just had a case of wine delivered from an old contact touting for business.'

'To be honest, I know bugger all about wine.'

'Doesn't matter. I just need to know that people will drink it.'

'I drink anything,' said Ettie. 'Dead common, me.' Definitely compared to someone like him.

'Why do you think that?'

'I'm not exactly what you'd call educated. I left school at seventeen and you've seen where I live. It's not posh. My mum's a dinner lady and a cleaner, and my sister's a single mum. And my grandad – well, whatever he gets up to, it's only this side of legal.' Grandad put Rodney Trotter to shame with his market-stall ducking and diving.

'Don't forget I inherited all this.' Dominic waved a hand around the study walls. 'And I've met your mum and your sister. They're lovely. Good people. Your mum gave me the last fish finger in the packet.'

Ettie spluttered out a laugh. 'You were lucky there.'

'No, I'm serious. They'd never met me before but your mum immediately offered me a meal, even though she doesn't have much money. And like I said before, you're clearly all close. I really enjoyed meeting them.'

Ettie shrugged, a little embarrassed that he'd seen so much in such a brief visit. They were still light years apart.

'How come you're so good with babies?' she asked him, remembering Tiffany Eight propped on his hip and wondering about what Gracie had said earlier. 'Do you have children?'

His face went blank. 'No,' he replied in the sort of tone that said he wasn't about to elaborate.

'Right,' she said, realising that she didn't know him that

well and he wasn't prepared to share. Back to business, then. 'Do you want me to ring Jonas with the good news?'

'Yes, that would be great.'

She picked up the phone, shutting his presence out, and made the call. His mobile rang and he picked it up and was soon involved in some conversation about ground maintenance.

The wisteria clinging to the wall of the house rustled in the light evening breeze as Ettie sauntered onto the veranda to where Dominic was waiting for her. She'd made a bit of an effort this evening, putting on a halter-neck jersey dress and twisting her hair up in a messy bun so that loose tendrils drifted about her face. She was aiming for bohemian chic, and from the sudden widening of his eyes as he studied her, she guessed she'd nailed it. Inwardly she high-fived herself. OK, if she were being honest, she'd been hoping to impress him. This afternoon, that flirty vibe between them had come back, and she wasn't one to sit around waiting for things to happen. She was attracted to him and there was no harm in finding out if it was reciprocated.

Dominic was sitting at a little bistro table that seemed to have appeared out of nowhere and rose to his feet when she approached.

'You look … lovely,' he said and pulled out the second chair for her in a chivalrous gesture that left her a little flustered. She wasn't used to that sort of treatment, nor did she expect it, but it was … well, actually, it was quite charming.

'This is nice, where did it come from?' She nudged the table with her toe, suddenly a little shy.

'The stable block – there's a storage shed full of outdoor furniture. I haven't had a chance to take a proper look but there's all sorts of stuff in there.'

'Ooh, I could do that,' said Ettie, immediately losing her self-consciousness, already wondering what they might find.

Dominic laughed. 'Why doesn't that surprise me?'

'I could go through and make you a proper inventory.'

'Actually, that's quite a good idea. There's probably a lot of stuff in there that might be quite useful, with the change of tack.'

'Excellent.' Ettie rubbed her hands together. 'It'll be like looking for treasure.'

'Each to their own. Now, let's see what this wine is like. One of the perks of the business, people giving you free samples. I thought we'd try this white wine, it's a New Zealand Sauvignon.'

'It could be a Welsh house wine, for all I know. I always buy whatever's on offer at the supermarket.'

He poured her a glass. 'Cheers.' He lifted his own glass, studying her face for a moment. 'And thank you, and I also owe you an apology.'

'Do you?' She raised a curious eyebrow, remembering their almost-encounter that morning.

'Yes. I'll be honest—' he gave her another assessing look

'—I thought you were going to be a bit flaky when we interviewed you.'

She laughed. 'Tell me something I didn't know. You did make it rather obvious.'

'Did I?' Quick horror filled his face. 'I thought I was being professional.'

'Not especially,' she said with candid cheerfulness. 'But it's OK, I've forgiven you.'

He burst out laughing. 'Thank you.'

'That's all right, although you can still tell me how you underestimated me and how fabulous you think I am now, if you like.' She raised her glass to him and sat back in her seat, crossing her legs. 'Gracie says you used to be married.'

'Did she, now?' If Dominic was surprised by her sudden change of tack, he didn't show it.

'I'm being nosy.'

Dominic smiled and put his glass down, the teasing glint in his eyes setting off a flutter low in her belly. 'At least you're honest about it. That's what I like about you, Ettie. You're so open. Honest to the point of being blunt sometimes, but I like that.' His voice lowered and like a magnet, her eyes were drawn to meet his gaze. 'I like it a lot.'

She swallowed, thinking of her swim earlier that day. Not telling him about it wasn't lying, was it? Just an omission. As was the planned swim next Wednesday. He didn't need to know about it. He'd be out, and there would be enough swimmers to assuage any worries about safety.

'So how long have you been divorced?' she asked in a chatty tone.

He folded his arms across his chest, his mouth twitching. 'You want the whole gory story?'

'Not particularly, just how you came to be here.'

'I met Paula at school. We went out, and then I went into the Navy. I joined up with the Fleet Air Arm – helicopters on search-and-rescue missions. I was away for long periods on deployment. We got engaged when I was on leave and I thought because she was used to me being away by that stage, it would be OK. It wasn't. She got lonely.'

'What sort of lonely?' Ettie asked, but she could read between the lines.

'The other-man sort of lonely. I decided if I wanted to save my marriage, I needed to come out of the Navy, except it didn't help. We discovered, when we actually lived together properly, that we weren't really that well suited. Our grown-up selves didn't have that much in common and there were other complications which I really don't want to go into.'

'I'm sorry.'

He shrugged. 'It happens. We married far too young. What about you? No boyfriend on the scene?'

'Nope. The last one cheated, so I have every sympathy. Although he was quite honest about it. I'm not sure that's any better. Said it just happened and he couldn't help himself.'

'Ouch. If it's any consolation—' he lowered his voice '—the man was an idiot.'

Her heart flipped at the expression on his face. He leaned closer to her and her breath hitched. Then he suddenly gave her a tight smile and the moment was lost. Disappointment pinched but her smile was smug as she said, 'Thank you, I think so too.'

He laughed and the intimacy that had sizzled between them vanished.

'How's the bookkeeping course going?'

She rolled her eyes. 'Painful. I've got to hand in an assessment on Monday and I haven't even started yet.'

'Last-minute merchant?'

'Always. So, I'm going to have to work every night and all weekend if I'm going to get it done.' She slapped her forehead. 'I never learn. At least at home, Mum will keep me supplied with fish fingers and tea and biscuits.'

'That's a shame...' He paused. 'I was ... well, I wondered if you fancied going out for dinner on—'

She beamed at him, confidence flooding back. She hadn't imagined that brief connection earlier after all.

'Hello, do you two want some snacks? I've made some parmesan cheese straws. They're fresh out of the oven.'

'Gracie!' Ettie feigned pleasure.

'I thought you might like something to go with the wine.'

'That's very thoughtful,' said Dominic. 'Would you like to have a glass? And perhaps we can talk about the new direction of the hotel and think about some of the activities we can lay on for guests.'

'That would be lovely. Ettie, it's a wonderful idea. I

don't know why Dominic didn't think of it before.' Gracie gave him an unexpectedly bold smile. 'See, I told you she was the right person for the job.'

'You did,' agreed Dominic, looking dutifully put in his place.

Gracie beamed at him and glanced at the table. 'I'll just go and get a glass.' She put the plate of crisp golden straws on the table and bustled away.

Ettie and Dominic burst out laughing. 'You were saying?' said Ettie, eager to return to the subject.

'Dinner, but it sounds as if you've got a lot on your plate.'

'I'd love to … but perhaps next week.'

'I'll check my diary.'

She snorted. 'I know your diary. I'm your PA. There's nothing in it.'

'Great then, it's … it's a date.'

She would have asked him if he meant a *date* date, but Gracie, who must have put an Olympic sprint on, reappeared before she had a chance.

Chapter Twelve

As soon as Dominic's car door slammed when he left for his physiotherapy session, Ettie ran down the stairs and then stopped on the landing above the hall. No sign of Gracie. With luck, she'd be able to sneak out for a swim. In her jeans pocket her phone vibrated and she pulled it out to check it.

There was a new WhatsApp notification.

Grandad has joined the group.

Grandad! What was he doing on here?

Hazel: *I invited Cyril the other day.*

Ettie was going to kill Grandad.

Hazel: *I've added him to the group.*

Ettie sighed. The group was growing faster than fungus, which was the last thing she wanted. With every new addition, the chances of being caught increased.

Stealthily, like a ninja spy, imagining herself dressed all in black, looking neat and elegant like an Audrey Hepburn-styled cat burglar, she crept down the remaining stairs, her ears straining to hear. She'd almost made it to the front door and was reaching for the door knob, when she heard Gracie's voice.

'Ah, Ettie. Are you still wanting a picnic for tomorrow?' Gracie appeared in the hall behind her, making her feel a bit like a burglar sneaking out minus the ill-gotten gains.

'Oh, yes,' Ettie feigned a quick smile. 'If you're sure you don't mind.' She hadn't wanted to put Gracie to any trouble, but the minute she'd mentioned her idea, the other woman had immediately started making suggestions.

'Of course I don't mind, it will be good practice for when we have real guests. I think a Prosecco date night in the tree house is a wonderful idea. I'm going to make some herb biscuits to have with a nice slab of mature cheddar, some home-made chutney, and I'll pop in some posh crisps and some mille-feuille that I've been practising for afternoon teas.'

'That sounds wonderful. Thank you so much.' Ettie hadn't even run the idea past Dominic; she thought she'd just take him to the tree house and present him with a fait accompli.

'It's fine, dear. And Dominic needs a bit of looking after.

He never got much tenderness from that wife of his.' Gracie gave her an arch look. 'You're so much better for him.'

'I'm just showing him the potential of the tree house,' protested Ettie.

'Of course you are, dear,' said Gracie. 'What time will you be back for breakfast?'

'Say an hour and a half?'

'Where are you going so early?'

A thump of guilt throbbed through Ettie's chest. What to do? She tried to come up with something. *I was just going out to test the temperature. I was going to do some meditation.* Or she could tell the truth. The idea was so novel, she turned it over in her head for a couple of seconds. *Tell the truth. It would make life a lot simpler.*

'Actually, Gracie...' She paused. 'I'm going swimming. In the lake. Sorry I didn't tell you before, but I didn't want Dominic to know.'

'I won't tell him, dear.' Gracie peered out of the window. This morning the weather was looking a bit murky. 'You swim in the lake? Isn't it very cold?' She gave a little laugh. 'I don't suppose it matters if it starts raining. You're wet anyway.'

'Exactly, and the water is lovely, once you're in.'

'What about fish and creatures?'

'I think the fish like to stay out of the way, and so far there's been no sight of the Loch Ness Monster or an equivalent.'

Gracie scrunched up her mouth. 'I'm going to come with you.'

'You are?'

'Don't you want me to?'

'No, no, it's not that at all,' said Ettie with a rueful laugh. 'I just don't want you to get into trouble with Dominic if he finds out. He's very anti swimming in the lake, for some reason.'

'I won't tell him. It can be our secret.' Gracie gave her a conspiratorial smile.

'Girls together.'

'Unless he asks me, of course. I can't lie to him. He's been very good to me, you know.'

'I know. I'm not asking you to lie to him, just not volunteer what we've been doing.' Ettie bit her lip. She might as well go for broke and be totally honest. 'There are other people as well. Is that a problem?'

'How many other people?' Gracie's forehead puckered.

'Only three, but it's a safety precaution. You shouldn't swim on your own.'

'Well, I never thought of that, but you're quite right. Safety in numbers, I always say.' She gave a little giggle. 'What fun. I've never swum in a lake before. I tell you, you're good for me, Ettie. I'm trying all sorts of new things.'

To Ettie's mild dismay, there were more than three at the lake when they arrived. Hazel and two other women were at the water's edge watching Grandad with his strong, unflashy crawl, making steady progress to the island, and paddling in the shallows was a skinny elderly woman in a neon-orange swimming costume and a swimming hat covered in rubber flowers in orange, pink, yellow and green. Even though Ettie was alarmed by the additional swimmers, the woman certainly brightened the morning up.

'Morning,' said Hazel. 'This is Rachel. You've already sort of met.' Ettie recognised her as the woman who'd been swimming with Hazel, the day Dominic had spotted them from the tree house.

'Hi,' said Ettie. 'Nice to meet you, properly. I'm Ettie.'

'Mm,' mumbled Rachel, her eyes not meeting Ettie's face. She was wearing some sort of waterproof-lined robe/poncho thing which she turned to peel off.

'Hope you don't mind, we've recruited Cyril. And this is Jane, my partner. She's not as keen as me.'

'You're obsessive about swimming,' said Jane in mild reproof. 'I'm a fair-weather swimmer, although this morning it's a bit grey, but warm enough. I hope you don't mind me joining in.'

Ettie shook her head. Jane had such a sweet smile, it was difficult to say otherwise. 'It's OK, but who's that?'

'Ah,' said Hazel, with sudden innocence. 'That's Hilda, she's our neighbour. Sorry, she followed us here.'

Hilda obviously had bat ears because she turned around and waved, coming towards them.

'Hello. I did not follow you. If I'd followed you, you

wouldn't have known anything about it.' She held out a hand to Ettie. 'Hilda Fitzroy-Townsend. Jane told me that you were swimming here and I haven't swum since my basic training. This is a lot jollier than skulking about in submarines in the middle of the night.'

Jane winced and whispered, 'I didn't tell her; she sort of interrogated it out of me. You don't say no to Hilda.'

Hilda smiled blithely as if taking her due and Jane had just complimented her. 'It's a wonderful way to start the day. I don't know why I didn't think of it before. I usually jog every day. This is a lot gentler on the joints.'

'We only swim on Wednesdays,' said Ettie firmly and she turned to Hazel. 'And no one else. We don't want Dominic to find us again, although that's not going to stop Grandad over there.' She nodded out towards where he was ploughing through the water.

'Don't be ageist,' said Hilda, her sharp blue eyes full of piercing reproof. 'Every wrinkle is hard earned and deserves respect.'

Ettie grinned at her, charmed by the woman's forthright feisty attack. 'He is my actual grandad.'

'Cyril's your grandad?' Hazel did an overt double-take. 'I had no idea. You were very discreet the other morning when you saw us.'

'I tend not to broadcast it,' said Ettie dryly.

'He's ever such a good swimmer,' Jane said, watching him, as he sped through the water.

'There was talk of him being good enough for the

Olympics back in the sixties, apparently, although that's what *he* says.' Her grandad had a habit of making up and embellishing stories, so she never knew quite how true this was, but he was certainly a good swimmer and had taught her from a very young age. 'He also says it's in the name. We're Mermans. He says he was destined to swim.'

'Mer-man. Oh yes! Got it,' said Jane. 'Wish I could swim like that.'

'I wish I could swim,' said Gracie.

Ettie shot her a *Whaaat?* look.

'Just joking, dear. I can swim, but not properly.'

'What do you mean, not properly?'

Gracie did some whirling windmill arms. 'You know, like that. I can only do breast stroke.'

'That's OK, that's all I do,' said Jane cheerfully. 'My partner here, Hazel, is the fast one. I'm Jane, by the way, and this is Hazel and Rachel.'

'And I'm Hilda.' The older woman nodded her head, the flowers on the hat vibrating, which seemed to mesmerise Gracie. It took her a second to focus and introduce herself.

'Gracie. I work up at the house with the owner.'

'What, old misery guts?' asked Hazel.

'He's not miserable. Just a bit… He worries, but he's got a very good heart. Bless him, he does have an overdeveloped sense of responsibility.'

Ettie felt she ought to defend him as well. 'He's all right, just a bit uptight sometimes.'

'I need to get on, I've got a lot to do today,' announced

Hilda. She was an announcing sort of person, decided Ettie. 'I'm organising a fun run for St Asaph's, the local hospice, although I'm wondering if perhaps we ought to consider a triathlon. This would be a perfect location.'

Ettie didn't like the determined glint in her eye. 'It's private property,' she reminded the older woman, 'and we're not supposed to be swimming here.'

'Hmm,' replied Hilda, as if that were totally immaterial, and she turned and walked into the water, the flowers on her hat bobbing with what looked like insouciant defiance. What was it Jane had said? *You don't say no to Hilda.*

'Come on,' said Hazel, giving Jane a nudge. 'Enough procrastinating. I know you.' She gave Jane a quick kiss, before the two women floundered their way into the water and set off swimming.

'If we don't get in now, Dominic will wonder what we've been up to. We need to be dry and dressed when he gets back,' Ettie said to Gracie.

'You're right, love.' She inched towards the water. 'Is it deep?'

'There's a shallow shelf here for a few metres and then it starts to slope.'

'Will I be out of my depth?'

'Not if you stay close to the shore – it gets deeper about six or seven metres out.'

'Are there weeds and things?'

'No, look – the water is beautifully clear. That's why this place is so popular.'

'OK.'

'Don't worry, Gracie,' said Ettie kindly, patting her on the arm. 'I'm a trained lifeguard. I'll stay with you. Come on,' she took the other woman's hand, 'we'll go in together. Just step by step.'

'Thank you, dear, but don't let me hold you back.'

'You're not.' She felt Gracie's grip on her hand tighten as they walked into the water.

'It's cold.' Gracie stopped dead as the water lapped over her ankles.

'Yup, but it gets better. Once you're in.'

'Mmm.' Gracie looked doubtful. 'Perhaps I'll just stay close to the shore.'

Ettie gave her a careful study, trying to decide whether to encourage her or leave her be.

'Whatever you want to do. There's no pressure.'

Gracie huffed out a big sigh. 'I'm here to swim.' She took a couple of brave steps forward and then turned with a cheeky smile. 'Come on, Ettie. What you waiting for?'

Ettie laughed and together they moved forward without hesitating until the water was at chest height.

'It's f-freezing,' squealed Gracie.

'Time to swim.' Ettie launched herself into the water, her body shuddering with the shock of the cold, smiling to herself as she heard Gracie's squeaks and squeals. The cold embraced her body with a frigid welcome that forced her to swim hard to fight against its icy bite. Grandad was coming towards her, and she glanced back at Gracie, who was standing in the water with her arms high above her head, still not fully committed to immersing herself. Ettie decided she'd ask him to keep an eye on her as well.

'You just have to be brave,' she called.

'Yes, dear,' said Gracie in her usual placid way, which made Ettie smile. Gracie would do things in her own time, in her own way. There was a silent stubborn streak to her.

By the time Ettie started swimming, Rachel was halfway to the island, doing a long, languid front crawl like a basking shark. There was no splash or wastage of movement as she glided through the water. Behind her by some way, Hazel bobbed along more slowly with her distinctive breast stroke. Ettie smiled; they both clearly loved their swimming and she could see why. It was so quiet without the constant whoosh and lap of a swimming pool. With each turn of her head to take in a breath she could see the trees on the edge of the east side of the lake, their leaves shimmering in perpetual motion in the light breeze. She felt the pull of the water against her hands and arms with each stroke, her muscles propelling her limbs in perfect symmetry.

When Grandad drew level, she stopped and trod water.

'Morning, flower, grand morning for a swim.' He shook water out of his face and gazed off into the distance. 'Funny how it gets you sometimes. Every now and then. I still miss her, you know.'

'I know, Grandad. I know.' She gave him a gentle smile.

Then with a deliberate wolfish grin as if he were thrusting the sad thoughts away, he pushed his goggles up to his forehead. 'Good to see you here. And you've brought someone along? I thought his lordship was dead set against it.'

Ettie grimaced. 'I couldn't stop her. Will you keep an eye on her? She's not a confident swimmer.'

'Good for her, coming then.'

'I wish she hadn't.' Ettie glanced back at Gracie. 'She works with Dominic as well. If he catches us, we'll be in big trouble. It's all right for me, if I lose this job I can get another. And if she drowns, I really will be in trouble.'

'Don't worry lass, I'll keep an eye on her.'

She reached the island before Hazel and was able to stand up in the shallows with Rachel, who was taking a quick break.

The other woman didn't turn towards her or say anything, but watching her profile, Ettie saw her swallow hard as she gazed out over the water. They stood in silence for a moment and Ettie almost felt guilty for disturbing her. She was just about to get back into the water when Rachel spoke.

'I bloody love this.' Her jaw was rigid, and she didn't look at Ettie. She seemed to be staring at something a long way out of sight. 'It's the only thing that keeps me sane.' There was another long pause as Ettie digested the words, realising that Rachel wasn't looking for any kind of response. 'Cheers for letting us come.' This time Rachel did turn towards her, her face sombre and those pale-blue eyes blank again.

Hazel swam up and joined them, her eyes sparkling with happiness as she asked, 'What do you think?'

'I'm hooked,' said Ettie. 'This is heaven.'

'There's nothing quite like it,' replied Hazel. 'You can work through your problems and it's bliss to get away from all the hassle. Jane's parents are doing my head in.'

'What have they done now?' asked Rachel, crossing her arms over her chest and rubbing her shoulders as her skin goose-bumped in the breeze.

'They're refusing to come to the wedding. Apparently they're worried what the neighbours will think.'

'Tell the neighbours to go do one,' said Rachel, with a belligerent scowl.

'I wish I could, and her folks. Jane's mum is like flippin' Hyacinth Bucket. The thought of saying "Jane's wife" is making her hyperventilate, and Jane's dad keeps asking if we can't just stay as we are, and her sister… Sorry, there I go again. Shouting my mouth off.'

'Hey, it's fine,' said Ettie. 'It's easier to unload with people who don't know all the people in the background. We don't need to take sides.'

'Thank God for swimming, otherwise I think I might go mad at the moment.'

'It's my safe place,' volunteered Rachel out of the blue, and then said nothing more. Ettie felt as if there'd been some kind of breakthrough when Hazel reached through the water and patted the other woman's arm.

'You're safe with us. Whatever we say here, stays here.'

Rachel gave her another one of those blank-eyed appraisals, her face remaining expressionless. Ettie wondered what had happened to her, but as she'd said, this was her safe place. The last thing Ettie would do was spoil that by asking prying questions.

After swimming for a good twenty minutes, Ettie returned to the shore to find everyone else had congregated, looking rather incongruous in their various robes. Hazel and Jane were wearing caped, hooded affairs in bright scarlet and emerald green, the colours reminding Ettie of a poinsettia. Hilda had a deep-violet cape/towel that came mid-calf, revealing sinewy calves and bony ankles. All of them were drinking from steaming cups and they offered Ettie and Gracie drinks.

'Yes, it's important to warm up,' said Hilda. 'You shouldn't really stay in the water for too long. The shock of the cold can be dangerous.'

Ettie remembered Dominic saying the same. She looked around the group; no one had turned blue. In fact, everyone was positively glowing, especially Gracie.

'But wasn't it fun,' said Gracie, her eyes shining. 'I'd never have done this before, not in a million years.'

Grandad was chatting to Jane about how to improve her breathing technique.

'You need to make sure, on the pull through the water, your elbows are high and your fingers down. This increases the surface area that moves the water.' Grandad demonstrated. 'If you do it like this,' he showed her flat hands and elbows, 'you're slicing through the water, instead of moving it behind you.' He changed the angle of his hands and elbows. 'Like this, and you're pulling the water, shoving it behind you.'

Jane was nodding and frowning in concentration.

'Tell you what. Next time you're here, I'll show you when you're in the water. Give you a bit of a lesson.'

'Oh, would you? That would be great. Next Wednesday.'

'I'll be here.'

'Do you think you could show me how to do the face in the water?' asked Gracie. 'I swim like a dog, trying not to drown.'

'You were doing just fine for your first time.'

'Look at the time,' Ettie reminded them, conscious that the longer they hung around, the more chance of being caught by Dominic. 'And make sure you don't leave anything behind.'

Grandad pulled a big fallen branch from the bushes and began to sweep it over the sandy surface of the beach, eradicating their footprints. 'That'll put him off the scent.'

Trust Grandad to have some trick up his sleeve.

They said their goodbyes and Ettie and Gracie headed back to the house.

'What lovely people,' said Gracie. 'Next time I'm going to bring some refreshments.'

'Glad you enjoyed it.'

'I did. It makes me wish that I'd been more adventurous when I was younger. I was always a bit too scared of trying anything new. I wonder what Bob would have thought.'

With a shake of her head, she added, 'Probably would have thought I was a bloody fool. He was proper conventional, our Bob. Rules and regulations. He liked everything to be shipshape, in its rightful place.' With a wiggle of her shoulders, she gave Ettie a conspiratorial wink. 'It feels good to be a bit naughty now and then.'

Chapter Thirteen

'So where are you taking me?' asked Dominic as they left the house in warm sunshine that evening.

'You'll have to wait and see,' Ettie said, lifting her nose with a prim expression, trying hard not to smile.

'Should I be scared?'

She shot him a quick wink. 'I'll be gentle with you.'

It really was turning into the most wonderful summer and Ettie was quite grateful that she wasn't living in London at the moment. The estate grounds were so beautiful, it was a real pleasure to be staying at the house and enjoying access to open space, without having to jump on a bus to find a park that felt safe to sit in, with no drug deals or snogging couples. There was a lot to be said for living in the country, which she'd never quite appreciated before – although, admittedly, the house was much more luxurious than her own home.

'Ettie?' She realised Dominic had asked her a question.

'Sorry, I was … miles away. Thinking about London and how glad I am I'm not there at the moment.'

'I asked why Gracie is so excited. What have you got planned? I'm starting to get quite nervous.'

'There's no need to be nervous. What's not to like about going to an Ann Summers party?'

'Sorry?'

'I thought it could be an evening entertainment at the hotel. They're very popular.'

He stared at her sober face.

'Great for couples on a get-away from it all – rejuvenate their sex lives.'

Dominic stopped dead and gawped at her, quite obviously lost for words. Ettie couldn't hold back the laughter. 'Your face, it's a picture!'

'That's because I've got a horrible image of orgies getting out of hand and the headlines in the local paper.'

'Don't worry,' Ettie waved an airy hand. 'Besides, I know enough about the editor to blackmail him. We were at school together.'

'You were at school with everyone. So where are we going?'

'We're going to the tree house. I had an idea for the hotel and I thought we could test it out.'

'What sort of idea?' His forehead furrowed. 'You're not going to have me doing naked yoga or anything, are you?'

'Now there's an idea.'

'Ettie,' he groaned.

'Don't you like surprises? I love them.'

'Not terribly keen, no.' He added, 'In my experience, they're usually unpleasant.'

Her heart went out to him; there was a wealth of sadness in his voice. She linked her arm through his. 'I promise… Well, I think you'll like this one.'

She swung the basket backwards and forwards, listening to the wicker weave squeaking in her hand, feeling like Little Red Riding Hood. She'd found it in the storage shed that afternoon, along with a cornucopia of items that she'd borrowed for this evening and lugged to the tree house on foot.

At the base of the tree, Ettie told Dominic he had to wait at the bottom until she told him to come up, and then she began to climb the ladder, the wicker basket bumping awkwardly against her thigh from where it was looped over one elbow.

'Are you sure you can manage that? Don't you want me to bring it up?'

'No,' she said firmly. It would spoil the surprise. She wanted to get everything set up before he came up. 'Give me five minutes.'

'Five minutes – what are you doing up there?'

She peeped back at him over her shoulder, a mischievous smile playing on her lips. 'You'll find out soon enough and it will be worth waiting for.'

The Prosecco cork eased out with a delightful pop and Ettie held out her glass, as the leaves fluttered around them, rustling in the gentle evening breeze. 'Now admit it, isn't this lovely?' she said, holding up the flute and admiring the flow of tiny bubbles fizzing up to the surface of her wine. 'The hotel guests are going to love it. Prosecco date night in the trees.'

'I have to admit, it's quite relaxing,' said Dominic. 'Although I'd still rather have a glass of red wine.'

She nudged his leg with her knee with a teasing, exasperated sigh. '"Red wine date night" doesn't sound anywhere near as sexy or as marketable.'

'True, but you've done a great job.' He looked around at her handiwork. They were sitting on a bright-turquoise soft-pile blanket in the early evening sunshine on the platform of the tree house, propped up on a pile of blue and pink silk cushions, all of which she'd found around the house. The previous owners had expensive taste and, in the brief rummage Ettie had had in the big walk-in airing cupboard upstairs, she'd had plenty of choice. She was rather pleased with the effect of the solar-powered fairy lights strung up across the roof trusses, as well as the battery-powered silk lanterns in vivid colours that hung from strategic points. She'd created a touch of oriental sumptuousness paired with *hygge* chic, and the finishing touches were the delicious contents of the wicker basket, which included a chilled bottle of Prosecco, complete with chilly sleeve, two glass flutes, a couple of damask napkins and pretty picnic plates loaded with Gracie's home-made crackers, crudités and cheese, along with a generous helping of grapes.

'Quite a feast.'

'I know, Gracie went to town. She really wanted to make it nice for us.'

'Her heart is well and truly in the right place.' Dominic caught his lip between his teeth before taking a sip from his bubbling flute. 'I hope I've done the right thing bringing her here. She doesn't know anyone. I worry that I've uprooted her. She loves having you around.'

'I know,' said Ettie, 'she's so kind. But I worry too – she's so busy looking after everyone else, but what does she do for herself?'

'She was devoted to Bob and, I know he was my friend, but he was the old-fashioned sort, expected her to do everything for him. I suppose it worked for them, though – they were married for nearly fifty years.'

They sat looking out over the lake and the grounds, and there wasn't another soul about. It felt as if they were hidden from the rest of the world in a secret place.

He took a thoughtful sip of his drink. 'I've been thinking about the name of the place.'

'Yes. Hepplethwaite Hall is all wrong. It sounds like an old-fashioned hotel or even an old people's residential home.'

Dominic's lips quirked. 'I wasn't going to go quite that far, but OK, smartarse.' The words were softened with one of his twinkly smiles that she was becoming more and more addicted to. When he smiled, his blue eyes crinkled and a rather sweet dimple appeared just to the left of his lips. There was a very slight scar that cut into his lower lip, which she found fascinating. Just as she was wondering what it might be like to kiss him, he asked, 'What would you suggest then?'

'Hmm, something current. I worked in an advertising agency for a little while.' Before he could ask why she left, she held up her hands to forestall the question. 'Too many divas.'

They both sipped at their drinks before Ettie said thoughtfully, 'Gracie wants it to be a home from home.' She wrinkled her nose for a minute before suddenly straightening up and spilling her drink with an excited jolt. 'Haim,' she announced. 'That's it! Haim. It's perfect.'

'What does it mean?'

'Nothing, as far as I'm aware, but it sounds sort of Scandi, doesn't it? As if it might be Danish or Swedish or something for "home".'

'Aren't you going to Google it?' Dominic asked with a teasing tilt to his mouth.

'No,' said Ettie, folding her arms and looking at him with a mutinous amusement. It was perfect and there was no need to look it up. It fitted, and if he didn't see that…

He grinned at her. 'You're quite stubborn sometimes.'

She raised a superior eyebrow. 'Only when I'm right.'

'Haim. Hmm.' He closed his eyes and then blinked them open again. 'Actually, on this occasion,' he paused with a nod, 'I think you've got it. I like it. I really like it. Haim.'

Ettie got her phone out.

'I knew you couldn't resist.'

'Danish for "home" is *hjem*, Swedish is *hem* and – aha! – Old Norse is *heim*. So pretty close, but made up, which makes it perfect. Original.'

He lifted his glass and toasted her. 'Haim it is.'

'What, just like that?' She beamed at him.

'That's the great thing about being your own boss. Also, I think it's perfect, don't you?'

'Of course I do, it was my idea. Do I get a raise?'

'No,' he said, hiding a grin.

'Worth a try,' she said.

'You never give up.'

'Course not. What would be the fun in that? Do you want me to have a go at designing a logo for you?'

'Don't tell me you worked for a graphic designer?'

'Well, funny you should say that, but no. But I sat near the graphics team at the agency. I'm quite good.'

'If you say so yourself.'

'If I don't, no one else will. At least let me try. What have you got to lose at this stage?'

'Nothing, I guess. I don't suppose you can build a website as well?'

She tilted her head on one side, as if giving it serious consideration, and he waited with a smile on his face. 'No.' She laughed. 'I mean, I could have a go, but it would take me forever.'

'But you'd have a go. Is there anything you haven't tried or wouldn't try?'

She scrunched up her mouth as if in thought and gazed at him. His eyes twinkled with amusement and a definite hint of admiration. 'Hmm. I'll have to get back to you on that.'

Dominic leaned over, grabbed the bottle and filled both their glasses before clinking his against hers. 'You really are amazing.'

'I know. You've said it before.' This time she gave him a knowing look, remembering how close she'd come to kissing him before.

'I did.'

'So, are you going to kiss me or not?' she asked.

With a sigh, his mouth twisted. 'I've certainly been thinking about it, but what about the rule about not mixing business with pleasure?'

She leaned back into the cushions, holding her glass, and, with a sultry smile, said, 'I have a rule too... Rules are made to be broken.'

He raised one eyebrow. 'How would that work?'

'You ask me out, I say yes.' She beamed at him.

'I meant working together.'

'I'm sure we could manage somehow.'

'I'm sure we could but … I'm your boss.'

'So?'

'You have to do what I tell you. It's inappropriate. I don't want to take advantage of you.'

Now she raised an eyebrow and then she snorted. 'Dominic. Seriously.'

'What? It's a consideration.'

'You honestly think I would take that sort of crap? Why do you think I've had so many jobs? I've told plenty of bosses to keep their hands to themselves.'

He laughed. 'I believe you.'

'If I choose to sleep with you, it's my choice, and I don't expect a pay rise. Well, not for that, any road.'

His eyes widened. 'You move quickly.'

'I didn't say I was going to.' She cocked her head to one side, like a cheeky robin. 'I'm considering it.'

To her satisfaction, she saw a faint blush tinge his cheeks.

'And do I have any say in the matter?'

'Hmm.' She pretended to give the question some thought, lifting her head and studying the leaves lifting in the breeze above them before letting her gaze rest on his face. 'Probably not.' Her mouth quirked as she tried to hold back her amusement.

'Have I just been propositioned?' he asked, feigning shock and clutching one hand to his chest.

'No, let's just say forewarned.'

'Thank you.' He studied her gravely for a moment, which made her heart flutter just a little. There was something about him that was so steady and strong. When he gave you his full attention it felt like being in safe water. 'That's very thoughtful of you.'

'I thought so,' she said with a perky smile which belied a tiny prick of uncertainty. The thought of going to bed with

Dominic set off a frisson of excitement dancing low in her belly, but at the same time he was quite a different frog from those she was used to kissing. Much more serious, more considered, but with darker undercurrents. Most of her previous relationships had been shallow, fun, flirty conquests, where neither side was prepared to step into deeper water. 'It's always best to be prepared about these things.'

'Are you always so matter of fact about…?'

She laughed at his sudden shyness. 'I don't have any hang-ups, but don't get me wrong, I *am* choosy. You should consider yourself lucky.'

He raised an eyebrow. 'Thank you.'

There was a pause as they stared at each other, and just before she wondered if she ought to make the first move, he took the wine glass out of her fingers and placed it next to his own, before turning back to her, and lying on his side facing her. His hand reached out to cup her face. 'I wanted to kiss you the first time we came here. And then I thought better of it. It could make things difficult. I … I find it hard to trust people easily.' His mouth twitched and his thumb grazed her cheekbone, sending a delicious shiver through her. 'I love how open you are, I can't imagine you're capable of keeping secrets. Like Gracie says, you are a breath of fresh air.' With a gentle smile, he lowered his head and kissed her.

Ettie closed her eyes, guilt prickling across her skin like ants on the march, but the beguiling touch of his lips pushed everything out of her head as every nerve ending sprang to life and she sighed with sheer pleasure, as his mouth seduced hers with softness and a deft, sure touch that, if she'd been standing, would have made her weak at the knees. Sometimes it was rather nice to let someone else take charge.

Chapter Fourteen

'Where are you off to?' asked a sleepy voice as Ettie crept out of Dominic's bed the following morning.

After leaving the tree house well after dark the previous evening, they'd snuck into the house, giggling quietly, grateful that Gracie appeared to have already gone to bed, and crept up the stairs to his room. Dominic in bed, to her surprise, was a delightful combination of masterful, which she'd expected, and at the same time tender and considerate. So while he took charge, he also listened and responded with definite skill to her every moan of pleasure. And when she flipped him on his back, he was quite happy to let her take control.

With the rain pattering against the sash windows and the sky outside a lifeless, flat grey indicating that the recent sunny weather had taken a break, it was very tempting to climb back into bed.

'Work. My boss won't be impressed if I'm late.'

'I've heard he's quite an understanding sort of guy.' Dominic propped himself up on one elbow, his dark hair and tanned skin a stark contrast to the white cotton of the rumpled sheets. Ettie couldn't help drinking in the sight of his broad chest and the rough stubble dotting his chin, and feeling just a little off balance and strangely possessive. He was so deliciously manly and at the moment all hers for the taking.

'I'd rather not take the piss just because I'm sleeping with him,' was Ettie's quick rejoinder.

Dominic sat up and she was hard pressed not to go back to bed and join him. His mussed hair made him look a lot younger and more carefree, and her heart softened. She skirted the bed and sat on the side to place a gentle kiss on his cheek.

'What was that for?' he asked with a dopey smile, which made her heart melt just a little more.

'Because you're cute.'

'Cute!' He wrinkled his nose in disgust.

'Very cute.' She poked his cheek. 'Dimples too.'

'I do *not* have dimples.' He squared his shoulders and straightened with mock affront.

'Do too,' she teased and was hauled in for a hug and a much longer, more thorough kiss, where things were starting to get delightfully out of hand as he wrestled her back down on the sheets, slipping one strong thigh over her leg.

'Dominic.' She pushed him away laughing, surprising herself by being the practical one, although part of her did want to prove to him that she could still be relied upon. 'I really do have to get to work. There's so much to be done.'

He rolled his eyes. 'You're no fun.'

'You're supposed to be the sensible one.'

He sighed, sobering quickly, and she regretted reminding him of his responsibilities. 'You're right. We have got a lot to do.'

She rolled over onto her side and dropped another quick kiss on his lips. 'But there's always tonight.'

'Are you sure?' There was a rather pleasing touch of uncertainty in his voice, as if he wasn't taking anything for granted, which made her like him all the more. He was a disconcerting mix of being very masculine and sure of himself, but at the same time wonderfully gentlemanly and a little old-fashioned. It made him even more attractive.

'Sure? About this?' She grazed a hand over the sheets. 'Yes.'

'But what about us working together?' He paused and pulled the sheet up over his hips and she wanted to giggle at his attempt to look serious, but he was so adorable with it, she decided to be good instead of teasing him some more.

'I think we should try and be professional in the office.' Her mouth quirked. 'No kissing.' She gave him another kiss on his mouth.

'No kissing.'

'No touching.' Her hand smoothed over his collarbone. He winced. 'No touching.'

'OK.' She sat up, folding her hands across her lap, with a

prim look down her nose at him. 'I think I can manage to keep my hands off you.'

His face lit with a sudden smile. 'You do like to put me in my place.'

'Of course. Now I must go.' With that, she left the room with a delighted grin on her face. Today was shaping up to be a very good day.

'You're in a good mood this morning,' said Gracie when Ettie bounced into the kitchen.

'I know.'

'Any reason?' Gracie looked out of the window. 'It's a miserable old day.'

'I slept well,' said Ettie, feeling a faint flush race along her cheeks.

'How did the picnic go down?'

'The food was amazing. Those biscuits you made were delicious and absolutely perfect.'

'Well, I've just taken a nice rye bread out of the oven and I'd like your opinion. Oh, morning, Dominic. You've timed it right. Would you like a poached egg on toast?'

'That would be great,' said Dominic, his hair damp and smelling of sandalwood shower gel. 'I don't know why, but I'm absolutely ravenous this morning. I feel like I must have burned a lot of calories.'

Ettie pinched her lips closed and avoided looking at him.

'It's all the fresh air, no doubt,' said Gracie, patting him on the arm. 'Now sit yourselves down, both of you, out of my way.'

'Do you want some help?' Ettie asked, although the other woman looked as if she had everything under control. There was a fresh pot of coffee on the side and several loaves of bread on a cooling rack.

'No, I'm practising for when we have guests,' said Gracie. 'There's nothing like fresh bread of a morning.' She shot Ettie a sudden smile. 'And I've decided that I'm going to try that dew dabbling.'

'Dew dabbling?' Ettie frowned, a little lost for a moment.

'You know, what you did the other morning. Rolling in the dew. Dew dabbling, that's the correct term. I reckon I ought to try all these new things, it might do me some good. Can't do any harm, unless you catch your death of cold. I might not be so keen, come winter.'

'Right,' said Ettie, sliding a quick glance at Dominic, praying that he hadn't heard or wasn't paying attention – a lost hope, as he was now staring at Gracie in bewilderment.

'Dew dabbling?' he asked.

Ettie stiffened. Of course he'd heard, he wasn't deaf or stupid.

'Yes, it's a wellness, mindful thing, isn't it, Ettie? And now that this place is going to be a get-away retreat, I ought to try it. Do you mind if I come with you, Ettie?'

'Er…' Her mind went completely blank. She was too busy thinking about 'get-away retreat' – that sounded like somewhere bank robbers came to recuperate after a heist.

'What on earth is dew dabbling?' asked Dominic, a confused expression on his face, as if he wasn't sure if she was winding him up, which was probably doubly confusing, because that wasn't the sort of thing Gracie did.

'You roll around naked in the morning dew,' replied Gracie with lofty, utterly misplaced superiority. 'Apparently milk maids used to do it to give them fair skin.' She turned to Ettie. 'I looked it up on the interweb, it's mentioned in an old English folk song.'

'Well, I never knew that,' said Ettie, brightly.

'Sounds very interesting.' Dominic eyed Ettie. 'Maybe I could come too, next time.'

Gracie hooted with laughter. 'I don't think it's your sort of thing at all.'

'No,' Ettie agreed gravely. 'You'd best stick to shelter building and other macho things.'

'Aren't you being a bit sexist?' he teased.

'Yes,' she said, looking down at her phone.

'You've come up with lots of original ideas – where do you get them all from?' asked Dominic with genuine interest.

She shrugged. 'Like I told you last night, my mind goes wandering all over the place when I swim.'

'Where do you swim?'

'The municipal pool,' said Ettie, desperately trying to think and give him a reassuring, nothing-to-see-here sort of smile. 'I did my lifeguard training there when I was a teenager. I did a season in a water park in Cyprus one year.'

'That wasn't on your CV either.'

'Wasn't it? That was … wild. I was only seventeen. I lied about my age to get the job. They never checked.' It had been the summer before she'd had to drop out of school.

Dominic raised his eyebrows as if he wanted to disapprove, but a smile tugged at the corners of his mouth. 'I can imagine. Although I'm not sure I want to know about you lying to get the job.'

'It's OK.' She beamed at him. 'I didn't lie about my age on my CV this time. I really am thirty and seven twelfths.'

'You really are something else too.'

'I know, it's part of my charm,' she said with a cheeky grin.

His face sobered and his eyes met hers with piercing intent. 'I know,' he said, in a low voice, almost as if it was the last thing he wanted to acknowledge.

She swallowed as her heart fluttered in her chest with feather-like disconcerting beats. He glanced around the kitchen. Gracie had disappeared and was banging about in the pantry, no doubt looking for jam pans. He rose and hauled Ettie to her feet, to give her a kiss.

'I thought there was no kissing at work.'

'We're not at work yet,' he said, nuzzling her lips.

'That's fine then,' she said, returning the kiss with enthusiasm.

Chapter Fifteen

'**D**amn.' Dominic read his phone and flopped back into his pillow with a groan.

'What?' asked Ettie, still groggy with sleep, her eyes blinking at the bright sunshine that poured in through the gauzy curtains at the window as she stretched, relishing the comfortable bed and the company. Sleeping with Dominic was a bit of a revelation. She wasn't used to men who didn't mind staying the whole night or weren't worried that they were giving her the wrong idea by having sex with her on consecutive evenings. She looked around at the pretty room that Gracie had made so welcoming for her, luxuriating in how good life was this morning.

'My meeting this morning with the website guy has been cancelled.'

'Oh good,' said Ettie, propping herself up on one elbow to look at him. Her heart did a funny little flip at the sight of his dishevelled hair and early morning stubble. She liked this private view of him. There was a softer side to him that, if she were completely honest, she would say she felt more at home with. Here they were equals, and although she was always quite bossy with him, if she let things get too serious between them, she'd have her heart broken – she knew that. Men like Dominic did not commit to women like her. He had a hard time trusting people and he needed to know exactly where he was with someone. He needed them to be steady, predictable and reliable. She was none of those things and at the moment he found that entertaining and perhaps a tiny bit challenging, but long term, Dominic wanted something a lot safer and more certain.

She reached out and ran a suggestive hand over his chest, her fingertips grazing the dark hair across the top of his firm muscles. Despite being so strong and commanding, he could also be very gentle and tender, especially in bed. It was a heart-melting combination that she'd never come across before. On the one hand he was very much assertive and masterful, but at the same time he listened to her and showed her the sort of consideration that made her feel treasured. A dangerous blend that was beginning to make her want things she had no business wanting.

She swallowed and gave him a cheery smile. 'I know what you can do today if your meeting's been cancelled.'

'Stay in bed?' asked Dominic, snaking an arm under her shoulders and pulling her towards him, placing a gentle kiss on her forehead. For a moment she wished they could stay there, but it was too tempting, and if she wasn't careful she'd get far too used to this.

Instead she said, 'Sounds like a good idea, except remember … my boss.'

'He's a boring old fart. I'd ignore him if I were you.'

Ettie narrowed her eyes and then couldn't help grinning. 'I do most of the time.'

He laughed and kissed her. She wriggled out from beneath him. 'I'm going in the shower.'

She skipped into the bathroom without a backward look, even though she would have liked to stay put, lying in his arms. For good measure, she slipped the bolt on the door into place. They'd showered together yesterday and although it had been wonderful, it had also, if she were being totally honest, scared her. *Too intimate.*

Three weeks of this and she was starting to get a little bit too used to being with him.

She turned on the shower and stepped in. *You mustn't get too attached, Ettie,* she told herself. *This is not serious.* She'd slept with him in the tree house because she fancied him something rotten and she was secure enough in her own judgement and body to enjoy herself. As usual, she hadn't given any thought to the consequences. She certainly hadn't thought it would develop into something deeper. It was supposed to be a bit of fun and because the job was temporary, there would be a finite ending.

In the meantime, there was no reason she couldn't enjoy herself, teasing Dominic and having fun, as long as she remembered he wasn't for keeps.

'What is that?' asked Dominic as Ettie gave a triumphant shout an hour later.

'It's a firepit!' she said, backing out of the shed, pulling the big circular piece of metal and wiping her rust-stained hands down her denim shorts. It was another beautiful sunny day and she'd dragged him out to the storage shed to do a long-overdue inventory of its contents. 'And there's another one in there. They'll be perfect. There's so much useful stuff in here, I can't believe it.'

'There's also an awful lot of junk,' he replied, touching a wheel-less wheelbarrow with one foot.

'You could plant flowers in that and put it somewhere in the garden. If it was filled with spring bulbs it would look fabulous.'

Dominic gave the broken wheelbarrow a dubious look.

'No, seriously.' She put her hands on her hips. 'It's perfect, and it's given me another idea. We could upcycle lots of things as part of the theme of the hotel. Not throwing things away but repurposing them. It's good for the environment.'

'Preserving a broken, rusty old wheelbarrow is not good for the environment.'

She rolled her eyes. 'It's better than throwing it into landfill.'

'If you say so,' he said with a long-suffering sigh.

'I say so,' she replied, cocking her head to one side.

'I thought you might.'

She grinned at him.

'In that case, I suggest that we empty the stable and sort it into two piles. Stuff we can use—'

'Stuff we can upcycle.'

'Stuff we can upcycle,' he acknowledged dryly, 'and stuff we can throw away.' As she went to open her mouth to protest, he added, 'Ettie, we have to throw some things away. Seriously.' He picked up a rotting hessian sack.

With a purse of her mouth, she nodded, accepting that he might be right.

A sweaty couple of hours later, Ettie was crowing with delight at the haul they'd found, including several wicker hanging chairs, an outdoor table set, a couple of parasols, a drinks trolley and a megaphone.

'That can go in the skip pile,' said Dominic, grasping the tarnished handle of the drinks trolley.

'No!' wailed Ettie, tugging it from him, squeezing her body between him and the trolley. 'This will clean up beautifully.'

'Are you sure?' he asked, doubt wrinkling his nose.

'Positive. Look, you just need to polish up the brass.' She pointed to the intricate filigreed metal around the edge of the glass top.

'I'm not sure it's worth the effort.'

'Of course it is. It just needs some tender loving care.'

'Does it now?' Dominic's voice dropped and his hands went to her waist, his fingers caressing the bare skin between her T-shirt and shorts. 'I know something else that needs some tender loving care.'

'You do?' She glanced up at him, her eyes full of mischief.

'Mmm,' he said, drawing her closer and nuzzling her neck with soft kisses.

She squirmed and giggled as his touch set her nerve endings tingling. She slid her hands down his chest, across the flat of his stomach, and paused, her fingers stroking the soft hair just above the waistband of his jeans.

His hands caressed her hip bone before cupping her bottom and pulling her against him.

'The wood will need special attention,' he muttered.

'It'll get it,' she whispered back. And then she giggled. 'There is no wood. It's all brass.'

He drew back and laughed. 'And you're distracting me.'

'I'm distracting *you*!' Ettie put her hands on her hips in mock outrage. 'Come on, back to work.'

'I thought *I* was the boss,' he grumbled, giving her a last kiss.

'Hmm, I just let you think that sometimes.'

He rolled his eyes and attacked the pile of rubbish again.

'Surely you're going to let me throw this away.' He held up a tin bucket with a hole in the bottom.

'Flower pot.'

He groaned. 'You said that about the chamber pot we found, the umbrella stand and that old colander.'

'Maybe not the colander.'

'You're ever the optimist.'

'Absolutely. If you spend too much time dwelling on the dark side, it will swallow you up.'

He glanced at her. 'That sounds … perceptive.'

She gave him a bright smile. 'Not really, but sometimes you have to fight through, don't you? Just because someone puts on a brave face doesn't mean we're always sparkly underneath.'

'Are you putting on a brave face?' He stepped forward and brushed her damp fringe from her eyes, his fingers smoothing over her cheek in an oddly reassuring gesture, as if he understood about putting on brave faces.

Ettie scrunched up her mouth and thought about her life and goals. At the moment she was just treading water, waiting for the next phase of her life. She might be enjoying herself enormously but at the back of her mind was always the knowledge that this was nothing but a no-man's-land between jobs. She was thirty and she still hadn't found an Ettie-shaped niche. At least she had her course to focus on, even if she found it deadly dull. It was a means to an end but it didn't fill her with joy.

'Not at the moment,' she said softly and then gave him a rueful smile. 'I'm having far too much fun. Are you putting on a brave face? Is your broken leg the reason why you left the Navy?'

She could see that when he tired, like now after a morning of carrying things to and fro, his limp became worse.

He stopped and put down the length of hosepipe he was carrying to the to-be-thrown-away pile and absently rubbed his thigh. 'The accident was a contributing factor, but I could have gone back after that. The main reason was for my wife. I thought it might…' His mouth twisted. 'As I said, my wife didn't cope well with me being away so much. And then there was…' Stopping, he looked down as if resigned to going through with this, before adding with a heavy sigh, 'She was pregnant. It seemed a good time to leave the Navy and stay at home.'

There was silence as they both turned back to the stable to separate a tangle of plastic chairs.

'Obviously, since we're now divorced, you can surmise that my being at home didn't suit her either.'

'I'm sorry.'

'Don't be. Turned out the baby wasn't mine. Although I didn't find that out for six months.' He grasped one of the broken chairs and hurled it through the door onto the rubbish pile. It landed with an angry clatter.

'What!' Ettie gasped. She couldn't help herself, she tossed the broken chair in her hand aside and in two quick steps crossed to put her arm around him and give him a hug. 'I'm so sorry.' She squeezed him tighter and was pleased when she felt the muscles in his arms beneath her fingers relax a fraction. 'How awful. For you, I mean.' She caught her lip between her teeth. That had to be the worst thing anyone could do to someone. 'That really is…'

'It was a bit shit. A lot shit, actually. Bryony, that was my … the little girl's name. She was…' He sighed and she could hear his pain in the sharp huff of expelled air, as if it hurt to release the breath. In profile his jaw was granite-hard, as if any more words were stuck tight behind his teeth.

She didn't want to fill the silence but at the same time

she didn't want him to suffer, which she realised was a little bit arrogant of her, imagining that she could help. 'I wondered why you were so good with Tiffany Eight,' she murmured, releasing him, realising he wanted to talk but guessing he felt more comfortable doing so as he worked. She picked up another chair.

'I had a bit of practice. More fool me, I insisted on being a hands-on dad. Wanted to be involved. Make up for being away so much.'

'Do you still see her?'

'No.' There was a world of sorrow in that one word. He kicked at a couple of loose bricks which had tumbled from the wall. 'Paula made it as difficult as possible. Moving to Scotland, for starters. Turns out that's where Bryony's real father comes from. I have no rights and Paula said it would be weird for me to insist on being involved with a child that wasn't actually mine, especially when her own father was on the scene. When she put it like that, all I could see was endless trouble ahead. Bryony isn't my daughter. I thought it would be easier to make a clean break.' He looked ahead, his eyes fixed on a distant point, and Ettie thought she could see a slight sheen to their surface. 'It wasn't.'

Her heart constricted and she put her hand out and took his, squeezing his fingers gently because it felt like the right thing to do. 'That is shit,' she murmured.

'Yeah, it is, or rather it was. I have to put it behind me, but it makes... Well, I find it hard to trust people.'

'Understandable,' said Ettie. She couldn't imagine not having contact with her niece. She might not have seen her very often but the little girl had stolen a piece of her heart the very first time she'd seen her. Poor Dominic.

'Actually, you're everything that Paula wasn't. Open, honest, you say what you think and you challenge me.' He looked at her, with a quick smile.

Realising that he was ready to move on from the subject, she grinned at him. 'Now what about this canoe?'

'It's definitely seen better days. There's a massive crack down the side and if you suggest we turn it into a planter, I'll make you fill it with compost using a teaspoon.'

She held up both hands in surrender. 'OK. I'll order a skip this afternoon.'

'Thank God for that. I mean, I'm all for a bit of upcycling, but I don't want the place to look like a jumble sale.'

Ettie had to admit he had a point. She nodded. 'I'll add this watering can to the out pile.' It was beyond both physical and cosmetic repair, and even she had to admit defeat sometimes.

Any chance you can keep your boss tied up for a few hours this afternoon?

Ettie glanced at the message on her phone from Grandad. What was he up to now? And why had he used the Wednesday message group? She huffed out a small sigh.

'Everything all right?' asked Dominic from the desk

opposite. They'd both had to have showers after clearing out the stable this morning, and now he looked neat and cool again. Ettie couldn't decide which she preferred – him hot and sweaty or neat and tidy, with that slightly stern frown as he worked.

'Yes, fine. My family driving me nuts as usual.'

'They do that?'

'Do they ever.'

She picked up her phone and typed back a short, brutal message.

No, why?

It's an emergency. I need to use the lake. And I need you to help.

How can that be an emergency?

Do you need any help? Hazel's message flashed on the screen.

Bums! That was all she needed. A three-way conversation.

Hilda: *I could stage an intervention.*

Grandad: *No, I just need to have the lake to myself for half an hour, with Ettie on standby as lifeguard.*

Gracie: *Half an hour? We can sort that, can't we, Ettie?*

Great, now Gracie had pitched in.

NO.

Ettie knew capitals were rude, but seriously!

'You're pulling an awful lot of faces for someone who is fine,' observed Dominic with a barely concealed smirk.

Ettie pasted a bland smile on her face and pushed her phone out of reach. She had work to do.

She ignored her phone, which vibrated with a series of new messages. Grandad's emergency would just have to wait.

'Ah, Dominic. There you are.' Gracie bustled in and gave Ettie an extremely unsubtle meaningful look. 'I need to go shopping.'

He looked up from his desk with surprise. Gracie rarely asked for anything, let alone made demands. 'What – now?' he asked with a frown and a glance back at his laptop.

'Yes, well, in half an hour.'

'What for?'

'What for?' she echoed.

'Yes, what do you need to go shopping for?'

'Er … ingredients. Yes, I need ingredients to … er … erm … to practise a new cake recipe.'

'This afternoon?' He scrunched his head in sceptical query.

'Yes,' said Gracie with a sudden burst of confidence. 'Vegan cake. I need to try some vegan recipes. I read an article and a lot more people, especially youngsters, are going vegan now. We need to be able to offer a good vegan menu. So, I need different ingredients and to cook a cake to make sure the recipe works. In preparation. You know.'

'What sort of ingredients?' asked Dominic, narrowing his eyes in interest. 'What sort of cake are you thinking of? Could you do biscuits as well? Perhaps we could offer vegan afternoon teas.'

'Oh,' said Gracie, clearly taken aback by Dominic's unexpected enthusiasm.

'That's a brilliant idea. You've got it exactly right. That's what our guests will expect.'

'Oh,' Gracie preened a little. 'Well, you know.'

'Yes, fantastic. Get right on it. And Ettie can take you.'

Gracie's eyes widened in horror and her rabbit-in-the-headlights appearance had Ettie focusing on her computer screen, in a desperate bid not to give in to the sudden bubble of laughter that rose in her throat.

'Oh, oh, oh,' Gracie spluttered, shooting a help-me-out-here look of panic towards Ettie.

Ettie frowned. 'I'm sort of in the middle of something,' she said. 'This spreadsheet is ... you know.' The spreadsheet was a pain in the butt because she was trying to consolidate all the different quotes from all the different suppliers so that Dominic could manage his cash flow over the next few months. It wasn't complicated, just dull.

'I'm sure Ettie's far too busy, aren't you, dear?' She turned to Ettie with a beseeching expression on her face.

Dominic stared at her but before he could point out, as Ettie was sure he would, that he was equally busy, Gracie added, 'Besides, I need a big strong man to carry everything.'

'How much are you planning to buy?'

Gracie shrugged. 'Enough. You don't mind, Dominic, do you? I'm sure you could do with a break. You're working far too hard. It can't be good for your eyes. On the computer all the time.'

'What about Ettie?'

'Oh, she's younger than you.' Gracie dismissed his concerns with a blithe wave of her hand.

Dominic sighed. 'Can you give me half an hour?'

'Oh, three quarters will be fine. I need to make some lists.' She disappeared back to the kitchen, shooting Ettie a quick look of triumph.

Ettie closed her eyes and breathed a tiny sigh. She didn't even dare look at her phone. It seemed Gracie had taken charge.

'Nice to see her so enthusiastic,' commented Dominic.

'Mmm,' said Ettie, her eyes glued to her screen. If she started laughing now, she'd give the game away.

A few minutes later, she got up, discreetly palmed her phone and went to the loo to catch up on the WhatsApp group chat.

I can get him out. Leave it with me, Gracie had messaged.

Grandad: *Great. Let me know timings. Ettie, get yourself down to the beach. Ready to swim if you need to.*

What the heck was he up to? Why did he need her?

OK. Thunderbirds are go. We have lift-off. Leaving at 3 hundred hours. Ettie will text you the minute we've gone.

Dear God, Gracie had gone full ninja.

Some of us have work to do.

Ettie's sarcasm went straight over Grandad's head.

See you at the lake.

Chapter Sixteen

The minute Gracie and Dominic left, Ettie raced up the stairs and put her costume on under her clothes. Curiosity had won and she was dying to know what Grandad was up to. Just as she approached the lake, she heard the familiar buzz of his decrepit motorbike haring across the grass towards her. Today, however, there was a sidecar attached that she was horribly familiar with, and in it was a small, begoggled, helmeted person reminiscent of a *Star Wars* character. Intrigued, Ettie picked up her pace and drew level with the beach at the same time as Grandad.

'Ettie, lass. Good of you to come.'

'I'm not sure I had much choice.'

'What's she doing here?' grumbled a sour voice.

Ettie peered at the person in the old-fashioned goggles.

'Shush lad, she's a trained lifeguard. I promised your mother I wouldn't let you drown.'

'I'm not going in.' The boy folded his arms and stuck his chin out.

'Course you are. That's why we're here,' said Grandad matter-of-factly, as if it wasn't even up for debate.

Ettie squinted again. 'Josh?'

'Yes.' The boy took off the goggles and helmet. 'Can you tell your grandad to eff off and leave me alone?' He folded his arms again, high on his chest, his shoulders hunched up round his ears, like a defiant toddler.

'I can certainly try,' said Ettie as pleasantly as she could. 'But he won't listen to me.'

'I'm not a kid.' He shot her a belligerent stare, obviously keen to remind her that her babysitting days were long gone. 'And I don't want to be *taken out for the day.*' He assumed a childish, derisive tone for the final phrase.

Grandad raised his eyes heavenward. 'Do you need a hand getting out of there?' He pulled out the crutches from behind Josh and held them out.

'No,' snarled Josh, snatching them from him. 'I can do it.'

Ettie covertly studied him as he arranged his arms into the cuffs of his crutches. She'd not seen him for a few years and puberty had burst on him with all the meanness that adolescent hormones could convey. He had a pathetic outcrop of fluff on his chin, a rash of spots across his forehead and lank, greasy hair that flopped into his eyes. Added to that, his face was twisted with an unfortunate sneer that deepened the lines around his mouth. Life had not been kind to him, that was for sure. His father had left when he was three and then the car crash a year ago had left him with his leg amputated below the knee.

Josh hauled himself up onto his crutches and manoeuvred his way out of the sidecar, with careful concentration and a whole lot of determination. Neither Grandad nor Ettie gave in to the temptation to try and help, but both stood by like a nervous mare watching her foal's first wobbly steps.

Once Josh was on firm ground again, Grandad turned to him. 'You're not being taken out for the day. You've come for a swim. Get some exercise.'

Josh's scowl deepened. 'I don't want to effing swim. I already told you.'

'Well, we're here now. You might as well give it a go. I said to your mam, I'd get you out of her hair for a while, give the poor woman a break.'

Ettie had to bite her tongue. Talk about tactless! What was Grandad playing at?

'All right,' Josh's voice rose in a burst of resentment. 'You don't need to go on about it. I'm a burden. I know that. Completely useless, aren't I?'

'All we're going to do is go for a swim. Or are you too chicken?'

Ettie's eyes widened but she held onto the gasp of 'Grandad!' that she'd been about to utter.

'I ain't chicken.'

'Prove it,' said Grandad. 'Bet you can't swim to that island and back before me.'

Josh glared at him, anger pooling and smoking in his

dark-grey eyes. 'Hello. One leg.'

'There are plenty of swimmers in the Paralympics with one leg. I'm not asking you to break a world record.' Grandad lifted one shoulder in an indifferent shrug.

'Yeah, to be fair, Grandad, how's he supposed to keep up with you, what with you being seventy and all,' said Ettie, catching on to what Grandad was up to.

Josh turned his angry gaze her way and she could guess from the high spots of colour on both cheeks that his blood was simmering. His fingers gripping the crutch handles were white, the tendons standing proud as if they might burst from under his skin at any second.

Without warning, he wheeled round and, swinging his crutches at a furious pace, hopped down towards the wooden jetty. She and Grandad followed, neither of them saying a word. It felt like they'd stirred up a hornets' nest and any moment they might get stung.

At the end, he tossed one of the crutches to the side, using the other to lower himself awkwardly down onto the edge of the jetty, his solitary leg hanging over the side. For a moment he hunched over, his shoulders rounded, and Ettie's heart went out to him. He looked so young and defenceless. Maybe Grandad was being too harsh with him. She bit her lip and gave Grandad a beseeching look. 'Don't you think you're being a bit hard on him?' she asked softly.

Grandad's faded blue eyes met hers and he shook his head. 'Don't worry, lass. I know what I'm about.'

'You'd better get a move on, Grandad,' said Ettie softly.

'Thanks, love.'

Grandad stripped off and sat down next to Josh. 'Coming in?'

Josh's thin shoulders lifted in a half-hearted shrug.

Ettie walked down the jetty and sat down on the other side of Josh.

'You don't have to go in,' she said. 'No one can make you do anything you don't want to. And if you can't do it, it doesn't matter.'

'I can if I want to!' Josh spat like a cobra striking, and in one fluid movement, he peeled off his top and began to wriggle out of his shorts. Then he paused and looked at the water. 'And I don't have to go in, if I don't want to.'

'Swimming's good for your upper-body strength,' said Grandad. 'No one's here. No one can see you. What have you got to lose?

'I might drown,' said Josh, although the petulance was fading from his voice.

'Doubt it. We won't let you. Your mother would have my balls on toast for breakfast if I let anything happen to you.'

His words brought a startled laugh from Josh. 'It's almost worth drowning to see that,' he said.

'Not from where I'm sitting,' said Grandad with a mock-dramatic shudder.

Suddenly he leaned forward and, as he went into the water, he grabbed Josh's arm and took him with him.

Ettie froze as Josh went underwater and came up spluttering, shaking the water from his hair like a dog.

'What did do you that for?' he yelled at Grandad.

'Didn't want you to chicken out.'

Josh pushed an angry hand through the water, sending an arc up to hit Grandad squarely in the face.

Grandad laughed. 'Come on, then.'

Ettie stood on the jetty and watched as Grandad set off with his usual powerful strokes. Every nerve was alert in case she had to jump in. At the moment, Josh was waving his arms about to help him keep afloat, bobbing up and down. Grandad certainly believed in throwing people in at the deep end.

She bit her lip, watching Josh floundering about. Then he put his leg down.

'I can stand here,' he said.

'That's good.'

'I'll never get out.'

'Yes, you will. Grandad and I will help you.'

'You're not carrying me. I'm not a baby.' He stood in the water, swaying slightly, but his face had relaxed. He hopped up and down experimentally, waving his arms backwards and forwards, a thoughtful expression in his eyes. Ettie could almost see him testing himself, trying to work out what he was capable of.

Grandad was now swimming back towards them.

'How's the water?'

''S OK,' said Josh. He spread out his arms as if practising his balance, moving them through the water to keep him upright.

'And how're you doing, lad? Up for a swim?' asked Grandad.

'I'm in the water, what more do you want?'

'That's a start. I'll leave you to it for a while.' With that, he turned and swam off again back towards the island.

Ettie realised that Josh might be feeling a little bit self-conscious, so she sat down, ducked her head and began studying her mobile phone screen as if she were totally absorbed. From under her fringe, she could just peek at Josh and keep an eye on him.

At first he just hopped about like a baby robin taking its first steps out of the nest. But then she watched as he firmed his mouth with sudden resolution and launched into breast stroke. She held her breath, poised to dive in if she needed to, but as she watched, she could see both his legs kicking out in rhythm with his forward strokes, and while his course was a little skew-whiff, he was swimming well and moving quickly through the water.

Ettie kept a careful eye on him as he struck out towards the island, but he looked strong and confident. She began to smile as he got closer. He'd done it. When he reached the island he turned round and began to swim back. This time he looked a lot more relaxed. He'd proved he could do it. Grandad waited for him, treading water.

'He's doing really well,' she said.

'Aye,' said Grandad, not looking her way. 'Isn't he just?' His voice cracked just a little. 'He were always … a good little swimmer when he were a kid. I knew he could do it.' A big broad smile wreathed his face, and Ettie was pretty sure that the sheen in his eyes had nothing to do with the lake water.

Josh swam closer, his strokes never faltering.

'Well done, lad,' said Grandad.

Josh's eyes were wide and his mouth was a little 'o' of wonder. 'I did it. I did it! I can swim.'

'You certainly did. I were a bit sad when you gave up swimming club when you were a kid. Always thought you had a lot of promise. You've always had good technique.'

Josh shrugged in the water but Ettie could tell he was pleased.

'Want to have a go at freestyle? That might be even better for you.'

Josh swallowed and gave him a nonchalant nod of the head. 'Might as well.'

He launched into front crawl. Ettie nodded to herself – the boy had excellent technique. He raised his arms nicely out of the water with a good clean stroke, close to his head, and he had good pull, although she could see that kicking with one leg meant he veered a tiny bit off course every other stroke. But given it was his first swim, he was doing well.

Grandad swam alongside him and from what she could see, he wasn't holding back but doing his usually powerful crawl, and Josh was keeping abreast of him.

They swam out to the island, turned and swam back. As they neared the jetty, Grandad slowed right down, letting Josh pull ahead. When he drew level with the jetty, and put his foot down, Josh allowed himself a small triumphant smile, the barest twitch of his lips, although his chest was heaving.

'Well done, lad.'

Josh simply nodded and concentrated on breathing, clearly out of practice. It was probably the first heart-racing exercise he'd done for a while.

'That's probably enough for one day,' said Grandad.

'But I've hardly done any distance,' protested Josh. 'I used to swim loads more than that.'

'You've got to take it easy to start with.'

'Eff that,' said Josh, and began to swim back out towards the island again. Grandad shot Ettie a smug grin.

'He's quite tired. He shouldn't overdo it,' said Ettie, a little worried.

'That's why you're here. But he wants to do it. I'm not going to stop him. First time he's wanted to do anything in a long while.'

Josh's initial speed faded quite quickly and although he made it to the island, his return journey was extremely slow. However, when he drew level with the jetty again, he held his head high, and his eyes shone with renewed light. His chest was heaving but there was a clear pride in his achievement. Ettie sniffed, swallowing back a tear.

'Right, lad. That's enough for me. I'm an old man, you know,' said Grandad. Ettie refrained from pointing out that Grandad could outswim most people and could easily have swum for another hour.

Josh nodded. 'Yeah, don't want to give you a heart attack or anything.' He grinned, he actually grinned. 'Now I've got to get out of here.'

'You'll manage, lad,' said Grandad. 'You can do anything you want.'

Josh looked at him. 'Not sure about that, but I can swim.'

'You certainly can.'

Ettie retrieved Josh's crutches as he swam towards the shore. Once he reached the shallows he swam right up until he beached himself, and then sat in the water until she waded out.

She handed a crutch to him and he took it.

'Hang on,' he said, still catching his breath. After a minute he inched his way to standing, holding onto the crutch, putting one hand over the other as he hauled himself up the stick before reaching out for the second one. Ettie handed it over and then stood back as he hopped his way up the beach. Grandad tossed a towel around his shoulders and led the way over to a flat rock. 'I brought hot chocolate. Thought you might like some.'

Josh leaned against the rock, dropping his crutches and taking the small plastic cup.

'That'll warm you up,' said Grandad encouragingly, but the boy didn't respond. He sipped at the hot chocolate, his eyes firmly fixed on the horizon.

Grandad poured one for Ettie too and the three of them stood in companionable silence. Ettie didn't say anything, not wanting to break the portentous feeling that surrounded them.

Eventually Josh turned to Grandad. 'You were right.' He paused and a slow smile lit his face. 'I bloody loved that. It's like being me again.' He swallowed hard and blinked.

'You're welcome, lad.'

'Can I come again?'

'Course you can,' said Grandad looking at Ettie.

'Here, I mean. I don't want to go to the pool. Everyone staring at me. I hate that.'

'You can come here as often as you like,' said Grandad.

'Grandad! You can't say that.'

'Why not? You can fix it for us, can't you?'

Ettie rolled her eyes.

'What's the problem?' asked Josh.

'It's private property,' explained Ettie. 'I work here, but no one is supposed to swim in the lake. We managed to get rid of the boss for the afternoon.'

'So I can't come again.' Josh's face fell.

'Yes, you can,' she said before she could think it through. 'We'll sort something out.' She had access to Dominic's calendar and she knew his general routine.

'Really?' His eyes met hers, widening with hope.

How could she possibly say no to him?

'Yes,' she repeated. She'd find a way.

'That'll be great, our Ettie. He can always come on a Wednesday morning, and all.'

She sighed. Wednesday mornings seemed to be taking on a life of their own, but she didn't seem to be able to stop it. All she could do was pray that Dominic never found out. How would he react when he discovered she'd been keeping things from him?

Chapter Seventeen

'What time is the tightrope man arriving?' asked Dom, a few days later.

'Two o'clock,' said Ettie, consulting her calendar.

'Can you handle him on your own?'

'No, I need you to come. He needs guinea pigs – quite a few, to simulate what a class might look like.' She paused. 'Gracie has invited a few people.'

'Gracie has? Who?'

'Er, just a few local people.'

'I didn't think Gracie knew anyone around here.'

'They're …' Oh God, how did she explain this one? '… friends of friends.' That was very nearly the truth, if you counted them as Ettie's friends in the first instance.

'Well, won't having them be enough? You don't need me as well, do you?'

'We need a full demographic; you'll plug the gap, as it will be all women.' Dominic had to come. Grandad was taking Josh for another swim this afternoon. 'Besides, you really ought to try it, so that if a guest asks about it, you can be informative.'

Dominic pulled a face.

'Don't be like that. You should be prepared to do everything that you're offering to your guests.' And Ettie could text Grandad and tell him that the coast would be clear. During the last few days Dominic hadn't left Hepplethwaite Hall and Grandad had been badgering her to let him know when he could bring Josh back. Unfortunately, he'd been communicating via the WhatsApp group, so now Gracie was in on the act, and right on cue, she marched into the office with a tray of coffee.

'I'm going to have a go,' she announced. 'So should you.'

'Are you?' asked Dom, surprised.

'Yes. I'm trying everything. And I need you and Ettie to come to the kitchen so that I can practise my breadmaking workshop out on you.' She winked at Ettie. 'That'll take a little while.'

'Do you need me as well? Won't Ettie do for your pet project?'

'No, she won't. I need to manage more than one person and I need to see how it's done. I was planning to limit the workshops to six people at a time. I think that will work.'

'Maybe we could do that on Tuesday afternoon,' said Ettie, mentally ticking off another day for Grandad and Josh.

'I am trying to set up a hotel here, you know.' Dominic's eyebrows drew together.

'And all work and no play makes Dominic a dull boy,' said Gracie. 'You need to enjoy yourself a bit more. In fact, I think you should take Ettie down to the pub, one evening after work. The Old Tradition is doing an exotic burger night on Thursday. They've got crocodile, buffalo, that sort of thing. You'd like that, wouldn't you, Ettie?'

'Yes, I've always wanted to try crocodile burgers,' said Ettie brightly, giving Gracie an I-don't-believe-you look. The woman had the subtlety of a sledgehammer.

'But seriously,' said Gracie, 'a break from this place would do both of you the power of good.'

Dominic glanced up. 'I wouldn't mind a pint and I'd quite like to check the pub out. If it's half decent, we could recommend it to visitors, but if it's awful we'll know not to.'

'Excellent idea,' said Gracie, her voice rising in mock enthusiasm.

Ettie could already imagine her triumphant messages to Grandad.

Marcus Marcusman rocked up at two o'clock on the dot wearing drainpipe blue-and-black tartan trousers hoisted a good three inches above his skinny bare ankles, a tight, pale-blue tie-dyed T-shirt which stretched over his broad but sinewy chest, with a red circus-ringmaster jacket slung over one shoulder. All this teamed with the barely-there

Rhett Butler moustache made him the sort of person you definitely took a second look at.

'Hello,' he bellowed with enthusiasm as if she was his new best friend. 'I'm Marcus. So good to meet you.' For a moment Ettie thought he was going to throw his arms around her and hug her on the front doorstep.

'Hi. I'm Ettie, we spoke on the phone.'

'Wow, this is some place! And I'm just so excited to be here. I mean, it's such a cool idea. No one else is doing this. It's going to be immense.'

'I certainly hope so,' said Ettie, smiling at his infectious enthusiasm.

'It will be, don't you worry. Marcus Marcusman will see to it!' He patted her on the arm. 'All my customers love me by the end. Especially the big burly men.' He winked at her. 'Especially them. So … where do you want me?'

'It's a bit of a walk, because we want to do it in a woodland glade. I think I explained we want to make this place a sort of back-to-nature retreat.'

'Cool.' His eyes shone. In fact, nearly everything about Marcus sparkled. He was one of life's happy, positive people. 'And perfect for setting up.'

'Yes. Have you got any kit or equipment?'

'Just this.' He nudged a big black bag with one of his feet.

'Is that all?' Ettie was intrigued.

'Yes. I'll just set up a slackline today. Easy to do between two trees. I do have a portable tightwire, but let's see how we get on today. That's a bit more advanced and heavy-duty.'

'Do you need any help? It's quite a long walk.' She was loath to suggest using the quad bike because it would give Dominic the chance to move quickly if he decided not to carry on, and she'd got Grandad lined up to take Josh swimming in about ten minutes.

'No, darling. It's fine. I'm a big strong young man.' He held up his arms and, though skinny, they were impressively muscular.

She led the way through the house, stopping at the office doorway to round Dominic up.

'Come on.'

'Give me a minute. Why don't you go on ahead?'

'No,' said Ettie firmly. 'You'll wimp out, find something important to do. This is Marcus, by the way.'

'Hi there,' trilled Marcus. 'A big strong fella like you isn't going to wimp out, are you?'

Dominic looked as if he might strangle Ettie. He gave Marcus a tight smile, while glaring at Ettie – it was quite an achievement, she decided. 'I'm not wimping out of anything. I'm just busy.'

'Not that busy,' said Ettie, marching over and removing the mobile phone from his hand. 'It's a gorgeous day and as Gracie keeps telling you, some fresh air will do you good.'

With a show of reluctance, Dominic got up from his desk and they walked through to the kitchen.

'Hello, dears, are we all set?' Gracie picked up her phone. 'You must be the tightrope man.' With her usual lack of subtlety, she tapped out a message on her phone, and Ettie felt a WhatsApp message ping on her phone in her pocket. She could only imagine what Gracie had said, probably something along the lines of *Thunderbirds are go*. The woman was enjoying this subterfuge malarkey a bit too much; Ettie might just have to rename her Jane Bond.

'I've arranged to meet the others at the stable block,' said Gracie. 'We'll scoop them up on the way.'

'Who are these friends of yours?' asked Dominic.

'Just friends, dear.' Gracie waved an airy hand. 'Now, young man, you must tell me, how does one go about becoming a tightrope walker? It's fascinating.'

'Well, the official term is a funambulist, and…'

Gracie led him off out of earshot and Ettie waited for Dominic.

'Come on, there's no getting out of this. It might even be fun. That *is* the whole point of it.' She paused and studied his face. 'Do you ever have fun?'

'Yes.' He raised an eyebrow.

'Outside the bedroom,' she said with a reproving smile.

'I've got a lot on my plate at the moment.'

'Maybe you need to be the first person on the retreat once it's up and running,' she teased with a mischievous grin. 'I think you're exactly the sort of customer we need.'

Dominic pursed his lips and then let a smile sneak through. 'Sometimes you forget who the boss is here.'

'Ah, he doesn't mind really. Come on, get your dancing shoes on, we're going tightrope walking.'

'Why does that fill me with a sense of foreboding?'

'What's the worst that can happen?'

'I can fall off.'

'It's only a foot or so off the ground.'

'Someone can drown in a few inches of water, so I suspect they could break their neck falling from a foot or so.'

Ettie stared at him, wondering why he'd chosen the example of water.

'Do you have a problem with water?' she asked suddenly.

He snorted. 'I was in the Navy. I have a healthy respect for the dangers of water.' There was a coldness to his words, intimating that there was perhaps a little more to it. Now wasn't the time to ask him.

'If we're going, we'd better go,' he said, interrupting her thoughts. 'I've got things to do today.'

By the time they reached the clearing, Marcus had already looped one end of a yellow rope around a tree trunk and was walking to a second tree with the other end in his hand. Gracie was standing with Hazel, Jane, Hilda and, to Ettie's surprise, Rachel. Ettie closed her eyes. What if Dominic recognised them? Surely he'd start asking questions. Luckily they all looked quite different in their clothes, with dry hair. Rachel actually looked stunning, with long, straight, silky dark-red hair and matching Lululemon leggings and running top. With her slim, lithe body she had the appearance of a proper athlete. Next to her, Jane, with a halo of grey curls and loose sweatpants, was the polar opposite, along with Hilda wearing a violet tracksuit and day-glo trainers. Hazel turned and smiled at Ettie, who held her breath. *Pretend you don't know me.*

'Ah Ettie, Dominic. This is Hazel, Jane, Hilda and Rachel.' Gracie did the introductions and Ettie breathed an internal sigh of relief.

'Hello,' said Dominic, barely registering them, his gaze fixed on the equipment that Marcus was setting up. 'I'll just see if he wants a hand.' Ettie grinned to herself.

A moment later she could see him asking Marcus lots of questions and tugging at the fixings around the tree. Dominic was the sort of man who wanted to know how things worked. Marcus was talking back to him animatedly, demonstrating the clips.

On the breeze she heard the sound of a motorbike and glanced at Dominic to see if he'd heard it, but thankfully he seemed absorbed in whatever Marcus was explaining.

Ettie wandered over. 'Oh, it's more like a flat tape than a rope,' she said when she got close enough to observe the thin yellow band.

'Yes, this is called a slackwire. Much easier for beginners. It's a training wire, helps you get your balance and centre of gravity. Once you've mastered this, you progress onto the tightwire. That takes a bit of skill and practice. I'm not sure you're going to want to offer that, but you can certainly see after today's lesson.' He beamed at Dominic. 'We've got a good selection of ages here. Shame we haven't got any kids, but they always pick it up quickly.'

Once the wire was secured to his liking, Marcus clapped his hands. 'Gather round, people. Welcome to the ancient art of funambulism, also known as tightrope walking. Anyone done it before?'

Everyone shook their heads, apart from Hilda. 'Back in the day, a team I was with was planning on storming a building in … well, I can't say where … but the access was difficult, and we considered doing it across two roofs, but we realised it would take too long to train and too much could go wrong.'

Everyone blinked at her.

'Right, who wants to have a go first?'

'I will,' said Hazel, stepping forward. 'In for a penny, in for a pound.'

Marcus stood beside her and helped her up onto the tightrope, taking a lot of her weight. 'All I want you to do is stand.'

Of course, Hazel was bending and bowing like a sail in the high seas, even with Marcus holding her.

'Try to stand as straight as you can, one foot in front of the other.'

Hazel continued to sway.

'Right. Next.'

One by one they all had a go, and not one of them could stand still, let alone take a step, except Hilda, who did manage to stay still for at least ten seconds.

'Bloody glad I didn't take the roof in Budapest,' said Hilda when she fell off the rope.

'Not easy, is it?' said Marcus when they'd all taken their turns. 'That's because you need to know the fundamentals. We're going to do a few exercises and then we'll try again, and you'll find it so much easier. Sorry, folks, but I want you to feel the difference and to realise you've actually learned something.

'First things first, you need to be relaxed. Most of you got on the wire and immediately tensed, and the minute you tense, you fire the wrong muscles. It's all about internal muscles. Your core needs to be strong, and those are the muscles that you'll be firing. Everything else needs to be loose. So, we're going to start by shaking all that tension out.'

For the next five minutes, Marcus had everyone shaking their hands, arms, legs and feet – 'shaking like snakes', he said with a gleeful gleam in his eyes. 'You gotta loosen everything up. Come on, Dom, man – give it a bit of welly. You won't lose a foot. Imagine you're trying to get a really stuck welly boot off. That's right, fling that welly off across the woods. Now Hazel, you can do better than that, those arms are stiffer than an ironing board, and who wants to be an ironing board? Jane, you're doing great! Rachel, darling! Don't think so hard about it. This is fun, fun, fun! That's the style, Hilda, I can tell you mean business!' Marcus used a lot of exclamation marks but everyone was responding; even Rachel managed a smile.

Next he had them all standing on one leg, which was fine until he asked them to close their eyes, and Ettie could feel herself wobbling all over the place.

'Now open them,' said Marcus. 'And focus on one spot, concentrate on drawing your stomach muscles in to strengthen your core. Doesn't that feel easier?'

'Not a lot,' said Jane, her right foot hovering a few inches from the ground.

They practised a few balancing exercises and then Marcus hopped up onto the slackwire. 'You need to keep your balance centred, so it's important to stand up straight with your arms equally outstretched on either side. It's all about keeping your weight centrally. Imagine you're a pair of scales and you need to keep the balance dead in the middle. Once you've mastered that...' He grinned at everyone and nimbly walked the full length of the tape, making it look easy.

'Right, who wants to have a go now? All I want you to do is stand and feel your centre. Remember how it felt when you were standing on one leg. Focus on a spot and on your core. You need to have one foot in front of the other, and you need to lead with your dominant foot.'

This time Rachel, who'd been the best at balancing on one leg, was keen to step up. Determination lined her mouth as Marcus helped her up onto the rope. After a few wobbles, she managed to stand quite still, her eyes glassy as she focused on the tree ahead. 'How does it feel this time?'

'Completely different,' she said, not looking round.

'Now, holding onto your core muscles, keep your range of movement very small. Take a step, sliding your foot forwards rather than out to the side. Believe it or not, it's actually easier to do it faster rather than slower.'

Rachel managed quite a few steps but each time she came off, she hopped straight back on. 'God, it's addictive,' she said when her turn was finally up. 'Each time I want to master it.'

'Your Pilates training has paid off – that's given you a strong core and excellent balance.' She also had the necessary mental focus.

No one else was quite as good as Rachel. Ettie was a complete disaster; she didn't seem to have any control over her limbs once she was up on the rope, even though she'd always thought, with all her swimming, her core was quite strong. But the great thing was how supportive everyone was of each other, cheering and clapping, laughing when they fell over.

At one point Ettie caught Dominic's eye and he gave her one of those smiles. He looked so much more relaxed. She felt she'd made a difference, not just to him but to all of them. Today they'd come together in rare accord, and something inside her brightened at the sight of them all standing companionably in one group.

It made her soul smile…

When Marcus wrapped up the session, everyone returned to Gracie's kitchen where she doled out freshly made scones and big mugs of tea.

'That was so much fun,' said Rachel, her cheeks glowing. It was the most alive that Ettie had seen her.

'It was hilarious, but I'm not sure I'll try it again,' said Jane.

'Don't worry, doll,' said Marcus, patting her arm. 'You tried and you had fun.'

'I definitely had fun.'

Everyone around the table had a smile on their face, especially Dominic, who hadn't been much of a slackwire walker. 'Marcus, this turned out so much better than I expected. I'd definitely like to make it a regular fixture for the first couple of months. Perhaps a session every week, on a Saturday or Sunday morning. Why don't you come to the office and we'll talk terms?'

Marcus jumped to his feet. 'Sounds like a plan. Lovely to meet you, ladies, and thanks for being such brilliant guinea pigs. It all went better than I could have imagined.'

Dominic led him away and everyone around the table visibly relaxed.

Gracie got out her phone. 'Josh and Cyril have just finished. Mission accomplished.'

'And Sir didn't recognise any of us,' said Hazel with a naughty gleam in her eye.

'Thank goodness,' said Ettie with a quick grin. 'And honestly, he's a good guy. He's just...' She shrugged, not finishing the sentence, not wanting to be disloyal. Yes, he had a bee in his bonnet about swimming in the lake but... 'He's got a lot on his plate, but he's kind, and when you get to know him, he's the sort of person you know you can rely on.' And he was honest and loyal, thoughtful and lots of things that she wasn't about to share, because she wanted to keep the warm glow about how he made her feel locked up inside her.

'So, who's up for a bit of bread-making, same time next week?' asked Gracie with a well-timed interjection.

'Yes, please,' said Rachel without a second's hesitation.

'Why not?' said Jane, nudging Hazel.

'I'll watch,' said Hazel.

'You could learn, you never know. You might be quite good.'

'I'm a disaster in the kitchen and you know it, that's why I'm banned most of the time.' Hazel turned to the others. 'Seriously, there's not much I haven't burned. She won't even let me make toast.'

'It's more the mess you leave. I'd let you in if you could make bread,' teased Jane, 'and tidy up afterwards.'

'I'm sure being messy is a sign of creativity,' said Hazel with a lofty smile, although her eyes were warm as they rested on Jane's face.

'In that case, Ettie is a creative genius,' said Gracie. 'You should see the state of her desk.'

'I know where everything is.'

'Just as well, because no one else does.'

Being tidy didn't come naturally to Ettie and some people – previous bosses – had taken it as a sign of being disorganised. She preferred to say she was too busy doing other things and getting things done to be bothered about tidying things up. In the vintage clothes shop, Sally had complained that there were clothes everywhere in the changing room, but what she'd failed to understand was that this also equated to increased sales. By being so amenable and bringing lots of things to try on, Ettie was very good at persuading customers to buy more.

'Talking of which, I need to get back to my desk. Good to see you all.' She included Rachel in her nod because Rachel had actually been quite bearable today. 'See you bright and early on Wednesday.'

'Enjoy the crocodile burgers,' said Jane as Ettie left the room.

Chapter Eighteen

The following Wednesday they were the first at the lake, which worried Ettie slightly as Gracie wasn't a particularly strong swimmer.

'Don't go out of your depth,' she said in warning.

'I'm not going to, dear. I'll just do my little doggy paddle.'

Perhaps because of the contrast of the warm summer sun, the water felt even colder than usual around her ankles, but Ettie still laughed as Gracie did her usual 'oooh' and 'aaah' wails, splashing water up her arms in the mistaken belief that it would make it easier to brave the temperature of the lake.

'It's best to get in quickly,' said Ettie, preparing to wade in and expose herself to the shock of the cold.

'I'm not that brave.'

Ettie clenched her stomach muscles and waded in, ignoring the quick icy bite against her skin, reminding herself that once she was in she'd soon warm up. During her first few strokes she gritted her teeth, swimming hard, and although it took a few determined minutes, gradually her body acclimatised and the temperature was bearable. Her breathing came slow and sure, and with it that wonderful confidence in the ability of her body as it glided through the water. The usual calm descended, her mind rounding up all its scattered thoughts, corralling them into one place, so that she could tick through them one by one.

She slowed to turn and check back on Gracie, who had now got into the water and was swimming with splashy uncoordinated strokes. Ettie had to admire the other woman's determined fortitude; she wasn't a natural swimmer, yet she was giving it a go. Ettie's heart clenched in sudden sympathy for her. Gracie was giving everything a go. She'd been uprooted from everything she knew but was still trying to carve a place for herself, pushing herself out of her comfort zone, making new friends. Gracie was stronger than Dominic realised, stronger than she perhaps realised herself.

Ettie began to swim back towards her and as she did, several familiar figures appeared on the lake's edge. She hailed them, her spirits immediately lifting at the sight of Hazel, Jane and Rachel – well, maybe not so much at Rachel, whose face, even from this distance, was masked in its usual scowl.

As they were disrobing Ettie swam to Gracie. 'You OK?'

'Yes, dear. It's been a few years, but I'm getting there.'

'Grandad's a swimming teacher, he might be able to give you a few lessons.'

'I think I'm a bit old to learn now, but I'm happy splashing about. Really happy.' She shot Ettie one of her shy smiles. 'Who'd have thought an old duck like me would get so much pleasure out of a bit of swimming? Goodness knows what my Bob would have said. I've never been the adventurous sort, but this feels like an adventure.' She added more quietly, as if to herself, 'A proper adventure.'

Ettie grinned. 'Grandad always says you're never too old to learn. Then again, when you're complaining to him about him leaving the loo seat up, he says you can't teach an old dog new tricks.'

Gracie laughed. 'Sounds like my Bob. I never did train him out of that habit.'

'And talk of the old devil.' Grandad and Josh were making steady progress down the beach, Josh on his crutches, walking as quickly as he could with his prosthetic leg on the difficult surface... Ettie couldn't quite believe the change in him. It was as if he couldn't wait to throw himself into the water.

Leaving Gracie puttering about, she swam to the shallows where she stood up. Josh had bypassed the others without a second glance and, balanced on one crutch, with Grandad hovering like an anxious hen behind him, was easing off his leg and placing it carefully in a big blue Ikea bag.

'Hi, Josh!' she called.

'Hmm,' he grunted, pulling his goggles into place and

shuffling forward crablike on his bottom until the water was chest height and he was able to swim, and then he was off.

Grandad, who'd stopped to have a conversation with the other women, still talking among themselves, waded in.

'Hi, Grandad, he's keen.'

'Huh, lad's cross because there are other people here.'

'Oh,' Ettie's face crumpled in sympathy. 'Feels self-conscious, does he?'

'No, he doesn't do small talk with old ladies, apparently.'

'Rachel's not old. In fact, neither are Hazel and Jane. They're probably in their fifties.'

'Anyone over twenty is ancient to Josh. And he's a grumpy little sod.'

'You must be prehistoric, then,' teased Ettie. 'Although I guess being grumpy is hardly surprising. He must be going through a lot.'

'No, he's just a grumpy teenager. He's still got his other leg.'

'Grandad,' Ettie gasped. 'You can't say things like that.'

'Why not? It's true. He wants to be treated like everyone else. He doesn't want special treatment or to be always thought of as that boy with one leg. He wants to be Josh.'

'You mean he doesn't want to be defined by his disability.'

'That too. Anyroad, he's taken to his swimming.' Grandad nodded and Ettie saw that Josh had already reached the island with a powerful and extremely smooth freestyle.

'He's good. Fast.'

'Always was. But he wasn't interested in training when he was younger. Preferred his football.'

'Is he enjoying it?'

'Huh, you think he's going to admit that? Of course the lad is, but he's far too proud to let on that an old codger like me might be right. He's still carrying on about being seen in the sidecar.'

'I'm with him on that.' Ettie grimaced, remembering the teasing she'd got when she'd been spotted in the infamous sidecar when she was a young teen. Although, to be fair, she had decked the girl that had taken the teasing too far.

'He's fast,' said Hazel, who'd waded into the water beside them, along with Rachel, who didn't say anything, just pulled her goggles down over the flaps of her hat and set off. 'How are you today?'

'Great, thanks. How are you?'

'I'll be better after a swim. The outlaws are driving us mental. That's why Jane's here today as well. We needed to get away from everything.'

'They'll come round, lass,' said Grandad.

'I'm not sure they ever will,' said Hazel with troubled eyes, glancing over at her fiancée. 'Poor Jane, she doesn't complain, but I know she's brooding about it. Not sleeping.'

'And what's bitten that one?' asked Grandad, watching Rachel slicing through the water.

Hazel lifted her shoulders in a puzzled shrug. 'No idea,

but she's got some kind of demon. She's been unhappy ever since I met her here.'

Ettie thought Hazel was being kind. Rachel was plain miserable. You could be unhappy but you didn't need to be rude with it. They all turned to watch the woman, who had caught up with Josh on his way back. Rather than swim past him to the island, she turned and said something to him, pointing to a tree that jutted out a few metres from the lake edge on the beach side. He paused, nodded and then across the water, Ettie heard, 'Three, two, one.' The two of them began to race across the water, their arms spiralling like water spiders.

'My goodness, look at them go,' said Hazel.

Grandad was beaming from ear to ear. 'He's taking her on. Look at him. He's a bloody marvel.'

Josh was already easing ahead although Rachel was giving determined chase, pushing him all the time. His arms moved rapidly, flashing in sharp rhythm, eating up the distance. Everyone turned to watch as he came closer.

'Come on son, keep it up.' Grandad's head was bobbing, his entire focus willing Josh on. 'That's a good hundred metres.'

Josh opened up the distance without slowing or even seeming to tire, and when he came level with the tree, just a few metres from them, he stopped and rolled onto his back, his chest heaving.

As Josh righted himself, standing up in the water, Grandad swam over and clapped him on the back. 'Bloody fantastic, boy!'

Josh looked up and grinned at the sight of Rachel swimming the last metre. 'I beat her. She bet me I couldn't. I wasn't going to let a girl beat me.'

Ettie rolled her eyes and Hazel caught her. 'He's fifteen.'

'Mmm,' she replied, glad when she heard Grandad say, 'Your attitude needs some work, lad, but you can swim. Let's see if you can beat our Ettie, next time.'

Josh looked over with a slightly contemptuous expression. 'Course I can. I'm not useless.'

'No one's saying you're useless.'

Josh stuck out a pugnacious chin, ignoring Grandad as he looked over at Ettie. 'Race you to the island.'

'Give yourself a chance to catch your breath, lad.'

'Well done,' said Rachel, arriving and holding out a hand to shake Josh's.

He shrugged gracelessly. 'I knew I could beat you.'

A smile actually crossed Rachel's face. 'Cocky little bugger, aren't you?'

Josh stared at her, clearly not sure how to take that, then turned to Ettie.

'Going to take me on?' he asked, confidently.

Ettie gave him a gentle smile, seeing through the bravado. He didn't want anyone to think he was going to back down from a challenge, but she couldn't help showing a touch of concern even though it would probably be a red rag. 'If you really want to. Are you sure you don't want to rest a bit first? There's no hurry.' Although that wasn't strictly true. Dominic would be back at some point and she shouldn't forget the time. She and Gracie had given themselves an hour to get back and get dried off. It would look a little suspicious if they both had wet hair.

'I'm not scared of you beating me. To the island.'

Ettie nodded. She wasn't scared of winning or losing. In fact, she was looking forward to the challenge. It was a while since she'd done any competitive swimming but back in the day, she'd done a mean hundred metres and she'd kept up with her swimming ever since.

'Ooh, this is exciting,' said Gracie, who'd swum to join them but her teeth were chattering. Rachel gave her a scathing glare as if she were too stupid to live.

'Why don't you go and get dry and watch from the beach?' suggested Ettie to Gracie, glaring at Rachel. 'You shouldn't stay too long in the water if you're not moving.'

'You're right, dear, and I've made a couple of flasks of hot chocolate for everyone to warm up afterwards.'

'What a brilliant idea,' said Hazel, narrowing her eyes at Rachel, who had the grace to look a little embarrassed.

Ettie waited until the older woman had returned to the shore safely before she turned back to Josh and Grandad, thinking that it was giving Josh some recovery time. Although he was young, the water was very cold.

'OK,' she said brightly. 'Be gentle with me. I haven't swum in a race for years.'

'You'll be sound, love,' said Grandad. 'You've always had good technique.'

Technique was one thing, stamina another. She could swim forty lengths quite happily in a twenty-five-metre pool, going at a steady pace, and sprint for two or maybe three lengths, but putting on a burst of speed for longer than that was something else. She only hoped her lungs would hold out.

She and Josh arranged themselves in readiness, which wasn't so easy as in a pool, where you had a hard surface to push off against.

'On your marks,' shouted Grandad. 'Get set. Go.' He brought his hand down and hit the water with a splash.

Ettie sliced out her lead arm and set off – one, two, three, breath, one, two, three, breath – her legs kicking as hard as she could as she pulled through the water. The first fifty metres were fine; years of practice and muscle memory aided her and she kept pace with Josh, although she was swimming as hard and fast as she could, driven by dogged determination. With every alternate breath she could see him beside her, a grim look on his face. The boy had that killer competitive instinct. He wasn't going to be beaten if he could help it. While she'd been competitive and wanted to do well as a teenager, she'd never had that desperate desire to win. Her driver was to be the best she could. She competed against herself rather than other people. It hadn't been enough to keep winning competitions, and she'd given up competitive swimming after a couple of years.

Halfway to the island, she could feel her lungs tightening, her breathing more laboured as she desperately sucked in each breath. Her arms felt like lead and her legs were starting to flag. Josh began to pull ahead and although she pushed herself as hard as she could, there was no way she was going to catch him. However, mindful that

Grandad was watching the boy to see just how good he could be, she continued to push herself, and therefore him. On this occasion she wasn't going down without a fight.

In the end Josh beat her by a good five metres and when she caught up with him, she collapsed on the shelf under the water leading up to the island.

'What kept you?' he drawled as she tried to draw in breath to her heaving chest. Despite his superior sneer, she was pleased to see that he was still breathing hard.

'You're over ten years younger than me.'

He gave another one of his surly shrugs. 'I've only got one leg.'

'One and a half,' corrected Ettie, and immediately felt a bit petty. He'd beaten her despite his disability because he was a good swimmer. 'You know, you're really good.'

'Like you said, you're older than me.'

'Josh, you beat me by five metres. I was the school swimming champion and I swim a couple of times a week. You're seriously good.'

'That's what Cyril says.' He narrowed his eyes. 'I figured he was just trying to make me feel better about myself.'

Ettie raised an eyebrow. 'How long have you known Grandad?'

This raised a half laugh from Josh. 'All me life.'

'Exactly. Have you ever known him not be straight with anyone?'

'No.'

'So, if he thinks you can swim, you can swim.'

'So what?'

'You could enter competitions. Have you seen those guys in the Paralympics?'

'Might have done,' he said, his face closing down quickly.

Ettie decided not to push it but she would talk to Grandad about what Josh might be able to do.

'What's your breast stroke like?' she asked.

His eyes gleamed for a second and dipped towards her chest.

'Ha!' said Ettie, rolling her eyes. 'I'd forgotten you're a teenager.'

At least he had the grace to look abashed. 'I'm not as good at it, but I can do it.'

'Let's try that going back,' said Ettie.

They swam back and he was still very strong, although she just about managed to keep up with him.

———

When Ettie came out of the water ten minutes later, followed by the others, Gracie was already on the beach waiting and had spread a blanket out and laid out mugs for everyone.

'Who wants hot chocolate and home-made brownies?'

'You angel,' said Jane, who was already wrapped in her robe. 'That sounds delicious.'

She dropped down onto the blanket, quickly followed by Hazel and Rachel.

Grandad had rescued Josh's crutches and he hopped out

of the water. As no one paid any attention to him, he crept closer, keeping a wary eye on everyone.

'I'd love some home-made brownie.' Grandad patted his stomach. 'I'm starving after all that swimming. How about you, Josh?'

Josh gave another of his laconic shrugs but Ettie could see his eyes hungrily watching as Gracie unpacked a big Tupperware box.

She patted a bit of the blanket on the edge and Josh came and sat down, keeping his head down.

'How are the wedding plans going?' she asked Hazel and Jane, deliberately focusing the attention away from Josh, not that the others were insensitive enough to stare at Josh, which she realised was what he was expecting.

'We found our dresses this week,' said Jane, a smile lighting up her tired eyes. She had shadows beneath them, testament to the lack of sleep that Hazel had referred to. 'But it was hilarious, because we both went to the same bridal shop, just for a look, you know how you do. The woman that runs the shop was so helpful and we started trying things on. And then it went tits up because I found the dress! I was in the changing room, about to come out, and I just knew, so I had to tell Hazel to go away so she didn't see it. Then ten minutes later she did exactly the same thing. The poor woman in the shop nearly had a nervous breakdown, trying to hide them away from both of us – it's only a tiny shop. But the fact that we found them so quickly feels like a good omen.'

'Or she was a really good saleswoman,' said Hazel in a teasing voice.

'We're only getting married once. We're doing it properly.'

'Are we ever!' Hazel pulled a long-suffering face as Jane poked her in the ribs, but it was clearly with affection.

'I don't know why you're bothering.' Rachel spoke with sudden bitterness.

'Because we love each other and we want our friends and family to celebrate that with us,' said Hazel, and Ettie realised it was a line she'd had to say on more than one occasion.

Rachel's mouth pursed like a small, hard raisin, making Ettie wonder what had made her so sour and miserable.

'Mainly friends,' Jane chipped in. 'Because, quite frankly, I'm only inviting my family because I have to.'

'Well, don't,' said Rachel.

'It's not simple.' Jane shook her head. 'They'd be even more insulted if we didn't invite them. I can't seem to win. Maybe we should have just eloped.' Her mouth took on a mournful twist.

Hazel took her hand. 'If you think I'm getting married by a dodgy Elvis impersonator in Las Vegas, you can think again. We've got plenty of supportive people coming and we'll find a reception venue soon enough.'

'I thought you'd got that sorted,' said Rachel.

'So did we. Unfortunately the place had double-booked.'

'Allegedly,' said Hazel, her eyebrows meeting in the middle and her jaw tightening.

'We can't prove anything.' This time it was Jane's turn to lay a hand on Hazel's.

'Bastards didn't want a gay wedding.'

'Seriously?' asked Rachel. 'I thought we'd moved beyond that sort of crap.'

'Nope, some people are still living in the dark ages.'

'Can they do that?' asked Gracie. 'Isn't it discrimination?'

'Officially, no, they can't, but if they say they've double-booked, what can we do?'

'Why did they take the booking in the first place?' asked Ettie.

'Because we both went to visit separately. It was only when we went together to confirm the booking, that there was a sudden about-turn.'

'When's the wedding?' asked Gracie.

'September,' said Jane, her lower lip trembling. 'If we ever get there. How are we going to find a venue at such short notice?'

'We'll get there,' said Hazel in a mild but determined voice.

'Why not have it here?'

Everyone turned to look at Ettie. 'The hotel won't be open but most of the rooms downstairs should be ready and even if not, we can do something. You can be our very first guests. Wouldn't that be wonderful?'

'Yes,' said Gracie, clapping her hands together. 'How many guests have you got coming?'

'Only about forty, it's supposed to be small and intimate,' said Hazel.

'And if my family don't come, it will only be thirty-three,' said Jane.

Josh was staring at Hazel and Jane, his eyes going back and forth with suspicious puzzlement. Ettie prayed he wasn't going to blurt out something inappropriate, but thankfully he kept quiet.

'We can accommodate that, easily,' said Gracie. 'If the chef hasn't been appointed by then we could get caterers in, or I could make afternoon tea for you, and Ettie can help me.'

'I'll help too,' said Rachel. 'I used to be a chef.'

'Did you?' asked Hazel a little too sharply. It almost sounded accusing and everyone turned to stare at Rachel. 'I didn't know that. I thought you worked in an office.'

Rachel reddened and swallowed. 'I gave it up. I'm not a chef anymore,' she said with a touch of defiance, brushing her long red hair impatiently over her shoulder.

'That would be wonderful, dear.' Gracie ignored Rachel's sudden awkwardness. 'I'm sure we can sort you out.'

'What about the owner? Don't we need to book or something?'

'No, it will be fine,' said Ettie, confident that Dominic would be pleased to get some early business. Hopefully it would kick-start word-of-mouth recommendations in the local area for functions at the hotel. 'It will be a great dry run. And I'm sure the hotel needs to start earning some money.' So far a lot of money seemed to have been spent, and at some point it needed to be recouped.

'The only thing is…' Jane paused and Hazel took over: 'We don't want anything too stuffy.'

'Ha! Then you'll be fine.' Ettie spent the next five minutes talking about their plans for Haim, as it had now been agreed the hotel would be called.

Everyone bar Josh, who was more interested in his phone, was enthusiastic – even Rachel, who asked a few questions without her usual scowl or negativity.

'I hate to say this, but we ought to leave,' said Ettie. 'We don't want Dominic catching us.'

Gracie scrambled to her feet. 'No.'

One by one they packed up their things and Hazel, Jane and Rachel left first, scurrying through the trees back to their car parked in the layby on the edge of the estate.

Grandad was careful to let Josh get up by himself. 'Let's be off, lad. Thanks, our Ettie, and you too, Gracie. Lovely chocolate brownie, and that hot chocolate was just what the doctor ordered.' He gave her a warm smile that brought a blush of pleasure to Gracie's face, before turning back to Ettie. 'Let us know when we can come back.'

'Will do, Grandad.'

'And I can leave you a little warm-up bundle on the beach,' said Gracie. 'I make a lovely rocky road slice.'

'That would be grand. It's Cyril, by the way.' He gave her a typical Grandad-style salute. Ettie refrained from rolling her eyes. He'd always had a way with the ladies, although he'd never strayed from Gran throughout their marriage, and, despite world-champion-level flirting, had never dallied with another woman since. He wasn't one for sentimentality but would occasionally say of Gran, 'She were a grand lass.'

'Come on Gracie, we ought to get back.' Ettie was also a little worried, because despite the sunshine, there was a chilly breeze and the other woman's face was starting to look a little pinched.

They headed up the slope back towards the house as Grandad and Josh crossed over to the motorbike and sidecar.

'I didn't know you were going to make me go swimming with a bunch of lezzers and geriatrics,' grumbled Josh as he slung his crutches into the sidecar.

'That's all right lad, they didn't know they were going to be swimming with a disabled moron,' said Grandad amicably.

Ettie bit back a smile as Josh glared at Grandad, but interestingly enough, the boy didn't say another word.

Chapter Nineteen

The trip to the pub for the much-discussed crocodile burgers merited a proper dress, Ettie decided, and she'd put on one of her favourites, a vintage scarlet crepe dress with a sweetheart neckline and a flared skirt.

As she finished tying her hair up in a high ponytail, complete with coordinating paisley scarf, she stared at herself in the mirror and wrinkled her nose at the underlying tug of guilt that haunted her. She was looking forward to going out on a proper date with Dominic but at the same time she was also horribly aware that the sole purpose of the date was to leave the coast clear for Grandad to give Josh an extra swimming session.

With a last look in the mirror, she gave a slight shake of her head, pushing her nagging conscience into submission. It was for a good cause. Josh needed the swimming, it was helping him, and if Dominic didn't have such a pig-headed attitude towards swimming, he'd understand, surely. What was the problem there, she wondered. When she thought about it, that first time he'd caught her swimming in the lake, he'd been cross, admittedly, but also extremely concerned about her safety and the dangers of swimming. Now that she'd got to know him, she realised that he acted on logic rather than emotion. But his response to people swimming in the lake seemed more of an emotional reaction, and he seemed terribly tense when Scrapper wouldn't come out of the water. With sudden awareness, she realised that she'd been guilty of dismissing his attitude because it didn't suit her, rather than asking him why he felt so strongly. There had to be more to it.

With that realisation buzzing around her head, she left the room and skipped down the stairs, enjoying the sensation of the skirt swishing around her knees instead of her usual jeans. Dominic was waiting in the hall and the flash of admiration in his eyes made her glad she'd made a bit of an effort.

'You look nice,' he said after scanning her very quickly, and she ignored the brief spurt of disappointment that she felt.

'*Nice*,' she teased him with a decided pout.

He laughed. 'You look gorgeous and you know it.'

She laughed. 'That's better. Thank you, and so do you. Come on. It's ages since I've been out, properly out. I'm looking forward to this.' She linked a matey arm through his. 'We both scrub up well.'

He looked more than nice, he looked positively edible. She might have been used to seeing him every day, but in navy-blue chinos and a button-down white Oxford shirt that emphasised the dark tan of his olive skin, he definitely brushed up nicely. Her hormones fluttered, making 'we want to come out and play' noises. They could flutter and mutter to themselves – she was on a mission this evening and needed to take him off the premises.

'I hope you're ready for exotic burgers,' he said ten minutes later as they walked between the wooden trestle tables of the pub garden towards the front door. They both had to duck as they crossed the threshold into the flagstone-floored saloon bar. 'God only knows where they get them from,' he whispered as they approached the bar.

Ettie squinted at the girl behind the bar, who looked vaguely familiar, someone who'd been in the year below her at school, as she replied, 'Who knows? I've not seen any crocodiles in the lake, so I'm guessing they're not locally sourced.'

'Now there's an idea. Perhaps I could introduce a few.' He chuckled to himself. 'That would give new meaning to wild swimming.'

Ettie pursed her lips. 'And would be very mean. They're not doing any harm.'

Dominic's lips tightened. 'I believe we've had that conversation.'

'We could have "catch your own crocodile for tea" events. Might be something we can add to the menus.'

'Given that I suspect a lot of our clientele might be vegan, or even mainly vegetarian, I'm not sure that's going to be a good idea.'

'Mm, you're probably right. Very millennial. You're going to need to source some craft beer and lots of different gins.' She nodded to a solitary bottle of gin behind the bar. 'They're missing a trick,' she whispered under her breath.

Dominic laughed.

They ordered drinks – a pint for him and a glass of wine for her – and he opened a tab.

As the barman handed their drinks over along with faux-leather-bound menus, Dominic lifted his glass and clinked it against hers. 'Cheers. You know, we do make a very good team.'

Ettie beamed at him. It was the second time he'd said as much in the last two days. It cheered her up no end, because last night's online evening class had very nearly bored her into submission. Bookkeeping was duller than dull. She was starting to have doubts that it was for her, but then, wouldn't that be giving up again? And she really wanted to prove that she could stick with something. The explosion in London was her wake-up call and she'd resolved to change. And here she was, being side-tracked by how well everything was going at the Hall.

'Yes, we do.' She led the way over to a table by the window, which offered a wonderful view of rolling countryside, dotted with sheep and criss-crossed with dry-stone walls.

'Have you been to this pub before?' Dominic asked, taking a seat opposite her.

'Not since these owners took over.' She looked around. The new owners had transformed the place by updating the décor, and the walls were now covered in wainscoting painted in pale green. Very National Trust, although the clientele hadn't changed much, she noted with a faint smile. Three familiar ruddy-faced farmers monopolised the bar stools in the snug at the back; one of them had given her a wave. A mate of her grandad's, she recalled. They'd all been coming here as long as Ettie could remember. There was something to be said for community, something she'd missed in London. She'd found something here, through the swimming. And there it was again... Just at the thought of Dominic, Gracie, Grandad, Hilda, Hazel, Rachel, Jane and Josh, she felt it again ... that sensation of the sun coming up inside her, lighting up her soul.

She turned to Dominic, holding up her hands as a precursor to an apology. 'Before you say anything, hear me out. I really think you should consider swimming in the lake. It would be a real draw.'

She watched as he stiffened, and before she could stop herself she asked the question that had been stumbling around in her brain for ages, which she'd refused to give credence to before because it sounded so ridiculous. He'd been in the Navy, for God's sake. 'Do you have a problem with water? Are you afraid of swimming?'

A guarded, wary expression gave her the answer.

His mouth crimped in a line as if it were firmly zipped and he was holding back the words.

She studied him and deliberately didn't fill the silence. Instead she kept her gaze on him, softening her expression.

Just when she was sure he wasn't going to answer, he exhaled a long breath through pursed lips.

'Not afraid. Cautious.' The words came out as if he were trying to extinguish any development of where that question might lead. 'Do you know how many people drown each year? Nearly six hundred. That's a lot of people. I think that would make anyone cautious.'

'Yes, but why you?' she asked, wondering at her own stupidity. It was so obvious now, that there was more to it. 'You were in Search and Rescue, you must have always been aware of the risks and dangers, and yet you still did your job.'

'*Did* being the operative word.' There was a haunting bitterness to his bald statement. 'You asked before about what happened to my leg. It was a rescue that should have been straightforward but went badly wrong.' She saw his brow wrinkle as he frowned, keeping his gaze fixed on the distant horizon. 'Since then, what with the divorce, losing Bryony, I just avoided the issue, and then the first time Scrapper ran off into the lake, I realised that I … that I have a healthy respect for the water.' The stiff, mechanical words spoke to Ettie of a deeper issue.

'When was the last time you were in the water?'

He closed his eyes and for a moment she wanted to take back the question. Was she being insensitive?

'The night of the accident. I haven't swum since.' He swallowed and she saw his Adam's apple dip and bob furiously.

'Have you tried?' she asked gently, remembering how

he'd sat at the water's edge and tugged at his socks while waiting for Scrapper to come out.

'A couple of times.' His face scrunched in a wince. 'It seems so stupid. Everything just freezes. I feel sick when I see other people in the water... People drown.'

'They do, but if you take proper precautions...'

He shook his head. 'You can take all the precautions in the world, but accidents happen, and I know it's not logical, but everything inside goes into freefall when I see people in the water. I'm better than I was...' He let out a laugh. 'Ridiculous, I know.'

'You're not ashamed, are you?' said Ettie, putting a hand on his arm.

His mouth crimped again, in a way that was becoming familiar to her, telling her that he didn't want to answer the question.

'Oh, Dominic.' She leaned over and kissed his cheek.

'It's stupid. I need to get over it, but I had other things to worry about and I've got so much on my plate, I'm not about to tackle it just now.'

She swallowed, realising that as they were sitting there, Grandad and Josh were probably swimming in the lake at that very moment. Beneath the table she twisted her hands while she nodded in agreement with him, feeling very uncomfortable. Now it made sense, and while she couldn't relate to his fears, she ought at least to respect them. Before she'd managed to justify things by telling herself that what he wasn't aware of couldn't hurt him. Guilt gnawed at her. On the other hand, like her, the others – Grandad, Josh, Hazel and Rachel – all got so much out of swimming. They all had their problems and their issues. Could she deny them the solace that she knew swimming brought? How could she ask them all to stop? She thought of how she unravelled things in her head while she swam, the feeling of ease she associated with stepping out of the water, the way that her anxiety was sliced away, like someone taking off the top of an egg, the second she reached out, stretching her muscles to take that first stroke. The way that she pushed her cares away as she felt her limbs move through the current. The knots in her stomach tightened. She hated not having any idea what to do.

She turned her attention back to Dominic, who had picked up one of the menus. She tried to push the myriad of jumbled thoughts out of her head and put on her happy face. She couldn't solve the dilemma now and she didn't want to spoil the evening with him.

'So, what about these exotic burgers?' He was clearly ready to change the subject too. 'What do you think we should go for?'

'I think you should definitely try the crocodile,' she replied, relieved to move on. 'Gracie would be so disappointed if we didn't have something weird and wonderful.' She perused the menu. 'Hmm … wildebeest, ostrich.'

The waiter came over to take their order and Dominic ordered the crocodile burger and two glasses of red wine, and then turned to look at Ettie, for her choice. 'I'll have the…' she held the pause deliberately '…ordinary cheeseburger.' She folded the menu and handed it to the waiter, hiding a smile as Dominic shot her a quick look of mock outrage.

'Hello, what happened to "Gracie will be disappointed", Miss I'll-give-anything-a-go?'

She lifted her shoulders in an insouciant shrug, giving him a cheeky smile. 'It's ages since I had a decent burger. I wasn't going to give up the opportunity, especially not when you're paying.'

'I'm paying?'

'This time. Next time I'll treat you. I'm not that flaky.'

He laughed. 'I don't think you're flaky.'

'Not now, but admit it, when I came for the interview, you did.' Now she felt back on safe ground, teasing, flirting with him and talking about inconsequential things.

'Yes, I did, but I've seen you in action – no one could ever accuse you of being flaky.' He paused and gave her a flirty smile. 'A bit bossy sometimes.'

'And what's wrong with that?'

'Nothing at all,' he said, laying a hand on hers, his face softening as he picked up his beer and sipped at it.

She watched his throat as he swallowed, and he caught her hand when he put the glass down. For a moment their eyes were locked on each other and her heart did one of those odd miss-a-beat hiccoughs of sudden awareness. Did she really just moisten her lips? And did his lips curve in a knowing smile?

When the burgers arrived, he insisted she try a piece of

crocodile, and they both agreed it tasted quite like chicken. In fact Ettie wasn't convinced it wasn't chicken.

'I think it's a con to bring the punters in,' she said, chewing and screwing her eyes up, trying to identify the taste. 'Definitely chicken.'

Dominic laughed. 'If you say so.'

'I do. I reckon I could make these.'

'I believe you can do anything if you set your mind to it.' His smile was gentle.

'That's what my grandad says.' She sighed. It just seemed an uphill battle to get anywhere.

Dominic leaned over and took her hand. 'Ettie, don't doubt yourself. You're smart, beautiful and you have a really positive can-do attitude. All those other employers must have been idiots not to see it.'

She gave him a twisted smile, wondering what he would think of her if he knew she'd been swimming in the lake and encouraging others to do the same. Who was she kidding? She didn't need to wonder what he'd think; she knew what he'd think if he found out. He'd been badly let down by his wife, lying to him, before; he wouldn't take kindly to her doing the same. She caught her lip between her teeth. What was she going to do?

Chapter Twenty

'See you later,' said Dominic. 'I'll be back around lunchtime. Off to the torture chamber.' He patted his pockets, checking for his phone, and shot a quick questioning frown at Gracie, who was tidying up the kitchen in her dressing gown. 'Not getting dressed today?' he queried.

'Eventually, dear,' said Gracie with a vague smile.

Ettie looked down into her tea mug, that familiar tug of guilt pulling at her, knowing full well that Gracie had her swimming costume on underneath her towelling robe in readiness for their morning swim while Dominic was at his usual physio session. She'd noticed he was walking a lot better these days and wondered how many more appointments he might have. That would solve the problem. If he was around on a Wednesday morning, they'd have to stop swimming then ... but she couldn't imagine not seeing everyone at the lake every week, and how could they give up something that had become so important to them all?

As soon as the sound of the Land Rover's engine faded, Gracie pulled out a big black insulated picnic bag, opened up the oven to pull out lots of foil-wrapped bundles and then disappeared into the pantry, re-emerging with several large thermos flasks.

'Are you ready, Ettie, dear?'

'No,' she said, sighing, guilt now burrowing a hole in her stomach. 'I need to get my cossie on and I'll just grab my goggles and my hat.'

She ran upstairs and rounded up her things from the back of the drawers where she kept them hidden from Dominic. She went to stand at the window; the lake was just visible. They had to stop swimming. Ettie couldn't keep lying to him. She didn't want to be that person. Foolish as it was, she was halfway in love with him. His feelings mattered. She dreaded to think what Grandad was going to say, or Hazel or Rachel or Josh for that matter. Swimming meant so much to them all. Still, she had to tell them today that it had to stop.

Fifteen minutes later she arrived at the lakeside. Unfortunately she and Gracie were the last ones. She'd hoped to speak to everyone before they went in the water. She spotted Rachel's familiar orange swimming cap coming towards the shore like a small torpedo. Beyond her in the distance Jane and Hazel were striking out parallel to the shore, and she could see Grandad giving some coaching to Josh.

As she watched Josh splashing Grandad, a big smile on his face, her heart hitched. He was almost unrecognisable now. The permanent sneer around his mouth and the suspicious, wary look in his eyes had been replaced with enthusiastic grins, cheeky sarcasm and sharp interest. Even Grandad seemed a little happier these days; there were fewer of those lapses when he'd stare into the distance thinking about Granny Cynthia. And as for Rachel – well, some days she was actually quite nice and stayed to talk to everyone. Hazel seemed more relaxed, and apparently on the days when she swam, Jane slept much better. Hilda, Ettie decided, was indefatigable whether she swam or not. She was the sort of positive person who would find something else to keep her busy and active.

Ettie winced. But not the others. How could she take this away from them?

Enjoying the flow of the water across her body, Ettie swam for another ten minutes, lost in her own world, as all the fractured pieces in her mind came to rest instead of swirling madly about. She'd put the case to the others. That's all she could do.

As the little grassy knoll neared, she revelled in the stretch and pull of her muscles and the sensation of the cold water sliding across her skin and the blood pumping around her system. Here she felt connected to the world around her, synced to nature and the ebb and flow of life. Choosing to take a quick break, she waded out of the water onto the tiny beach, her whole body tingling with that magical life-affirming sensation that nothing else could match. Could she really give this up? Could she try and make Dominic understand? She stretched, pulled off her swimming cap, letting her damp hair fall free, and threw back her head, enjoying the moment, looking up at the deep blue of the sky, dotted with scudding clouds, her feet grounded into the sand. There was nothing quite like it. She closed her eyes and took several deep breaths, her chest rising and falling, her pulse thudding in her veins. Alive, every part of her buzzed with the feeling of being alive. When she was here like this, all the day-to-day worries faded away and she could just be, here in this moment. Why did she have to go and fall for Dominic? With a heavy sigh she balanced her elbows on her knees. Why was life so flipping complicated?

She looked out across the water towards the beach where Gracie was already out of the water; ten minutes was usually enough for her. Ettie suspected that she was here for the social aspect and the opportunity to feed people rather than the actual swimming. No doubt she'd already unrolled the picnic rug and was starting to get out the bacon butties. Ettie was looking forward to the first bite of the soft home-made bread rolls and the salty kick of bacon, along with the ultra-dark hot chocolate that had quickly become addictive.

Time to go back.

As she neared the beach, she lifted her head to see how much further she had to swim, and to her horror she spotted a figure striding across the sand towards the water.

'Hey. What do you think you're doing!'

In sheer shock at both the sudden bellow and the

recognition of who it belonged to, Ettie stalled and went under the water, swallowing a massive mouthful.

No, it couldn't be. Oh shit, it was.

Dominic.

Coming up for air, spluttering and coughing, she paused, treading water as everyone in the lake swung their heads in one direction, like sunflowers tipping up to the sun's rays.

What was he doing here? Now?

Instead of being miles away at the physiotherapist's, Dominic was marching across the beach to the water's edge, at such a rate that he'd stormed right past Gracie.

Ettie's stomach tightened, almost cramping in sudden apprehension. He wasn't due back for another two hours. She bit her lip. Even from this distance she could see he looked furious. Oh God, what had she done?

At his peremptory tone, the others nearer the shore began to wade sheepishly out of the water. Ettie tensed. Hurrying, she swam back, reaching the shoreline in time to hear Dominic shouting at Hazel and Grandad.

'I've told you two before! This is private property. You're trespassing.' He took his phone out of his pocket. 'I'm calling the police.' Ettie closed her eyes with a shudder. Oh hell.

One by one the others clambered out of the water.

Gracie rose to her feet behind Dominic, who still hadn't noticed her – he'd been so focused on the swimmers in the water.

'Dominic, dear. Are you sure you want to do that?'

He whirled around. 'Gracie!'

If she hadn't been so shocked by his appearance, Ettie might have laughed at the flabbergasted expression on his face. With her stomach roiling and her limbs rather shaky, she pulled herself together and put her head down and sped up with quick, fast strokes.

She was just nearing the beach when Dominic spotted Josh in the shallows. 'And you. Out. Now.' He pointed a firm finger at Josh. Ettie sped up. Oh no, this had *disaster* written all over it. She waded towards Josh as fast as she could, clumsy and off balance, hoping to divert Dominic's attention and also to help the boy up to his feet. As she approached Josh she saw the smirk on his face. Oh God, the boy was going to milk this. For a moment, she actually felt sorry for Dominic.

'I said, out, now! Are you listening to me?' Dominic's face darkened with anger but he sounded calm and extremely authoritative, with that expectation of being obeyed without question.

Josh gave him a cocky, defiant glare. 'Make me.'

Ettie winced. She knew that Dominic would be mortified when he realised the true situation. Josh was deliberately goading him and doing nothing to make the situation better.

'Oh, for God's sake,' she muttered, marching out of the water, straight past Dominic to Grandad, who held Josh's crutches in his hands.

She grabbed them from him and stalked back into the water to give them to Josh. It was at that point that she realised that in her swimming cap and goggles, Dominic had yet to recognise her, perhaps because he was so focused on Josh's apparent display of defiance. She thrust the sticks at Josh, saying under her breath, 'Don't make this any worse than it already is.'

'He can't do nothing,' Josh replied. 'We've got nothing to lose and he ain't going to call the cops on you, is he?' He paused. 'Or me.'

'I wouldn't be so sure about that,' said Ettie, as much to herself as to him, while sneaking a peep at Dominic's stern face. There was no getting out of this one.

Using his crutches, Josh hauled himself upright and shot a challenging look at Dominic.

Ettie saw Dominic take a couple of deep breaths as Josh gave him a triumphant smile as if to say, 'Now what?'

Dominic swallowed and his cheeks burned red. He transferred his attention to her and as his gaze came to rest on her face, an uncomfortable flush of shame rushed over her body. What had she done? Every fibre of her being boiled with regret. Why hadn't she thought this far ahead? It was inevitable that they'd be caught one day.

His face cleared for a moment but then confusion quickly followed. 'Ettie?' Her heart sank at the sound of disbelief in the solitary word. 'Is that you?'

Heat flooded into her cheeks as she pulled off her hat and pushed her goggles up onto her forehead.

Dominic's eyes flashed with hurt and it stabbed right into her chest. 'Ettie?' This time the word was soft, full of disappointment.

For once all her bold sass deserted her and she knew she'd done wrong. It must have been awful for him to see them all in the water – to feel that rising panic that something terrible was going to happen. The danger he felt they were in. She couldn't even raise a smile or attempt to charm him. She was too ashamed of herself to speak. Instead, she stood, shifting from one leg to the other like an awkward flamingo.

She nodded. His mouth closed, his lips compressed. Their eyes met and held for several seconds. Her heart thudded in her chest, so hard she thought that the echo might bounce across the lake. All she could see was the depth of his hurt. It was as if he didn't recognise her. In that moment, the enormity of what she'd done came crashing over her in a tidal wave of regret and self-recrimination. She might not have lied to him, not directly, but she hadn't been honest with him.

She had split a hair that wasn't as fine as she'd once imagined. It wasn't a hair as much as a chasm, both deep and wide.

Without saying another word, he shook his head and turned his back on her, walking back up the beach. He didn't spare a glance at any of them, just walked at a steady pace back towards the house. The bow of his shoulders brought a lump to her throat. She'd really messed up this time.

Hollowness carved out a hole in her chest, rendering her as immobile as a statue and just as heavy. The weight of what she'd done threatened to sink her. Her legs didn't seem to want to work. Once upon a time, she'd have raced after him, apologised and tried to make him see that no harm had been meant. That she hadn't meant to go behind his back. She would have laughed it all off as a mistake, an error of judgement, a slip-up – but this time she couldn't do any of that. She couldn't even apologise because from day one, she'd known that she was going against his wishes. She'd conspired with the others, led and encouraged them, told herself he wouldn't really mind when she knew full well that he would. She'd lied to herself for her own convenience, when she knew how strongly Dominic felt about swimming in the lake.

With a shiver she realised that she'd grown cold and strode out of the water, as everyone stood in silence.

Ettie wrapped her towel around her and walked to the rug.

'Oh dear,' said Gracie softly.

'He wasn't very happy,' said Hazel. 'I think that might just be the end of us.'

'He seemed a little too calm. Reminds me of my son, the bottled-up type,' observed Hilda, pulling off her ridiculous flowery cap. 'Not good at letting go of their emotions.'

Ettie blinked back a tear, hoping that no one would notice.

Everyone was subdued and even Gracie's bacon butties did little to lighten the atmosphere.

'This could be the last time we all meet up,' said Jane, her eyes starting to well up. 'And I've found it so good for me. It feels like we can share here.'

'Yeah,' said Rachel, her angry face screwing up. 'I can be a complete bitch and none of you ever call me out on it.'

'It's all right,' said Hazel, 'we talk about you behind your back.'

'No, you don't,' replied Rachel. 'But I am a cow. I probably deserve it. I need to swim to make me feel almost human.'

Ettie glanced at her and for the first time realised that it was self-loathing that drove Rachel. She felt bad about all the uncharitable thoughts she'd had about the other woman.

'I swim because I can,' said Hazel. 'It reminds me I'm alive and that I have all my faculties and my body still works. I don't want to slow down as I age. I look at my parents, who barely leave the house because they can't anymore, and I want to be as active as I can for as long as I can.'

'I swim because it makes me feel better,' said Jane, 'although I've no idea why.'

'I started because I'm so boring,' confessed Gracie.

'No, you're not,' said Ettie, whirling round to look at her.

'Yes, I am. I haven't been anywhere or done anything. I was just a wife. When you started at the house, so bright and bubbly, you inspired me to try new things. I was never that keen on swimming, but it's nice being here with you all. I feel like one of the gang. I've never been in a gang.'

Out of the corner of her eye, Ettie saw Josh frowning, as if it hadn't occurred to him that other people had their problems. She caught Grandad's eye and wondered if he might make his own confession. They were two of a kind. He'd introduced her to swimming when she was a child, when she carried the weight of the world on her shoulders, worrying about everything for the whole household. Mum and Lindsey had always been happy-go-lucky characters, never too concerned about what the future might bring.

'I swim because it stopped me feeling lonely,' said Grandad unexpectedly. 'My wife died and it helped.' He exchanged a glance with Ettie, a silent acknowledgement that they were the proverbial two peas.

'I had a miscarriage,' blurted out Rachel. 'It was my own fault. I was working too hard. I didn't take care of myself. I hate myself for it and I'm so horrible to my poor husband, I think he's going to leave me.' Her lip curled. 'And I don't blame him. I just want to swim into oblivion. Sometimes I imagine getting into the sea and just swimming for ever and never coming back. Swimming here stops me doing that. I have to turn around and come back.'

She shuddered and gave a half-sob as she realised the enormity of what she'd just said.

'No, Rachel,' said Jane, immediately putting her arm around the young woman. 'You mustn't think like that.'

'But I do.' Rachel broke down, sobbing as Jane hugged her, rubbing her back.

'I hate to ask this, but have you thought about counselling?' asked Hazel.

Rachel shook her head. 'People have miscarriages all the time. You just have to get on with it.'

'No, you don't,' replied Hazel. 'You need to heal. All of you. Not just your body.'

Rachel wiped away her tears and leaned into Jane's hug.

Josh lowered himself to the rug. 'You're a very good swimmer,' he offered with a hopeful smile, as if desperate to say something but fearful of saying the wrong thing.

Rachel raised her head and looked at him, a slight smile curving her lips. 'Thank you.'

'That's all right.' He screwed up his face as if steeling himself. 'Do you want to know why I swim?'

'Yes.' She nodded, actually coming across as human for once.

'Because when I'm in the water I feel as good as any of you. You're all older than me but I can swim the same as any of you.' He gave a sudden grin. 'And you're all too polite to say anything about me leg. You all just pretend like it's not a thing, and I like that. You all treat me like I'm an annoying teenager.'

'That's because you are,' said Rachel. 'Really annoying.'

'Well, you're a stroppy cow.'

'I know. But swimming makes me less stroppy.'

'Bloody hell. Really?' Everyone burst out laughing at Josh's heartfelt comment.

'Well, this is all very nice,' said Hazel, cutting to the chase in her usual forthright fashion. 'But what do we do now?'

'I must go and face the music,' said Ettie, lifting her chin. 'This time he's going to sack me, for sure.'

'I won't let him sack you,' said Gracie, her mouth setting in a mulish line. 'He needs you. We need you.'

Ettie's smile was forlorn. Dominic had every right to sack her. She should have put a stop to this when he told her how he felt about water. She wouldn't blame him at all for dismissing her. She'd done what she'd always done – did what she thought was best and assumed she knew better. It had been the same in every job. Each time, her own blithe confidence that she knew better was the cause of her downfall. She'd probably have been sacked from the vintage clothes shop eventually because of her timekeeping. Sally wanted the shop opened at 9.30 but Ettie had always been late because customers didn't rock up before 10.00, but that hadn't been her call to make, she realised. Just as swimming in the lake hadn't been her call to make, and certainly not encouraging and facilitating the others to come too. Dominic had made it quite plain that he didn't want people using the lake. That should have been enough, even before he'd laid out his reasons, but she'd ignored his wishes, even when she was sleeping with him. Even when she'd fallen for him.

She owed Dominic an apology and more. He had trouble trusting people at the best of times, and now she hadn't given him any reason to change his mind.

Chapter Twenty-One

Every step she took up the stairs seemed heavier than the last as Ettie headed up to the bathroom to shower and change. She knew she had to face Dominic straightaway, and as soon as she was clean and dry she donned her favourite shirt (bright red for a bit of courage) and her favourite cut-off denim shorts to show that she wasn't completely intimidated by him. She owed him an apology. A dressing down was well deserved but there wouldn't be any grovelling. She'd admit her mistake, say sorry and accept whatever he said. That was the bit she was dreading. Now that whatever they'd had between them was in jeopardy, her stupid heart had woken up to the fact that she was halfway in love with him. She'd let him down so very badly.

Steeling herself, she opened the study door. Dominic sat behind his desk, his face impassive as he tapped away at the keyboard on his laptop. He didn't look up.

Her heart clenched a little as she looked at him. She'd really blown it and now, as she took in his handsome face, regret kicked hard. Dominic wasn't the sort to give second chances and he'd been betrayed by his wife before. The thought made her stomach a little nauseous as it brought home the gravity of what she'd done. Ettie had betrayed him as well. She'd slept in his bed, all the while going against his wishes. She had no excuses. She'd known exactly what she was doing and had chosen to ignore what hadn't suited her.

She couldn't even use the excuse that she'd been trying to help the others. The plain truth was, she'd done what she wanted to do for herself.

She pulled up a chair and sat down on the other side of the desk. Dominic looked up, his mouth pinched and his eyes wary.

'I've come to apologise.'

Surprise flickered in his eyes and he leaned back in his chair. After a brief hesitation he folded his arms.

'I'm really sorry. I knew you didn't want people swimming in the lake and I ignored it. I shouldn't have done that and I don't have a good excuse. I went behind your back and I'm sorry that I did that.'

'Sorry that you were caught.'

She deserved that. 'Yes, but sorrier that I didn't appreciate how much I was letting you down.'

'You haven't let *me* down,' he said, the words tumbling out quickly.

The lump in her throat threatened to choke her as she

realised his meaning. You had to matter to someone in order to let them down.

'I take it you and your band of merry swimmers made hay while I was out at physio every week. Bad luck that my therapist cancelled this morning when I was halfway there.'

Ettie looked him straight in the eye. 'Actually, it was every chance they got.'

He let out a laugh. 'Had fun, did you?'

'I'm not making any excuses. At first it was just the Wednesdays, but then Grandad brought Josh along.'

'Grandad? Iggy Pop is your grandad?'

She nodded. His mouth pursed. 'Funny you didn't mention the familial relationship the first time I caught him.'

'No.'

Shamefaced, she looked down at her hands. This was more painful than she'd expected, having become used to Dominic's admiration of her skills and talents. She didn't like this stern disapproval.

'And Josh? The boy. Am I supposed to be charitable about him? Despite the fact none of you were supposed to be swimming there, he's going to melt my heart, is he?'

'No, but the lake is the only place he feels comfortable swimming. Grandad thought it might help boost his confidence and give him something to do. I'm not using that as an excuse, because we were already swimming on Wednesdays.'

'Even though I made it totally clear that I didn't want people swimming on my property.'

His eyes bored into her and she shuffled in her seat.

With a mirthless smile, he steepled his fingers. 'Actually, to my surprise, I'm reluctantly impressed that you've owned it. You haven't made any excuses or tried to justify yourself. In that you have been honest.'

She gave him a strained smile but he wasn't being complimentary and his expression remained implacable.

'I think we both know it was a fair cop. I have no excuses.' She laced her fingers together on her lap, meeting his impassive gaze. And that was possibly the worst thing. She didn't have an excuse. No good reason for going behind his back. She'd known all along that what she was doing was wrong, but she'd told herself over and over that because he didn't know, it was all right. But it wasn't all right. It was worse. She'd betrayed his trust. Deliberately. When she knew he had trust issues. And she'd proved him right – people weren't to be trusted. She might not have lied outright to his face but she had gone out of her way to plan things when he wasn't around. In lying by omission, she'd been deceitful. And how she hated that word. It spiralled out to suggest other less palatable attributes: unscrupulous, dishonest, devious, when she'd always prided herself on being a decent person – good, kind, loving, supportive. She'd been guilty of a kind of arrogant contempt for Dominic, being so sure that what he didn't know wouldn't harm him. Choosing to ignore his wishes for what she wanted. Shame licked at her like encroaching flames, bringing self-condemnation.

His eyes flashed. 'I'm bloody furious with you,' he said,

his words cold and contained, and all the more powerful for it. His mouth firmed. 'You're not the person I thought you were.'

She grimaced, swallowing hard. There was a horrible air of finality about his words.

'Sorry, Ettie, you're going to have to pack your bags. I'll pay you until the end of the week but it's probably for the best if you leave now.'

She sat frozen to her seat, unable to do more than nod at him. Her voice couldn't be trusted at that moment; it would crack and her words would wobble. The worst thing was that it was no more than she deserved. There was no point trying to argue, even if she'd wanted to.

'Gracie?' Ettie dropped her case at the front door; the taxi was due any minute. The sweet smell of vanilla greeted her as she entered the kitchen. The entire counter was filled with pale biscuits in a variety of shapes – diamonds, clubs, spades and hearts, along with dogs, shamrocks and dinosaurs.

'You've been busy,' said Ettie, inhaling the delicious sugary aroma filling the room. God, she was going to miss this; she'd grown so fond of Gracie.

'Yes?' said Gracie, her face full of worry, wiping her hands on her apron. 'Come and have a cuppa. Are you all right? Was Dominic very cross? I'm sure he'll come round.'

Ettie felt stupid tears well up in her eyes. Annoying

things. She'd been trying to hold back her emotions, lacing them tightly out of bounds, but Gracie's words unpicked her defences. 'I don't think he will,' she said in a small voice. 'He sacked me.'

'No!' Gracie's face crumpled. 'Oh Ettie!' she wailed and began to cry. The knots in Ettie's stomached tightened. In a flash she crossed the kitchen floor to wrap her arms around Gracie's waist.

'It's OK,' she whispered to the weeping woman, rubbing her back ineffectually.

Gracie sniffed and hugged her back. 'No, it's not.' Then she straightened and blew her nose. 'I'll go and talk to him. He'll change his mind. That's typical Dominic, he'll calm down and see it doesn't make sense.'

For a foolish moment, Ettie almost believed Gracie, but Dominic was a man of strong principles; she couldn't see him forgiving her and she didn't want to give false hope to the other woman.

'He's not going to change his mind, Gracie. You know his wife lied to him. Well, so did I, and I went behind his back. He's not going to trust me anymore. I knew how and why he felt the way he did about the lake, and I wilfully ignored his feelings. His trauma.'

'Well, that may be, but he's an idiot as well. Anyone can see that you were doing a good thing for people. And for him, if he let you.'

With a scrunch of her face, Ettie shook her head. 'The principle isn't that different.' Not to a man like Dominic, with strong values and high standards.

'Yes, it is.' Gracie folded her arms stoutly. 'It's a lot different. We were swimming. Not breaking marriage vows. And we never lied to Dominic about it. We just didn't tell him what we were doing.'

'We lied by omission.' Ettie stared out of the kitchen window. 'It's just as bad.'

'We all conspired. In fact, I was the one that sent him out the other day. He hasn't sacked me.' She drew herself upright and turned as if going to face the dragon's heat.

Ettie grabbed her. 'Don't, Gracie, please. I think once the hotel is up and running, you're going to love it here.'

Gracie pulled a face. 'Not without you,' she said, shaking off Ettie's hand with surprising steel. 'I'm going to talk to him right now.'

Ettie put a hand on Gracie's arm again. 'Please don't. It's fine. It really doesn't matter for me, but you need this job and you want to stay here, don't you? And I was only ever going to be here for a short time.'

'But you fitted in so well, and you and Dominic... I'm not stupid. You seemed so good for him. I thought you might stay.'

Ettie's stomach hollowed out at her words. Deep down, she'd thought she might too. For the first time ever, she'd found a job she was good at and she enjoyed. Even though she was officially only an assistant, she'd felt part of something, and Dominic had listened to her and respected her judgement. He'd treated her like an equal and not just at work. She closed her eyes, thinking of him in bed this morning. Slow welcome-to-the-day kisses, his arm heavy over her waist, their legs entangled. A shaft of pain lanced through her, yet more regret exploding with a vicious kick. She almost doubled over and had to hold the sob in. She didn't want to make Gracie any unhappier.

'In fact, you *should* stay. He doesn't know a good thing when he sees it.' Before Ettie could stop her, Gracie stormed out of the kitchen, her head held abnormally high, and went down the hall towards the study. Ettie hesitated, torn between admiration for Gracie's determination and fear that the other woman might put her own future in jeopardy.

Gracie flung open the study door.

Ettie rushed after her.

'What are you doing, Dominic?' Gracie demanded, with both hands on her hips, standing over Dominic, who was sitting at his desk.

'What do you mean?'

'You idiot. Sacking Ettie. What's come over you?'

Dominic looked up at her, his eyes wary. 'I...'

'You're making a big mistake. She's the best thing that's happened to you for a long time. The best thing that's happened to *us*. This place would never have got off the ground without her and you know it. We'd both still be dithering about.'

'Gracie, she's broken my number-one rule. I said no swimming.'

'Oh tosh!' snapped Gracie, much to Ettie's amusement as she stood out of Dominic's eyeline in the hallway just beyond the door. 'You're cutting your nose off to spite your face. It's not about the swimming at all, is it?'

'I don't know what you mean,' said Dominic's voice, stiff with denial.

'Tell him, Ettie,' said Gracie, whirling round and furiously beckoning her in.

Ettie couldn't let the other woman down, but she could do without this. Dominic had every right to sack her, but for someone who was a stickler for honesty, she ought at least to put it to him. With a resigned sigh she entered the room.

'She's right, you know,' said Ettie, giving him a weary smile. 'This isn't about the swimming. It's about trust. You're using the swimming as an excuse because you don't want to trust me. You know perfectly well that we're all experienced swimmers, and two of us are trained lifeguards.'

Dominic glared at her, his mouth doing that crimping thing again before he said in a low voice, 'You lied by omission. You went behind my back, even after I told you why I don't want anyone swimming.'

Ettie opened her mouth, about to explain that she'd had every intention of winding the swimming up this morning, but looking at his thunderous face, she decided there was absolutely no point. Instead she turned to Gracie. 'Sorry, Gracie.' Then she walked out of the room to go and collect her things.

Ettie clambered into the back of the taxi and kept her head held high just in case Dominic happened to look out of the window. Whenever she'd been sacked before, it had come as a relief. Not this time. Not by a long chalk. Regret was a terrible thing. As was *If only...* There were too many things to wish undone. She had to console herself with the thought that, long term, Dominic wouldn't have stayed with someone like her, and besides, once she'd completed her qualification, she'd be going back to London. Perhaps this was for the best; she'd been getting a bit too settled. Even so, the thought of not seeing Dominic again, never kissing him again and never sharing his bed again, cracked her heart, and the pain of it forced a sob from her. She'd really messed up this time.

Chapter Twenty-Two

Ettie, pulling her suitcase behind her, pushed through the back door into the kitchen and sighed. Mum, Grandad and Lindsey, with Tiffany Eight on her knee, were all sitting around the table.

They looked at the suitcase.

'You've not been sacked again,' said Lindsey, pulling a face of overdramatic disbelief.

'He weren't best pleased,' said Grandad, nodding slowly. 'But I didn't think he'd sack you.'

Ettie heaved out another sigh. 'Yes. I've been sacked. Again.' As Lindsey opened her mouth, she added, 'And I don't want to hear one word about the sodding mustard factory.'

'Oooh, Auntie Ettie's in a snit,' said Lindsey, cuddling her daughter.

'Let me get you a cuppa, love,' said her mum, jumping to her feet.

'I'm sorry, lass.' Grandad stood up and came to give her hug. 'You right enjoyed that job.'

'Happen, I did, Grandad,' said Ettie, teasing his lapse into proper Yorkshire, which he tended to revert to when he was upset. 'But I'll survive. It's just a job.' She gave his wiry frame a gentle squeeze back.

'You're a good lass. I don't understand what his problem is.'

She knew he was talking about Dominic. 'I think it's not being able to control the environment properly. He's worried about the health and safety aspect.' She sat down in her usual place at the table.

'Well, I'm sorry. Maybe if I hadn't brought Josh—'

'It's not your fault, Grandad.' It had been inevitable the minute she started swimming behind Dominic's back.

'Don't fret,' said her mum, opening a pack of chocolate fingers. They were the standard Merman treat when anyone needed cheering up. 'You've still got your bookkeeping.'

'Not sure what we're going to do about young Josh, though,' said Grandad. 'He'd just got a taste for it.'

'Can't he just go to the pool?' asked Lindsey.

Ettie and Grandad exchanged a quick smile and he snorted. 'He's a stubborn tyke. He's not having any of it. He says he'll only swim at the lake.'

'He might change his tune when autumn comes,' observed Mum.

'That's a while off and in the meantime, he'll be back on that Xbox of his, staying indoors all the time.'

Ettie took a chocolate biscuit and drank her tea. It was a

shame about Josh, about all of them really, but if she was worried about anyone, it was Gracie. She'd seemed to have come out of her shell a little and she'd made some friends. Ettie hoped she wouldn't lose that.

'Eh, Ettie?'

'Sorry.'

'I said we should start a campaign.'

His words filled her with unease. 'What do you mean?'

'Campaign to let Josh use the lake.'

'I'm not sure that's a good idea. Dominic's pretty angry right now. I think it's probably best to let sleeping dogs lie.'

Grandad let out a cackle. 'And where's the fun in that? Dogs need keeping busy.'

'Grandad, please. Just let it go.' Ettie didn't want to think about Dominic; if she did, her brave face might crack. 'I'm going to go upstairs. Do a bit of studying. I've got exams coming up.'

For the next week, Ettie kept herself to herself during the day, trying to work on her modules and sleeping on the sofa at night because she couldn't bear being in a double bed with someone that wasn't Dominic. Needless to say, she didn't get much sleep; most of the time she gazed into the darkness. Never before in her life had she wished she could turn the clock back as much as she did now. She couldn't deny she'd enjoyed swimming in the lake, but she would have gladly sacrificed it to stay with him. Part of her ached with regret, but at the same time she knew it was her own stupid fault. She'd fallen into the same old pattern: Ettie knew best and she'd done what she wanted, ignoring the consequences. Except this time, she hadn't foreseen how much the consequences would affect her. She'd fallen in love with Dominic but she hadn't realised it until it was too late. The strength of conviction that made him so adamant he didn't want anyone swimming in his lake was the very thing that she found so attractive. He was a man of his word, with values and principles. He took things seriously and made things happen. He looked after people and felt responsibility keenly. Look how he'd looked after Gracie when he didn't need to; how he'd admitted openly that he'd been wrong to doubt Ettie's employability. She liked that he took charge but didn't try to handle her. He'd never made her feel less than his equal even though he was her boss.

The following Wednesday afternoon, she was sitting cross-legged on her bed with her laptop in front of her, when her phone began to buzz. She ignored it at first; she had to get some work done, although the module on documentation of accounts preparation she was supposed to be studying wasn't exactly holding her attention. Her thoughts kept straying to Dominic.

Her phone buzzed again. It was starting to sound like a hive of bees. She shoved it away and picked up her textbook, marking a passage about bad debts with a yellow highlighter pen. Screwing up her face, she re-read the paragraph and sighed as her phone buzzed yet again. What was going on?

Finally, in frustration, she grabbed her phone. Twenty-six alerts on WhatsApp.

Hilda: *Hello everyone. I have an idea.*

Gracie: *Hello Hilda :)*

Grandad: *Hello Hilda*

Jane: *Hello Hilda xxx*

Josh: *S'up Hilda.*

Ettie groaned as everyone greeted Hilda.

Hilda: *We need a council of war.*

Now Ettie regretted not looking at her phone earlier; she would have nipped this in the bud. But judging by the number of comments, that boat had sailed into the sunset the equivalent of three weeks ago.

Rachel: *What do we need a council of war for?*

Hilda: *To swim!*

Gracie: *Dominic's still very angry.*

Hilda: *He'll come round; we're going to make him.*

Ettie shuddered. What on earth had Hilda got up her sleeve?

Grandad: *Keep talking. Let's meet.*

There followed a lengthy discussion about where and when, which Ettie scrolled through with resignation. Trying to stop them would have been like trying to halt a tidal wave with a bulldozer. Absolutely no chance.

'No,' she moaned when she reached the current end of the chat.

Grandad: *See you later. The address is 65 Acacia Avenue, just off Craven Street. Anyone fancy fish and chips?*

Ettie closed her eyes as another flurry of messages arrived and then stared disconsolately out of the window before finally looking back at the phone.

Looked like it was fish and chips for seven downstairs in just over two hours. Josh had declined the invitation.

'Where's Grandad?' she asked, coming downstairs at six-thirty, following the strong scent of batter. The fish and chips had arrived.

'He's gone to pick up the woman from the Hall on his motorbike, should be back any minute,' replied Mum, standing in front of a mound of newspaper-wrapped parcels that she was putting into the oven to keep warm.

'What's going on?' asked Lindsey, who was feeding Tiffany Eight from a small bowl of fish and chips slathered in tomato sauce. It smelled delicious and if it hadn't been for the fact that it would probably make the baby cry, Ettie might have stolen a chip.

'Grandad and his mates have called a council of war,' said Ettie. 'How come you missed that?'

'I've been out. Seeing Darren.' Lindsey's lips curled. 'Except he'd forgotten. I found him in the pub.'

'Bet that went down well,' said Ettie, shooting a quick glance at her mum, who pulled a face.

'I don't want to talk about it. So what's this mothers' meeting about?'

'We're going to swim at the lake again,' announced Hilda, sweeping in through the open door as if she were a regular visitor. 'Hello, Ettie. This must be your mother. Lovely to meet you. I'm Hilda Fitzroy-Townsend and this is Claire. My chauffeur.'

'There's posh,' muttered Lindsey.

'Hello.' Mum looked up. 'You're Harold's wife, aren't you? He plays bowls with my dad.'

Hilda gave a slight sniff. 'Not yet. Harold wants to be my husband but I'm not the least bit wifely.' She grinned. 'My last four husbands have found that out to their cost, although technically I wasn't married to number three, but I didn't find that out until he was dead and his first wife showed up at the funeral. You'd have thought she'd have more taste.'

Mum nodded, her eyes widening in bemusement.

'Hi.' Claire's eyes danced with amusement; she was clearly used to Hilda. 'I'm apparently just the chauffeur today, but I also helped to set up the parkrun. Hilda has decided—' she shot Ettie a wry smile '—you need her help. She's very bossy and I thought I'd make my life a lot easier by agreeing to Hilda's command that I bring her here forthwith.'

'Forthwith,' said Ettie, pinching her lips together.

'Exactly,' said Claire. 'Basically, Hilda never takes no for an answer and I run interference where I can. You're doomed.'

'Claire! You do exaggerate. And you must be Lindsey. I heard you called the baby after a jewellery store. Isn't Ernest Jones a strange name for a little girl?'

Lindsey opened her mouth and made a strange wheezing sound. She was rarely lost for words.

'You get used to her, after a while,' said Claire, as Hilda paused for breath.

Hilda looked down her nose.

'Actually, scratch that. You never know what she's going to say next.' Despite her words, Claire hooked her arm through Hilda's with an affectionate grin. 'She's a menace.'

'Huh, I'd rather be a menace than an invisible old woman. I still have things to say and do. And my newest mission, should the rest of you choose to accept it—'

'You will,' said Claire. 'You don't have a choice.'

'We,' Hilda declared, ignoring her friend, 'are going to turn Josh into a Paralympian.'

Ettie raised her eyebrows. This was news to her, but given Hilda's booming assertion, she had no doubt the woman could probably make it happen.

'What, that lad with one leg?' said Lindsey, focused on wiping tomato sauce from around Tiffany Eight's mouth.

'It's one and half,' said a voice.

Everyone turned around to find Josh standing in the doorway.

'Ah, lad.' Grandad appeared behind Josh, Gracie behind him, still wearing an old-fashioned motorbike helmet on her head that gave her a bug-like appearance. He put his hands on the boy's shoulders. 'You decided to come after all.'

Josh gave one of his familiar laconic shrugs. 'Nowt better to do.' He turned to Lindsey. 'And it's *amputee*.'

Lindsey blushed. 'Sorry.'

Josh gave her an insincere smile.

'Come sit down, lad. I've been doing a bit of research.'

Gracie gave Ettie a shy smile. 'Are you all right? I'm so cross with Dominic, I'm not talking to him, you know.'

'Oh, Gracie. Don't take my side. I was in the wrong and I don't want you to spoil your relationship with him.'

'Huh, chance would be a fine thing. He's as grumpy as a bear who's stuck his head in a wasps' nest. And he's not eating.' Gracie looked appalled by this. Ettie tuned back into the conversation around her.

'Cup of tea, Josh?' asked Mum. 'How's your mum?'

A rare brief smile flashed across Josh's face. 'She's good. Finally gone back to work full-time instead of fussing over me. Gone back to fussing over her animals. She likes them better than people. They don't answer back.'

Everyone laughed. Josh's mum was a veterinary nurse

and for as long as Ettie could remember, she was the first point of call if anyone found a stunned bird, a hedgehog with a broken leg or a bleeding cat.

His expression saddened. 'She can't fix me and it upsets her.'

Sandra looked at him. 'Are you broken? Doesn't look like it from here. You're getting around just fine. You walked here, didn't you, on that thing.' She nodded to the prosthetic leg.

Josh lifted his chin in surprise. 'Yes. Yes, I did.'

'Well then, you're not dead, are you? There's a lot of folk worse off.'

Ettie winced at her mum's forthright observation.

'I know you had a tough time in hospital and that, and I'm sorry for that,' continued Sandra, 'but you got to get on with it now, and from where I'm sitting, you're doing all right.'

Josh laughed. 'I'm not getting any sympathy from you, am I?'

'Do you want it?'

He shook his head.

'Well, that's that, then. You stopping for fish and chips? There's plenty.'

'Yes, please.'

Sandra busied herself making a cup of tea.

Ettie was wondering where everyone was going to sit when Hazel, Jane and Rachel turned up, each clutching two foldaway picnic chairs.

'Me and Lindsey and the baby will go in the other room,

out of the road ,' said Mum, reading Ettie's mind.

Even so, the small kitchen was pretty crammed and Josh, Ettie and Grandad sat in a line in front of the sink and the cooker, eating their fish and chips out of the newspaper on their laps because there wasn't room at the table for everyone or enough plates. The others squeezed around the table, their elbows in tight as they awkwardly ate, but there was plenty of noise and good humour. Ettie smiled. It was the most people she'd ever seen in the kitchen, but no one seemed to mind. Gracie seemed to be in her element, chattering away as if she'd been starved of female companionship for most of her life and was making up for lost time.

'So, me and Josh had a bit of chat on the way back from the lake the other day. Didn't we, lad?'

Josh smirked. 'I think it were more you talked and I had to listen.'

Grandad grinned at him. 'And what do you think?'

With a lift of his shoulders, Josh said, 'Why not?' But there was a light in his eyes that suggested he was far from indifferent.

'So, I've been talking to Hilda—' said Grandad.

'And I've talked to someone I know,' said Hilda.

Ettie looked from Grandad to Josh. 'What are you talking about?'

'With a bit of serious training, I reckon Josh can go all the way. He's got grit, determination and he can bloody swim. When he was racing you, he upped a gear in a way you rarely see ... and that's without training.'

JULES WAKE

Josh looked down at the table, his ears turning pink.

'OK,' said Ettie, smiling at the teenage boy's downturned head.

'So,' said Hilda, as imperious as a queen, 'I've been talking to my friend Johnny – he swam in the Paralympics in London in 2012. First thing we need to do is get you classified. Apparently it's all about the drag. How much your leg increases your drag in the water is how they classify you. There's a waiting list but that's all right. In the meantime we can get you some training and then you can start entering some competitions.'

Hilda made it all sound so straightforward, but then she explained that there were programmes he could apply to, but he'd need to build up points from entering in races.

'It's going to take some time and a lot of hard work to get you on one of these programmes,' said Grandad.

'Don't you think I can do it?' Josh clenched a fist on the table.

'Nay, lad. I know you can. You've got that killer competitive edge. That leg of yours isn't slowing you down. I've trained champions before and it's up here.' He tapped his forehead. 'Winning is in the head. You've either got a will to win, or not. Our Ettie never had it.'

'Thanks, Grandad.'

'Well, you didn't. You liked the swimming and you were good at it, but winning wasn't that important to you.' He was right. She'd enjoyed the camaraderie of the pool, pushing her body as hard as she could, but she didn't care enough about the winning. 'Josh here is a barracuda in the making. You wait and see.'

'There's one thing, though,' said Josh. 'Isn't this going to cost money? The training. And where am I going to train? I'm not going to the pool here. And then getting to competitions. My mum can't afford anything extra. It cost her a fortune in taxis getting me to all my hospital and physio appointments last year. I can't ask her again. And who's going to give me a job?'

'Don't you worry about that, lad. We'll come up with something. There must be lottery funding or something.' Grandad lifted his tea mug. 'In the meantime, we need to get a proper training schedule going.'

'I'm not going to the pool,' repeated Josh stubbornly.

'We're going to get you back in the lake,' said Hilda.

Ettie rolled her eyes.

'Shame you're not still working there,' said Lindsey, who'd appeared in the doorway with two empty plates.

'Yeah, we could have got you to do something to keep him out of the way permanently,' said Grandad.

Gracie lifted her head. 'I might—'

'No,' said Ettie firmly. 'You can't risk it.' The last thing she wanted was Gracie losing her home. 'He's made his views more than clear and he has good reason for them.' She wasn't about to betray his confidence about his fear of water. 'It's not right to go behind his back.'

'I bet we can think of something.' Grandad's eyes gleamed like a feral fox's.

'Oh yes, I'll just shove him down the stairs so he breaks

his leg again. Or better yet, why don't I finish him off and bury him under the patio?'

'You always have to be so dramatic,' complained Lindsey, her daughter on her hip. 'Just seduce him.'

Ettie opened her mouth but nothing came out and her sister, who never missed a trick, pounced.

'You minx! Have you already done the dirty?'

'Lindsey,' muttered Ettie.

'You have. Go on, tell. What's he like in the sack? Is he all masterful, like in that film *An Officer and a Gentleman*? Did you make him wear his uniform? I bet he's got a good bod, hasn't he?'

'I'm not having this conversation in front of Grandad and a teenager.' Ettie tried to sound haughty, which was a little difficult when every head in the room had turned her way; even Tiffany Eight was gurgling at her.

'Shame,' said Josh, leaning on the table, putting his chin into both hands with interest.

'I used to babysit you,' said Ettie, folding her arms and staring down the teenager, who simply grinned at her. As it was the first time she'd seen him smile properly for a very long time, she huffed out an exasperated breath. 'Shall we change the subject?'

'Anyone for more tea?' Ettie's mum came bustling in like a busy moorhen and Ettie could have kissed her.

'I think we should have a campaign of civil disobedience to make our point,' said Hilda. 'Be a thorn in his side until he reconsiders, and kill two birds with one stone.' Ettie was about to object and point out that it was Dominic's lake, and he could do what he liked with it, until Hilda added, 'We'll get Josh back in the lake and we'll start a campaign to raise some sponsorship money for him.' There was a chorus of approval and agreement around the table, rather like MPs cheering in the House of Commons.

'What do you have in mind?' asked Hazel.

'I like the idea of being a thorn,' said Rachel, her mouth twisting at the thought.

'Does anyone know anyone on the local newspaper?' asked Hilda.

'What are you up to?' asked Claire. 'It will be legal, won't it?'

'Of course it will,' said Hilda, lifting her head with all the arrogant serenity of an elegant swan. Claire muttered something under her breath and Ettie saw Hilda elbow her in the ribs.

'Ettie does. You went to school with that Mark Armstrong,' pointed out Lindsey, as helpful as ever. Ettie flexed her toes with relish, deciding that her sister was going to get one heck of a kick in bed tonight.

'Excellent,' said Hilda, her eyes full of mischief. 'I've got just the idea. Mr Villiers isn't going to know what's hit him and it will make a lovely photo story in the local paper. And it will kick off a fund-raising campaign to get Josh some sponsorship to pay for some proper coaching. I know the paper's photographer, Harold's son, Adam. Between us we're guaranteed to get some interesting press coverage. Although, Josh, we're going to need your help. Would you be willing to have your photo taken?'

Everyone straightened up with sudden interest but tactfully didn't turn to Josh.

Josh stared at her for a minute. Ettie could almost see the debate going on in his head, as his mouth pursed and then firmed and then opened. Eventually he swallowed. 'I'll do it. If it helps us get the lake back.'

'Good lad,' said Grandad, patting him on the back. 'What have you got in mind, Hilda?'

Everyone turned towards Hilda as if she were their commanding officer. 'A publicity stunt.' She went on to explain her idea, which was daft, harmless and in some ways quite amusing except – Ettie closed her eyes – Dominic was going to hate it. She had to say something.

'Look, it's … a clever idea, but I don't want any part in it,' said Ettie, knowing she had to make a stand. She'd let Dominic down once; she didn't want to do it again. And she knew him well enough to know that any kind of action would only make him more angry and even more reluctant to let them use the lake.

Everyone turned to look at her and she felt like a traitor. 'I'm sorry.' She held up both hands.

'But it's worth a try, isn't it, Ettie?' said Josh.

She heard the plaintive note in his voice and saw the rare animation in his face. Grandad was watching the boy like a proud father.

'For Pete's sake,' she said irritably, 'I'll help but I'm not going in the water.' It was a compromise. Dominic wasn't going to forgive her anytime soon, so what was one more transgression?

Chapter Twenty-Three

The white van that had been travelling up the long drive towards the house suddenly veered off the tarmac road and careered across the grass towards Ettie, who was at the lakeside. The van slammed to a halt, went into reverse and circled round before backing up to the beach. It was hardly stealthy or subtle. Luckily, Gracie had confirmed that Dominic was out at his physio session, having changed it to a Tuesday afternoon, which, unfortunately for him, rather handily coincided with the local newspaper's deadline.

The driver's door opened and out jumped Hilda in a lime-green tracksuit and her favourite day-glo trainers, as Grandad staggered out of the passenger side, his face a similar shade of green. Then a young girl of about thirteen or fourteen hopped out after him.

'Dear God, woman, where the hell did you learn to drive like that?'

Hilda waved a dismissive hand. 'This is nothing, you should try driving in Egypt across the desert in the dark without headlights. Hairy, I can tell you. This is my friend Poppy. She's come to help.'

Ettie gave the girl a friendly smile and received a shy smile back.

'I didn't think you drove,' said Ettie, thinking of Claire bringing Hilda over the other day.

'I don't. Haven't had a licence for years,' replied Hilda with a blithe toss of her head.

'Hilda,' squeaked Poppy. 'You didn't tell Claire that.'

'It's best if she doesn't know. Now, we'd better get started. Where is everyone?'

'Jane and Hazel are on their way,' said Ettie. 'They'll be here in five minutes. Rachel is picking Josh up and they'll be here a bit later. Gracie will be another forty minutes and she's bringing the swimming hats.'

'Right, action stations.' Hilda marched around to the back of the van and threw open the doors. Inside were piles and piles of brightly coloured plastic. Poppy and Ettie helped her while Grandad pulled out a couple of foot pumps. 'These'll save us a lot of time. For once that useless oik Darren came up trumps, although why anyone would have a lock-up full of foot pumps is anyone's guess,' grumbled Grandad. 'What's first? Flamingos, pizza slices or T-Rexes?'

'Where did you get all these?' asked Ettie.

'The swimming pool ordered a job lot a couple of years ago. They were going to do fun inflatable sessions but then they realised there was nowhere to store them, so they would have needed blowing up every time, and no one fancied that. They've been sitting in a storage shed ever since. Never been used. I didn't think anyone would notice if I borrowed them.'

By the time Gracie arrived, the beach was covered in every shape and size of blow-up swimming toy imaginable and Grandad had tied them all together with yards and yards of string. 'We don't want them drifting off to all corners of the lake.'

The plan was to fill this section of the lake with them and take a photo with the swimmers in the foreground. As Ettie had refused to go in the water, she'd been designated to meet the journalist, Mark, and the photographer, Adam Benton.

'I love this one,' said Jane, picking up a bright-pink swimming ring with a mermaid tail sticking up. She slipped it on around her middle and began prancing and posing, simpering at Hazel, who burst out laughing and began taking pictures. Their giggles lightened the strain on their faces.

'Is everything OK?' asked Ettie, when Jane finally relinquished the ring.

Jane puffed out a long breath. 'No, not at all. We still haven't found a venue for the wedding.'

Ettie slapped a hand across her mouth. 'I'm so sorry! I completely forgot. I was going to ask Dominic... Oh Jane, I'm so sorry. With everything that happened, I clean forgot.'

'Ettie, don't worry. Getting sacked like that must have

been awful. Besides, I'm not sure Dominic would want us – he certainly won't after today. And that's the least of our problems. Bloody family. Oh, look, here's Gracie.'

'Isn't this marvellous,' said Gracie, coming to stand next to them, staring round at the colourful display. 'The poor ducks and moorhens aren't going to know what's going on.'

'There's plenty of room in the rest of the lake for them,' said Hazel, putting a supportive arm around her partner. 'How do the hats look?'

'Perfect,' said Gracie, rummaging in the bag at her side. 'Here.' She pulled out a jumble of neon-orange hats.

'Great,' said Hazel. 'They look really good. Hopefully they'll get the message across.'

Each cap featured a large letter which Gracie had stencilled onto the silicon surface with a Sharpie.

Rachel walked over wearing a llama swim ring around her shoulders, her face, for once, lit up with a rare mischievous smile. 'This is a laugh. I think my husband thought I was off to meet a fancy man this morning. Although he'd have a shock if he saw me with Josh.'

'It's nice to see you smile, Rachel,' said Hazel.

'I didn't know you cared.' Rachel's mouth twisted with a sardonic, humourless smile.

'Of course we care,' said Jane, reaching out to her with both hands and taking her forearm, pulling her in for a hug. Rachel froze for a moment and then it was as if someone had popped a balloon and she sagged for an instant, letting herself be enfolded into an embrace, although the llama got in the way, bashing Jane in the nose. They both laughed.

'Well, this is all lovely,' said Hilda, making them all jump. 'But we've got a job to do, and I think that might be your journalist chappie, Ettie.' She pointed to a man standing on the edge of the beach.

Ettie jogged over to greet him. 'Mark, hi.'

'Hey, Ettie.' He dropped a kiss on her cheek. 'You're looking good.' There was no mistaking the admiring gleam in his eye.

'You're not looking so bad yourself,' she teased. 'Nice.' She tugged at the smooth supple leather of his jacket. Mark Armstrong had definitely improved with age. 'How long is it?'

'Must be a couple of years.' He grinned at her, his chestnut eyes warm as they checked out her face. 'Fancy a drink later?'

'I'd love to, but I've got an assignment to hand in.' Mark was lovely but he wasn't Dominic.

His face fell. Had Dominic spoiled her for anyone else? Lifting her chin, she suddenly said, 'But once that's out of the way, I'm free.'

'Great. Dinner?'

'That would be lovely.'

His eyes sharpened as there was a flurry of activity on the beach. 'So what exactly is going on?'

Ettie steeled herself, her heart pinching with guilt. Dominic was going to hate this. 'Let me introduce you to Josh.'

The photo shoot was all set up, and Mark had interviewed Josh to tease out the details of his accident and how he found swimming in the lake so much more appealing than in a pool. Ettie watched as Hilda, Gracie, Grandad, Hazel, Jane and Rachel, all in borrowed wetsuits, pulled on their hats and waded out into the water. Imagining the cool water, she almost wished she'd chosen to swim with them, but there was still some vestige of loyalty to Dominic that stopped her.

The swimmers arranged themselves in a line.

'What are they doing?' asked Adam the photographer.

'Just wait a minute,' said Ettie, choosing the video option on her phone as Josh moved into place. Hilda had choreographed things beautifully.

One by one the swimmers turned around and Ettie filmed the scene as the words on their hats spelled P L E A S E and to their right, strung between two of the inflatables, was a large banner which read *Let Josh swim*. And there in the foreground on the grassy ledge in front of the beach stood Josh in a pair of shorts, defiantly showing off his prosthetic leg.

'Brilliant.' Adam took dozens of shots. 'Inspired idea.'

'I have to agree, this is going to make a great story.' Mark took out his phone. 'I wonder if I can get an interview with the owner.'

Ettie winced. 'He's away at the moment.'

'That's a shame. Do you know when he'll be back?'

She shook her head. It was the truth. It could be five

o'clock, it could be six o'clock. She wasn't about to disabuse Mark of the assumption that it might be several days.

'I can hang on, it's not going to go into this week's paper, I'm afraid. A local councillor has been caught receiving back-handers, it's going to take centre stage. I'll try and get this in the following week.' He winked at her. 'Special favour to you.'

'Thanks,' said Ettie with a wan smile, wishing he could bury the story altogether.

'Wait up!' said the photographer, suddenly grabbing Mark. 'Look.'

Dominic's Land Rover Discovery was charging towards them, Scrapper's head hanging out of the back window, his ears flapping and his tongue lapping at the wind. Ettie froze. Oh hell. She wished she were anywhere but here. Luckily for her, he drove straight past and screeched to a halt beside the white van.

He jumped out and ran down to the beach. 'What the hell do you think you're doing?' he roared at the swimmers, who all spotted him at the same moment.

'Hello, Dominic,' said Hilda. 'How are you today?'

'What are you doing, and what's this?' He flung out an arm towards the inflatables, his eyes widening in horrified disbelief.

'Staging a swim-in,' said Hilda with a charming smile, her blue eyes twinkling.

Dominic was speechless as he took in the inflatables strewn across the surface of the lake. 'What ... what?' Hilda waved a pink llama at him, taking advantage of his momentary incapacity.

He shook his head. 'I don't believe this.' Once again he surveyed the rainbow of plastic shapes bobbing merrily on the surface of the lake. 'How am I … are you going to get all of these out?' He folded his arms. 'You can start right now and then you can get off my property.'

'Don't fret, lad,' said Grandad, tugging at one of them to show they were all linked.

Josh was walking towards Dominic and the photographer had his camera lined up ready for the perfect shot. Ettie couldn't bear it. She stood in front of the photographer.

'Don't,' she said. 'Don't turn him into the villain.'

'What are you doing?' asked Mark, tugging her away.

'This isn't fair.'

'I thought you wanted a story.'

'Not like this. He's not a bad person. This isn't his choice. This was Hilda's idea. He's not supposed to be involved, not like this.'

She pulled herself out of Mark's grasp and tore across the grass down to the beach, intercepting Josh before he reached Dominic.

'Don't,' she muttered. 'They'll make a story of it. It will be ugly.'

For once Josh seemed to understand the wider consequences and he nodded and held his ground.

'Ah, Ettie, why am I not surprised to see you here?'

'This is nothing to do with Ettie,' said Hilda, taking charge.

'That's right,' said Grandad, coming to stand behind her, suddenly flanked by Gracie, Rachel, Hazel and Jane.

'It was my idea,' said Hilda. 'Josh needs somewhere to swim, somewhere to train.'

'What's wrong with a bloody swimming pool?' asked Dominic, turning to look at Josh.

'Everyone stares at me,' said Josh with sudden vehemence. 'This lot are ... well, everyone's different here. They don't stare and whisper. They accept me.'

Dominic swallowed and shook his head. 'What safety precautions would you take?'

'What?' Josh goggled.

'I'd be here,' said Grandad.

'And what if you both got into trouble?' Dominic put his hands on his hips.

Grandad pulled a *Seriously?* face and huffed out a breath. 'Our Ettie's a trained lifeguard. What if she came too?'

Dominic's mouth pursed. 'How often would it be?'

Josh and Grandad looked at each other and Josh lifted his shoulders in a shrug.

'Not sure, we could discuss it.' Grandad's voice held a hopeful question in it.

Ettie watched Dominic's jawline firm, his expression stern and thoughtful.

'I'll need to know when you're coming, what time and for how long.'

There was a collective gasp as the words sank in.

'Thank you,' said Josh fervently, quickly adding, 'Sir,' which made Ettie smile.

'Now get these bloody inflatables out of my lake.'

With that, Dominic turned around and stomped back to the Land Rover, where Scrapper began to greet him with ecstatic barks. Behind him there were silent celebrations, as if they all knew they were pushing it and he could still change his mind.

Chapter Twenty-Four

In a triumphant mood, Gracie, Grandad and Josh came back to Ettie's mum's house and Sandra Merman had to crack open her secret stash of chocolate fingers and Fox's Favourites biscuits.

'I tell you, Gracie. Those hats were inspired. You've got a steady hand on you.'

'Thank you, Cyril. It comes from years of icing biscuits.'

'I don't suppose you know how to make a rhubarb crumble, do you?'

Gracie beamed. 'I've got a special family recipe. I put a bit of ginger in the crumble.'

Josh rolled his eyes and helped himself to another biscuit.

Grandad grinned. 'Heck, I might be in love.'

With a giggle, although blushing furiously, Gracie said, 'Don't take on, you haven't tried it yet.'

'Why don't I bring you some rhubarb from my allotment and see how you get on?'

Ettie and her mum exchanged a quick stunned look, before Ettie dropped her eyes, studying the tea in her mug to hide a smile. Grandad was very choosy about who he shared his prize-winning rhubarb with. Gracie had no idea just what an honour had been conferred on her.

The sharp rap at the door startled all of them and Ettie's mum frowned. 'Who can that be? Not next door again. They're always losing that little dog.' She yanked open the door and everyone at the table froze when she exclaimed, 'Dominic. Mr Villiers! What are you doing here?'

'Is Ettie in?' he asked. All of Ettie's senses prickled into life at the sound of his low voice.

She swivelled round as he stepped into the kitchen, her heart bungee-jumping halfway up her throat, thudding in recognition and unexpected longing. All she could do was stare at him, drinking in the sight of his face as dozens of memories flooded back. It was a physical effort to anchor herself in the chair when everything in her wanted to go over and hold him, be held by him.

Dominic's eyes sought hers and she saw a flash of what looked like relief and panic, before a guarded look fell into place as he realised he had an audience. Then his eyes zeroed in on the clearly surprising sight of Gracie sitting there in the thick of things.

'Gracie,' he said, as if swallowing a frog.

'Dominic! Fancy seeing you here,' she said bravely.

His mouth pursed and Ettie couldn't tell if it was with disapproval or disappointment as he turned to her.

'I ... I wondered if I could have a word.'

'Er ... yes.' She stood up on suddenly wobbly legs.

He glanced at everyone avidly watching the exchange. 'In private?'

'Sure.' She glared at the others, their faces bright with unashamed curiosity. 'Shall we go for a walk?'

'Probably a good idea,' said Dominic, his confidence leaking back as he straightened and his shoulders lifted. He held the door open for her and, without looking at the others, she made her way across the room and out into the low evening sunshine.

She led the way through the narrow alleyway to the street. 'Where do you want to go?' she asked, keeping her voice as bland as possible, although a thousand butterflies were trying to beat their way out of her chest.

He shrugged.

'We'll go down the allotments. It's only a minute's walk. There's a bench on Grandad's plot.'

They walked side by side in silence, with Ettie wondering what on earth he wanted to say to her. He hadn't made any move to touch her and she couldn't help the foolish thought that he'd come to tell her that he missed her as much as she missed him. Ettie hated being in the weaker position, not knowing what was going on. Normally she could read people but with Dominic, this evening, she had absolutely no idea what was going through his mind. The not knowing made her uncharacteristically ill at ease, and her nerves and anticipation built with each step.

When they reached the allotments, she led him down a grassy path through the patchwork of plots, some beautifully neat with soldier-like rows of strawberries and tidy wigwam bamboo sticks holding up peas and beans; others a blowsy mass of overgrown flowers and long-seeded vegetables; and some that had been neglected and were sorry sights of broken chairs and abandoned plastic sheeting.

Grandad's plot was a halfway house: his rhubarb bed was immaculate, while the beans needed a good weeding, and there was a pile of pallets with a broken watering can and half-full compost bags that needed a good tidy. Ettie sat down on the wooden bench, which had a couple of slats missing and a couple that had been replaced in a completely different colour. Dominic followed, and for a moment both of them stared out at the view of the grey-blue hazy Dales in the distance on the horizon.

'So what do you want to talk about?' The words tumbled out without finesse, clumsy and blunt, and she sneaked a peek at his profile.

Dominic's head lifted and he turned to look at her, eyes troubled.

'I came to ask you why you weren't in the water.'

Ettie faltered; she hadn't expected that and she answered without thinking. 'I knew you wouldn't like it, but I couldn't stop the others.'

His brows lifted in surprise. 'I wasn't expecting that. You normally do what you want.'

She shrugged. 'I couldn't stop them but I had to be there in case anything went wrong.'

'Good of you,' he said with a touch of acid, and any hope Ettie had that he might have missed her evaporated.

'I wondered if you wanted your job back.'

'*What?*' she spat the word out in utter surprise.

'Gracie is moping around like a wet weekend. She misses you.'

'What about you?' asked Ettie, figuring she had nothing to lose.

He closed his eyes and shook his head. 'What do you want me to say?'

'I'd have thought that was rather obvious,' she replied, the old Ettie reasserting herself.

'Ettie, I miss you...'

Her heart leapt.

'... but I can't trust you. If you come back, there are no more lies. You have to be completely honest with me.'

An uncomfortable lump lodged itself midway down her throat. 'Fair enough,' she said in a croaky voice.

He winced. 'Sorry, but ... you knew how I felt about people swimming, and you still did it. I'm not happy about Josh swimming, but I can see that he needs it, though the thought fills me with terror.'

'Why? He'll be perfectly safe with me and Grandad.'

'Logically, I know that, but...' He lapsed into silence for

a few seconds before lifting his head and looking away into the distance.

'It was a calm day. A bit like today. A light breeze, nothing more. We were called out to a boat that was in trouble, taking on water. It was sinking, but slowly. We had plenty of time. We needed to get the crew off. One of them panicked, went overboard. Two of us went in to rescue him, only one of us came out. A freak wave. Came out of nowhere. That's what a freak wave is,' he added with an almost disbelieving shake of his head. 'Slammed me against the hull of the boat, portside, twice, hence the multiple breaks. Dave, Dave Shipley, my crewman, went under.' Dominic's jaw tightened. 'We found his body the next day.' He leaned back on the bench and tilted his head to look up at the sky. 'Before we'd always been in control, even if people died. We, the rescue team, had a procedure, protocols, we knew what we were doing. That day it didn't work – all the training, the planning, the practice, none of it was worth anything against the water.' Ettie's heart ached at the distraught lines on his face as his mouth crumpled.

She covered his hand resting on his thigh with hers and gave it a gentle squeeze.

'It was a calm day,' he repeated, as if he still couldn't believe it had happened. 'Good conditions. No more than twelve knots. I still don't understand to this day what went wrong.'

He slumped, putting one elbow on his thigh and covering his face with his free hand. Ettie sat and waited, leaving him to talk, and watched as he fought with himself.

Finally, he lifted his head and looked directly at her, his mouth working as if he couldn't find the words or rather didn't want to.

Ettie tensed, guilt swamping her.

'Why didn't you say anything to anyone? Get help?'

Dominic retorted, 'What, that the big macho ex-Naval officer is scared of water? Ettie, I haven't admitted it to anyone, let alone myself. I kept telling myself it was nothing, it would pass – but it hasn't. That's why you have to promise that you won't let Josh go in without you and your grandad being there. If anything happened … to him … to anyone, it would be on my conscience because I know how dangerous water is.'

'I'm really sorry for going behind your back. I shouldn't have pushed things, the way I did.'

The corners of his mouth turned up. 'Then you wouldn't be you.'

'There is that,' she conceded. 'In fact, I'm thinking I'd better come back. You'll be lost without me.'

'I think I might manage, but it would be helpful. Plus you seem to know where everything is. I can't quite follow your filing system.'

'What filing system?' she teased, her eyes twinkling at him.

She saw the barrier go up, as his face shut down, sobering. 'It will be good to have you back but… It doesn't change anything between us, you know that. I need you to know, there is no *us* anymore.'

She nodded bravely, ignoring the recoil inside her as if

all her veins had constricted. Dominic had made it quite clear he couldn't trust her, but she was going to do her best to make sure he didn't regret his decision to reinstate her. From now on she was going to stick to the truth, the whole truth and nothing but the truth. She was an idiot, torturing herself, but she knew she couldn't stay away.

Chapter Twenty-Five

When Ettie rocked up at the house at nine o'clock on Monday morning on the back of Grandad's motorbike, she wasn't sure who Gracie was more thrilled to see, as the older woman fluttered around in the kitchen, making tea and insisting that Grandad have a piece of her latest bread experiment – a light rye loaf, apparently – which had just come out of the oven.

His eagerness to offer her a lift now joined up a lot of dots, especially since Grandad was more morning zombie than morning person.

'That's grand, lass,' he said, slathering the bread with butter that melted quickly in swirls around the glossy spots of Marmite. 'I haven't had proper bread in a long while. Ettie's mum likes that cotton-wool stuff that comes in plastic bags.' He pulled a face. 'Plays havoc with my digestion. Makes me—'

'Too much information,' Ettie warned, praying that he didn't start on about his flatulence.

Gracie laughed. 'My Bob was the same. Ettie, are you stopping?'

'Stopping?'

'Or are you starting work?'

Ettie shot Gracie a cheeky smile. 'I know when I'm not wanted. I'll go get started. Where's Dominic this morning?' She was thoroughly disconcerted to find that her good spirits at returning to the house had nose-dived in disappointment at the sight of the empty drive.

'He's gone to see someone over in Harrogate.' Gracie was vague, far more interested in offering Grandad another slice of bread.

Ettie left them to it, amused by the pair and irritated by herself. She prided herself on her ability not to mope or sulk or pout or be a princess, but this morning she felt irked. Yes, *irked*. Good word. It summed up that off-centre, not-quite-right sensation.

Even Dominic's empty chair rubbed at her mood. She hadn't realised how much she'd been looking forward to seeing him, and that foolishness bugged her too. With rare moodiness, she threw herself into her own chair and glared down at her desk. It was almost as she'd never left it, apart from a large stack of post.

Attacking the post, ripping open the envelopes with perhaps a bit more brutality than required, she began to sort it into piles: invoices, bank stuff, quotes and supplier catalogues, of which there seemed to be dozens. It was only when she reached the very bottom that her phone pinged with a text from Dominic.

> Hi Ettie, sorry I'm not there this morning but you know what you're doing. Can you pick up where you left off on arranging the activity schedule? I'm happy to leave it to you and I'm happy with all the ideas we discussed (except perhaps the naked dew dabbling).
> Dominic

'Morning,' she said with a chirpy smile when Dominic turned up later, determined that there should be no awkwardness between them.

'Morning.' His greeting was a little more reserved but she refused to let that affect her.

'You'll be pleased to hear I've paid all the invoices that you've approved. I've put the next lot that came in on your desk in the yellow folder. I've spoken to the gin guy, who is called Guy. He's coming tomorrow evening and wants me to round up some volunteers for a demonstration tasting.'

'You have been busy,' said Dominic, blinking at the deluge of information.

'I know,' she said. 'I've made great progress. Will you be around for the gin tasting? I've got a couple of people to ask.' He didn't need to know… Yes, he did. She'd turned over a new leaf. No more lies, half-truths or fibs. 'Actually,' she lifted her chin slightly, 'I've already asked a few people to come along. Two of them are looking for a wedding venue. This might suit them down to the ground.'

'Great. I should be back in time.'

'And Josh would like to swim today, this afternoon, if that's all right.'

There was a brief flicker of something in his eyes but he nodded. 'Fine. What time?'

'Four o'clock, for half an hour. So I'll work until six to make up the time.'

'You don't need to worry about that,' he said. 'Is there anything else you need to tell me?'

She tilted her head upwards as if giving the question serious consideration.

'No, I think that's everything. Would you like me to take Scrapper down to the lake with me? Give him some exercise, and he does love to swim.'

'Fine.'

'You could come, perhaps de-sensitise yourself.' OK, she might have done a little Googling on phobias. And while she was being honest: 'Apparently, the way to get rid of a phobia is to gradually get used to it.'

He whirled round. 'You're not trying to cure me, are you?'

She swallowed, realising she'd pushed too hard, but she wasn't one for giving up. 'I'd be lying if I said no,' she watched his jaw tighten, 'but it's a lovely day and it would be a shame not to enjoy being outdoors.' Her voice took on a cajoling tone.

When she saw his shoulders relax, she sent a winning smile his way.

'You never give up, do you?'

With a shrug, she handed him a stack of catalogues. 'I try not to.'

———

At a quarter to four, having changed into her swimming costume and pulled a T-shirt dress over the top, she headed for the office to collect Scrapper, who was curled up in the flood of sunshine streaming in through the French windows. She could already imagine the sunlight dappling the clear water and the feeling of swimming in the warmer, shallower patches of the lake.

'You off?' asked Dominic, as if he needed to say something but it was all he could manage.

'Yes, sure you don't want to come?' She waved a hand at the blue sky, slashed across by the fading airstream of a plane. 'It's a glorious day, far too nice to be inside.'

'I've got work to do,' he said, bending his head back over the computer on his desk.

'OK, then. See you later. Come on, Scrapper. Fancy a swim?'

Dominic rolled his eyes and muttered, 'Stupid dog' as Scrapper leapt to his feet with a delighted whine.

Ettie left via the French windows, crunching across the

gravel with the dog running in manic circles of pure happiness, diving off one way and then coming back, as if to chivvy her along because she just wasn't walking quickly enough. The dog's infectious mood made her smile and tilt her face up to the sunshine. Dominic's loss – she couldn't force him to accompany her but it was a terrible shame.

Grandad and Josh were waiting for her when she arrived at the beach.

'What kept you?' asked Josh, his arms folded, the assumed bored expression not hiding his latent excitement one little bit. Scrapper dashed past him with his usual over-excited yips and barks, his tail thrashing through the water as he ploughed through the shallows.

'I'm on time, you cheeky beggar. And I'm here now, what you waiting for?' She sank down on the beach to watch as the two headed into the water. Hearing Grandad coaching Josh brought back lots of memories of being at the pool in her teens. Being good at swimming had given her confidence and had really helped in those difficult teenage years, giving her a place of her own away from the competitive bitchiness of classmates at school, which she'd mostly ignored anyway.

Her daydreams were interrupted when a shadow fell over her, and she looked up to find Dominic standing behind her.

'You came,' she beamed at him.

'Mmm, just to make sure everything's OK.' He sat down beside her, crossing his legs, and the two of them watched Josh. The whites of his knuckles shone through clenched fists.

'You OK?' She wanted to put an arm around him, give him a hug.

'Fine, a bit on edge just watching Josh.'

'Look how well he swims.' She pointed to the water as Josh streaked past, his elbows dipping in and out of the water with textbook-perfect strokes. 'He could be a champion. Hilda's talking to some Paralympian to try and get him some professional coaching. I think he's going to need some money to do that at some point, but he's a great swimmer and completely safe.'

'I know that but … it doesn't stop the panic inside.'

She reached out because she couldn't stop herself and laid a hand on one of his taut fists.

'Funny, because I'm the opposite – swimming stops the panic inside.'

'You? Panic?' He raised sceptical eyebrows. 'You're the most positive, can-do person I've ever met. Nothing seems to faze you.'

Something squirmed in the bottom of her stomach. 'Well, that's where you're wrong. I need to swim. I do it for head space. And if that sounds pretentious, I don't mean it to, but I don't know how else to explain it. I do it to stop myself falling into the pit.' She faced him, focusing on his chin, before adding, 'To stop everything getting too much.'

'Too much?'

She risked a look at his face and saw quiet sympathy rather than the incredulous disbelief she'd received the only time she'd ever shared this before. He'd been one crappy boyfriend.

'When I was a teenager my mum was ill.' She spoke quickly, the words tumbling out so she didn't have to dwell on them. It was easier that way. Then the memories couldn't bite her. 'Mum was the sole breadwinner and money was always tight but then...' Money had been so tight, it had squeezed the very breath out of Ettie. Every night she'd worried about the bailiffs turning up, like they had at the Braithwaites' down the road one year. 'I had to leave school and get a job. There was no back-up plan. No savings. I worried about everything and it was like I had this huge ball of anxiety inside my stomach, threatening to consume me. If I looked over my shoulder there was this shadow of dread. Swimming was my escape. I had to breathe at a sensible rate, it allowed me to temper my thoughts. Breathe and slow them down. Whenever things start to get out of hand, I know that swimming will help. Just being in the water, on my own, I feel like it's an escape from everything, but when I get out of the water, I know I can cope again.'

She finally looked up into his eyes, feeling that she'd bared far too much to him, but she'd been determined not to lie. He'd had both barrels of honesty fired at him. 'And that's when I started to tell lies. To the teachers at school, telling them I didn't want to stay on. To Mum, telling her I'd had enough of school, telling her that we had enough to pay the rent, when I'd begged the bank for an overdraft. Telling Lindsey she didn't need to hand over her pay packet. The problem is, once you start it's like dealing with

the Hydra – you cut one head off and another two appear.'
What she didn't add was that lies smoothed the edges of life
and often made things easier. Sometimes people didn't
want to hear the truth and over the years Ettie had become
adept at telling people what they *needed* to hear.

Chapter Twenty-Six

When Josh and Grandad came out of the water, Dominic rose to greet them.

'Afternoon,' he said.

'Afternoon,' said Grandad, nudging Josh in the ribs.

Josh looked at him as if completely baffled.

'What do you say, lad?'

With an exasperated huff, Josh spoke: 'Thanks for letting us swim.'

Dominic just nodded, and some of his unhappiness must have conveyed itself to Josh who added, with unexpected maturity, 'I know you're not keen on this but … I like swimming here.'

'I understand that,' said Dominic, 'but promise you'll always be with Cyril and Ettie.'

'I'm always with Cyril, I can't get here without him, although I ruddy hate going in that sidecar. Look a right prat. Lucky, with them goggles and that stupid helmet, no one can recognise me.'

'That is fortunate,' said Dominic gravely. 'You know you're going to have to swim in a pool eventually if you're going to compete.'

'I get that,' he said, as if Dominic were stupid. 'But I don't want to do that until I'm … trained. You know. I want to be good first. Don't want any of those tossers from school to say owt.'

'Would they?'

'Not to my face.' Josh's mouth compressed. 'But you can tell when someone's talking about you.'

'You can, the trick is not to give a shit,' said Dominic.

Josh's head whipped up at the sound of an adult swearing. 'Easy for you to say that.'

'Why?'

'Because…'

'Because I've got two legs?' Dominic suggested.

Josh's sullen glare brought the attention of Grandad, who must also have been listening with half an ear.

'Given you don't go to school, there's not much chance of anyone saying owt.'

'I'm not going back to school. What's the point? Who's going to give me a job?'

Dominic stared at him, and Ettie almost giggled at his over-the-top dumbfounded expression.

'What on earth are you talking about?' Dominic put his hands on his hips, shaking his head in disbelief. 'You need to go to school.'

'Why? What's the point? I'll just have to do exams and no one'll give us a job,' Josh pointed out.

'Of course they'll give you a job.'

'Doing what?' scoffed Josh.

'You've got a brain, two arms and you're mobile. I'll give you a job, here,' said Dominic. 'You can help me on the estate at the weekends. I need someone to check the fencing and the woods, make sure there's no trees down. No holes in the fences.' As Josh was about to object, Dominic added, 'You can use the quad bike.'

Ettie's mouth twitched but she held the smile in.

'Quad bike,' said Josh, half hopeful and half derisive.

'Yeah, you can drive one, can't you?'

'Course I can,' said Josh, with the scorn of someone who, Ettie could bet the last chocolate in the box, had never been on a quad bike in his life. 'But I don't want your charity.'

'That's all right. I can't afford to pay you.' Dominic's satisfied grin suggested Josh had walked right into his trap. 'In return for a couple of hours on a Saturday morning, you and Cyril can come and train in the lake twice a week. But you have to tell me when and check in and out with me, so that I know you're there. And you have to go to school.'

'But…' Josh's face crumpled in annoyed disbelief.

'Your call. If you want to swim, you'll have to work for it.'

'But's that not fair. You already said I could swim.'

'This way you can swim twice a week instead of just once.' Dominic lifted his shoulders. 'Who said life was fair?

You want to sit around feeling sorry for yourself for the rest of your life?'

Josh glared at him but sensibly shut up. 'I'll think about it,' he said, folding his arms.

'Great,' said Dominic. 'If you're all done, I've got work to do. I'll see you on Saturday at ten.'

Ettie closed her laptop and checked the time on the clock opposite. Six o'clock. Time to find Gracie in the kitchen and find out what the plan for dinner was, and hopefully scrounge a glass of wine from the fridge. She felt she deserved it after sitting on the beach having to watch Josh and Grandad, when she couldn't go in and swim. Her shoulders could have done with it, she thought wistfully as she rolled them back, but she'd made good headway today and the gin guy was booked in to come and do a trial tasting and provide recommendations for stocking the Haim bar. The whole place was really starting to feel like a proper hotel and the activity schedule was coming along, although it was quite a headache sorting everything out. A little too much like dominoes, where one fell and took the next lot tumbling.

'You all right, dear?' Gracie pushed her towards one of the kitchen chairs.

'Yes, and I'll be even better with a glass of wine.'

'How about a glass of Prosecco and we'll take it out on the veranda?'

'Sounds wonderful.' Ettie smiled at her, wondering at Gracie being so uncharacteristically assertive. Normally she waited to see what everyone else wanted to do. Was Grandad having a good influence? He'd always insisted Ettie stand up for herself and make known what she wanted. Gracie had spent her whole married life doing what Bob wanted; it must be hard for her to break the pattern.

Once they were seated in the shade of the veranda, glasses in hand, watching the bees buzzing about the roses, Gracie surprised her again.

'I've been thinking. About Josh. Well, me, Hilda and Cyril.' She ground to a halt.

'And?' prompted Ettie.

'We've come up with a fund-raising idea for Josh.'

'What's that?'

'An open swim event.'

'What, here?'

Gracie nodded. 'We'll serve refreshments, cakes, hot chocolate and everyone will pay an entrance fee. You and Cyril can be lifeguards and Cyril can get some of the canoe club to come and marshal the lake so that people swim in the right area. Hilda can rope in volunteers from the parkrun to help.'

'You've got it all figured out.'

'Yes,' said Gracie, puffing her chest out with a touch of pride.

'One small matter. What about Dominic?'

'He'll come round. Look how he's warmed to Josh

already. Cyril says he offered him a job and is going to let him swim twice a week now. Hilda reckons if it's all organised properly, Dominic won't mind.'

Ettie went to open her mouth but before she could say anything, Gracie said with a touch of defiance, 'I'm going to invite everyone to dinner next week to discuss it.'

'You are?'

'Yes.'

Dominic was just going to love that. Perhaps in the meantime, Ettie could find some way of dissuading her.

Chapter Twenty-Seven

A s Ettie busily filled ice-cube trays with water, concentrating on not spilling the brimming trays en route to the freezer, she still managed to register that there was something a bit different about Gracie, but she was focused on the evening ahead.

'Have you seen this?' asked Ettie, shutting the freezer door and pointing to her work of the last few days. The ancient drinks trolley had taken quite some cleaning but it had come up rather well.

'Very nice, dear. You know I won't be there until later.'

'Mmm,' said Ettie, picking up the next ice-cube tray. 'Where are you going?' she asked, not really paying that much attention, as her mind was on where she should set up the gin tasting. It would have been nice to do it in the tree house, although getting the trolley up there could be interesting. It also brought back unwelcome memories. But she also wanted to show off what had once been the morning room because that might make a nice reception venue for Hazel and Jane.

'I'm going to Cyril's allotment.' Gracie patted her hair. 'He's picking me up.'

That was what was different. Gracie had had her wispy blonde hair done and the streaks of grey had been replaced with subtle blonde highlights. It shaved a few years off her age. 'Your hair looks nice.'

'Thank you, dear. I fancied a change. Do you think it looks all right? Not too mutton dressed as lamb?'

'No! Not at all.' Ettie smiled at her, hearing the note of uncertainty in Gracie's voice. 'You look lovely.'

'Thank you.' She tutted at herself. 'I know I'm probably being daft. It's not like it's a thing or anything. I'm just going to look at vegetables.'

'Grandad's marrow,' said Ettie with a wicked glint in her eye.

'Ethel Merman, what would your mother say?'

'She'd probably say you're far too good for Grandad.'

Guy, the gin man, turned out to be every bit as charming in real life as he was on the phone, and rather handsome with floppy dirty-blond hair and blue eyes that seemed to be permanently laughing. He was a welcome relief after two days spent in the office with Dominic being excruciatingly polite and friendly in a faux-brotherly way, which was really starting to get on her tits – and Ettie never used that phrase, which just went to show how pissed off with him she was. She was feeling distinctly frozen out and she could do with a bit of light-hearted cheer.

Guy arrived with a big box of gins and the biggest selection of Fever Tree mixers Ettie had ever seen, as well as a very welcome flirtatious manner that made her spirits perk up no end.

Rachel's appearance at the front door, as Ettie was helping Guy carry in a case of tonic water, brought her back to the present with a bump.

'Rachel!' Her long red hair shone as if it had been brushed a hundred times a night, and she wore a long patterned silk tunic over pale-pink three-quarter-length leggings. With glowing skin and made-up eyes, she looked the picture of health. She was even smiling.

'Hi, Ettie. Thanks for inviting me.'

'No problem,' said Ettie, smiling back at her, stunned by the transformation. To be honest, she'd felt obliged to invite Rachel because she'd invited Hazel and Jane.

'I brought you these.' Rachel handed over a bunch of stocks that she'd been holding, which Ettie hadn't noticed.

'Thank you. You didn't need to bring anything.'

'Well, I wanted to say thank you for the swimming. I kind of forgot, until your boss rocked up, that you were risking things for us. I never said it, but I was really grateful and those swimming sessions were life-savers. I've been to see a counsellor this week. She insisted I took my husband with me. Turns out he doesn't hate me at all, he blames himself for not making me rest more when he could see how exhausted I was. All this time, he's felt responsible. The counsellor reminded us that one in four pregnancies end in miscarriage in the first twelve weeks.'

Ettie stared at her, amazed by the transformation, and then Rachel laughed. 'Don't worry, I'm having a good day today. I'll be back to being a miserable bitch again tomorrow, no doubt.'

'Ah well, as long as we know where we are with you, that's fine. Come on in.' She peered out of the door. 'How did you get here?'

'My husband dropped me off. I think he was so relieved that I actually wanted to go out that he'd have driven me to Timbuktu. Hazel, Jane and I are going to get a taxi back.'

'Where do you live?' asked Guy, cheerfully swinging by with a cardboard box of clinking glasses.

'Churchstone End.'

'Oh, I live in Lower Hookleigh. I can give you a lift back.'

'Thank you,' said Rachel, looking bemused, as if she wasn't used to people being nice to her, which wasn't surprising, given how grumpy and rude she normally was to others.

Hazel and Jane arrived by taxi, clearly prepared to tuck into the gin, just as Guy was unpacking his boxes and setting everything up on the drinks trolley.

'I must say, this is an absolute beauty,' said Guy, patting it. 'Absolutely perfect. I'm going to have to recommend this place to my customers as somewhere to stay when they come up and see me.'

'Thanks,' said Ettie, a little sad that she wouldn't be here to see guests crowding around the glass-and-brass trolley with bulbous gin glasses in hand.

Guy had brought a selection of gins. 'I'd recommend you offer a selection of fruit, aromatic, herbal, spicy and classic dry gins. And of course make them local. I've brought you a Northern Fox, which is a honeyberry gin, the only one in the country. Then there's Hooting Owl spiced blood orange gin and Harrogate blueberry gin. Then you've got the classic dry gins with Yorkshire Dales Purple Ram gin and a lovely aromatic one from Whittaker's, made in Nidderdale.'

'What gorgeous labels and colours,' said Jane. 'I love a fruity gin, but Hazel prefers a classic London gin style.'

'Well, I'm going to get you to try a selection, so that you can taste the difference.'

And he was true to his word. They started with each of them tasting their choice of gin on its own, just taking a quick mouthful and discussing the flavours, before adding several chunks of ice to show how the flavour changed again. Then they added the best mixers and finally the suggested garnishes, which Guy had also brought along with him, including everything from lemon and orange peel right through to cardamom pods and pink peppercorns. He really knew his stuff and Ettie was very grateful for the detailed tasting notes he'd brought with him, which she could show to Dominic later.

'Gosh, who'd have thought that the mixer and the garnish would have made such a difference,' said Jane, bubbling with enthusiasm. 'Oh, taste this, Hazel, it's gorgeous.'

They swapped drinks as Rachel took a taste of her gin and tonic – she'd chosen the Northern Fox, garnished with a slice of lime. 'This is lovely. I've never even heard of honeyberries before.'

Ettie was drinking the Purple Ram gin just because she liked the name. She knew nothing about gin, but was happy to learn as much as she could, even if she wouldn't be here in the future. It was a shame; she wouldn't have minded running gin tastings. Guy made it all sound so interesting, she was sure she could copy him, and she might not be as knowledgeable but most people wouldn't know any better. If she recommended pink peppercorns with aromatic tonic and a blueberry gin, how many people would really know any… She caught herself. Hadn't she learned anything? Here she went again, telling little white lies. Assuming that what people didn't know wouldn't hurt them. It probably wouldn't, but at the same time, it wouldn't take that much more effort to learn the flavours that did go together, especially after Guy had gone to all this trouble to showcase the gins.

'What would you suggest is the maximum number of people to run a tasting?' she asked, putting her work head back into gear.

'It doesn't really matter, but I think you want to give people an experience and make it feel personal, so I would recommend no more than eight people. You could also create a gin board, so everyone tastes the same four or six gins. It means you don't have lots of bottles in your stock open at the same time.' He winked, his blue eyes twinkling at her. 'And you can always foist the less popular gins on people during a tasting. It's also a good way of seeing what is the most popular, then you can stock them in your bar and people will come back for them.'

They talked pros and cons of different ideas while the others tasted each other's gins.

'You've got a great set-up here,' said Guy. 'If you wanted you could really expand the gin selection in the bar and become a draw for local people. There isn't a decent gin bar for miles – you'd have to go to Harrogate or Leeds or York.'

'That's not my call,' said Ettie with a regretful smile. 'You'll have to talk to the owner. I'm not going to be here for that much longer.'

Guy managed to look disappointed. 'Oh, that's a shame. Moving on?'

'Probably, but I'm not sure where.'

'Well, you've got my business card. If I can help in the future, you know where to find me.' His accompanying smile suggested that he'd welcome a call, gin-related or otherwise.

Just then the door opened and Dominic strolled in, his face immediately darkening at the sight of Ettie smiling up at Guy. *Good*, she thought. *See what you're missing.*

She turned to him, all smiles. 'Dominic, this is Guy, who's been giving us a gin tasting. He's very good.'

Dominic gave her a taut smile and held out a hand to shake the other man's.

'This place is going to be fantastic,' said Guy. 'I was just saying to Ettie that you should target local people.'

Dominic nodded and frowned as he spotted Hazel.

'You remember Hazel, Jane and Rachel from the tightrope walking,' said Ettie hurriedly, and where once she might have avoided the truth, this time she added, 'and they're swimmers.'

His mouth tightened fractionally but then, to her surprise, he relaxed and asked with a long-suffering twist to his mouth, 'No Iggy Pop this evening?'

'Not tonight,' she said, slightly bemused and giving him a cheerful grin. Now wasn't the time to tell him that Grandad was out with Gracie. 'And Josh is underage, so we didn't invite him.'

'Glad to hear it.' He paused before adding with a saccharine-sweet smile, 'Although I'm surprised. Who'd have thought a pesky thing like the legal drinking age would stop you?'

Ouch! 'Who, me?' She put a dramatic hand on her chest and shot him a winsome smile, refusing to let him see that he'd scored a point.

Ha! She saw it. His mouth quirked, just a tiny fraction. With a lift of her chin, her eyes met his and with an eye roll, he acknowledged that he might have found her just a little bit amusing. In that moment Ettie vowed that she wouldn't give up on him. They might not be lovers again but she'd like them to be friends – who was she kidding? They made a good team in and out of the bedroom and she still fancied the pants off him, even with that glower. Admittedly, she'd done wrong, but he wasn't going to hold it against her for ever. Eventually he'd come round and see that she was basically a good person. She just had to rebuild his trust and not lie to him again.

'Now you're here, you must try some of this gin. The Northern Fox is delicious.' Ettie nodded to Guy who'd picked up the bottle.

'Why don't you talk him through the tasting? I've got a feeling you'll be good at it,' said Guy, handing over the bottle and a measure.

'OK. So Dominic, we have here a local gin – well, localish, it's distilled in Beverly, so still Yorkshire.' And she was off, talking him through the tasting notes that Guy had shared with her, repeating much of what he'd said earlier but with her own embellishments and chirpy asides, urging Dominic to try the gin unadulterated before adding the ice, the tonic and the garnishes.

Dominic played along, making all the right noises, and seemed to be entertained by her patter, but it was difficult to tell from his impassive expression.

'You're a natural,' said Guy with an approving nod and blatant admiration. 'Want a job?'

'I might.' Ettie turned her mouth up in a merry smile, knowing it would irritate Dominic.

'Give me your number.'

'She's got a job,' growled Dominic to her delight. His grumpy tones made her stomach fizz.

'For the moment,' replied Ettie a touch primly.

'Well, you know where to find me.' Guy winked at her.

'Where did the trolley come from?' asked Dominic suddenly. 'Did you bring it with you, er...?' He turned to Guy and Ettie had to swallow back a laugh. It was as if Dominic couldn't bring himself to say Guy's name.

'No, Ettie provided it. Although I'm rather taken with it. I might have to find one for the showroom and for evenings like this.'

'Remember, it's the one we found in the stables. I gave it a bit of a spit and polish.' Actually, it had been two hours of hard graft with the Brasso, to bring the metal up to a golden gleam and get into all the nooks and crannies of the filigree detail around the edges, and hot soapy water to clean up the glass.

Dominic did a double take. 'Seriously?'

'Yes,' she said, proudly.

'You've done a cracking job, Ettie,' said Guy with another of his admiring smiles.

'There's no end to your talents,' observed Dominic wryly.

'No,' she replied, raising her near-empty glass in a cheerful salute. 'Aren't you the lucky one?'

Again there was a tug at the corner of his mouth, as if he really wasn't sure what he was going to do with her. He very nearly cracked a smile. She rather liked keeping him on his toes. Whether he realised it or not, Dominic needed a bit of a tickle. He was so busy being responsible for everyone else, he'd forgotten how to be playful and take things less seriously. He might still be mad at her but she wasn't done with him – not yet. Besides, she was having too much fun teasing him.

Behind his back, Hazel was smirking at her.

'Oh,' said Ettie. 'Hazel, Jane, I was wondering if this room might make a good wedding venue for the ceremony or the reception.'

The two women turned to each other, their eyes suddenly lighting up.

Ettie turned to Dominic. 'It would be a good opportunity to showcase Haim before it officially opens.'

'It could work,' said Hazel, cutting across Dominic before he could speak again. 'What do you think, Jane?'

'I think it's perfect,' she replied, turning round in a circle to take in the full proportions of the room. 'Absolutely perfect.'

'When are you thinking?' asked Dominic, reverting to business mode. 'And what are you thinking?'

'As soon as possible,' said Jane with sudden loud assertion that clearly took Hazel by surprise. 'I'm sick of kowtowing to my family. Sod them. They either come or they don't, but I'm not waiting anymore for them to agree on a date. They've been filibustering for weeks now.'

'Great word,' said Hazel, swooping in and giving Jane a big kiss on the mouth. 'And yes. Let's go for it.' She turned to Dominic. 'We're looking for a venue for the ceremony. We've already got a celebrant in mind and then a reception afterwards.'

'The ceremony's no problem but the reception might be. I haven't got a chef lined up yet.'

'I can do it.' Everyone turned to Rachel, who gave them a wide-eyed look. 'What?'

'Are you sure?' asked Jane.

Rachel grinned at her. 'I have to get back in the saddle at some point.'

'You're a chef?'

'Yes, used to work at The Olive Tree before … before I had a bit of a breakdown. But I'm ready to get back to work now.' She gave Dominic an arch smile. 'The swimming helped.'

He shot Ettie a dirty look. 'So I'm hearing.'

'Well,' said Hazel. 'That all seems to be sorted, then. Now all we need is to agree on a date.'

Chapter Twenty-Eight

G randad was ensconced in one of the pine chairs at the kitchen table, polishing off a plate of eggs, bacon, sausages and mushrooms, when Ettie walked in the following morning.

'Hello there, Ettie, lass. How are you today?' She noticed him quickly snatch the notepad beside him and slip it onto his lap under the table. What was he up to?

'Morning, Grandad, fancy seeing you here.'

'I was just passing and I thought I'd pop in,' he said with a perfectly straight face.

'Oh really. Just passing on the way to where?'

He waved a dismissive hand as Dominic walked in and turned to Ettie.

'Good job on the gin tasting last night. I think that's going to work well.' Despite the praise, his tone was completely business-like, almost as if he'd been reading a book on good management and was going through the motions rather than actually celebrating her success.

'It did go well, didn't it?' she said, determined to make him acknowledge it properly.

'I just said so.'

'So you did,' said Ettie with a demure smile at his clipped words. She was rather enjoying herself, subtly winding him up.

'Well, when you're ready…' He held the door open as if to usher her towards the office.

'I'll be right with you, I just need to finish my coffee.' The clock on the wall was a few minutes shy of nine.

He disappeared and she winked at Gracie.

'You are naughty, Ettie.'

'I think he finds me amusing, really. I'm just trying to lighten him up a bit.'

Gracie scrunched up her face. 'He's gone back to being serious and responsible again. I do wish he'd remember that I'm not his responsibility. I know when I first came here I was a bit of a fish out of water, but I've found my feet now, or rather my fins.' Gracie chuckled at her own joke.

'That you have, lass. Your swimming was coming along nicely.'

'Never thought I'd be swimming in a lake or living here and making new friends, and it feels like I've got a proper job now, instead of just being Dominic's burden.'

'You were never a burden,' said Ettie, going across and giving her a hug. 'So what are you up to…' She deliberately paused before adding, '… today?'

There it was, that quick guilty exchange between the two of them.

'We might pop over to see Hilda later,' volunteered Grandad suddenly.

'You two are up to something, aren't you?'

Gracie managed to feign outraged innocence, Grandad not so much.

'Before you say anything, I don't want to know. I don't want any part in it. You're on your own now.' She poured herself a cup of coffee, very aware of the silent non-verbal conversation going on behind her back, and went through to the office before Dominic came in search of her again.

'Oh look, they're here.' Gracie untied her apron, her face wreathed in an anticipatory smile as wide as the Grand Canyon as she pointed through the window, where Hazel's Volvo had pulled up on the drive along with Grandad's bike. She'd been cooking since lunchtime, and delicious smells had permeated the office, making both Dominic and Ettie take frequent breaks to quell their constant hunger and, it had to be said, curiosity.

Ettie hid her apprehension. As far as Dominic was concerned Gracie had decided to practise her cooking skills on a larger number of people. With Hilda and Claire coming, as well as the Splashing Around group and Dominic, there would be ten of them for dinner.

Despite all her hard work – she'd been on her feet since

seven – Gracie glowed and Ettie had a hard time remembering the wan, almost listless character she'd first met in this very kitchen.

'Everything under control?' asked Ettie, slightly tongue in cheek.

Gracie flapped a scolding tea towel at her. 'Of course it is, dear.' She drew herself upright. 'This is my watch. Everything is ship-shape.'

Ettie giggled. 'Yes, General.'

'You mean Admiral, dear.'

With a salute, Ettie looked out of the window to see Josh emerging from the back of the car, laughing at something Rachel said as she stepped out of the door behind him. Ettie stared for a moment, pleased to see the easy smile on his face.

They all trooped into the kitchen, laughing and joking, and Gracie fussed around everyone as they handed over flowers, chocolates and bottles of wine. Grandad outdid everyone with an enormous bunch of his prized dahlias. Gracie was honoured indeed; usually he never picked them, saying flowers last longer in the ground.

Ettie took drinks orders, getting a glass for Grandad's four-pack of Tetley's and opening the bottle of Chardonnay that Rachel had brought.

'Come sit down, everyone,' said Gracie, keen to feed them. 'We'll eat and then we can have a proper meeting.'

'Meeting?' Dominic's brow furrowed and he glanced at Ettie, who gave him a shrug, as if to say, *Don't look at me.*

'Yes, dear.' Gracie patted him on the shoulder. 'Come on,

you sit here next to Josh. Rachel, you next to Jane and Cyril. Ettie, you can sit there, next to Hazel. Claire and Hilda, you over there.'

Ettie did as she was told, enjoying watching Gracie gently bossing everyone about, telling them what was in the big ceramic dishes on the table.

'Do help yourselves, everyone. Does anyone want bread rolls? They're just warming in the oven.'

'Sit yourself down, lass,' said Grandad. 'You're going to wear yourself to a frazzle. We've all got two legs.' There was a pause and everyone avoided looking at Josh, but Grandad grinned. 'Except you, o' course, Josh, but you're a youngster and with that probotic of yours, you can still get around faster than most.'

Josh sighed dramatically and shook his head. 'Prosthetic. You're losing it, Cyril. Probotic is yoghurt, innit?'

Everyone laughed and Dominic looked on with faint surprise.

Finally everyone was seated and began helping themselves to the food.

'Good God, Gracie. This is amazing. You said it was just going to be salad,' said Jane. 'This is salad par excellence delicious. What is this?' She pointed to one of the many dishes on the table.

'Bulgur wheat with pomegranate and pistachio. That one is home-made coleslaw, that's beetroot, goats' cheese and walnut and this is a potato salad with greens and crispy bacon.'

'Gosh, you've gone to so much trouble,' said Jane.

Gracie blushed. 'It's a pleasure. I've always liked pottering in the kitchen.'

'It's grand, lass. You can come and potter in my kitchen any time you like.'

'If you supply me with more of these lettuces, you're on.' Was Gracie flirting with Grandad?

Ettie caught Dominic's eye; he was looking more and more surprised.

After a dessert of meringue and passionfruit with whipped cream, Gracie got up to make coffee which Jane insisted on helping her with, while Ettie and Dominic put the plates in the dishwasher and the few leftovers in the fridge.

'How do you all know one another?' asked Dominic, quietly. 'Have you been friends for a long time?'

Ettie raised an eyebrow, wondering how he was going to take her answer.

'Actually, we only met a few weeks ago.'

'Really. How did you meet?'

'At the lake.' She caught her lip between her teeth before adding, 'Illicit swimming.'

'What? All of you? But you all seem to know each other so well.'

He glanced back at the table where Rachel and Josh were teasing Grandad about never having seen a *Star Wars* film, while Hazel was defending him, and then over to Gracie and Jane who had their heads together and were giggling about something.

'It's amazing what strangers will tell each other when they're all in their safe place together,' said Ettie.

'Safe place?' Dominic looked genuinely bewildered. No wonder, Ettie guessed, when he only saw the dangers of water.

'It's our safe place. Where we feel free from judgement. Away from people who know our back stories. They have no basis to judge us. When we're swimming we're just us. People in our own right. It sounds odd, but it's easier to talk about things together, or not talk about them if we don't want to.' She looked at Rachel, who'd been the most reserved and prickly of all of them. She'd just needed time to herself. 'We each have our own reasons for swimming. No one needs to know them and it's up to us to choose whether we share them.' She gave him a candid look.

Once the kitchen had been tidied and tea and coffee dished out, Hilda pulled out an A4 lined hardbacked notebook. 'Right, shall we start?'

'Start what?' asked Dominic.

'I've been speaking to Johnny Wagstaff and it's quite a complicated process.'

'What's a complicated process?' Dominic frowned.

'Getting Josh into the Paralympics,' replied Hilda, as if it were completely obvious. 'First of all, Josh needs to get an official classification, which is an application process supported by his medical consultant. He also needs to join Swim England and start competing. Johnny says he needs a coach.'

'And how much will a coach cost?' asked Grandad.

'Johnny's prepared to do it, but he charges by the hour and it's not cheap. Not if he needs to be coached for a couple of hours a week.' Hilda mentioned a figure that had them all wincing. 'So we need to drum up some finances. Hopefully the piece in the newspaper might get some support, but we need a fund-raiser of some sort.' Everyone shuffled in their seats and looked down at the table. If it wasn't so mortifyingly obvious, it would have been amusing. Ettie pursed her lips, waiting for the performance to unfold.

'I've had an idea,' said Gracie, without a trace of her usual diffidence. In fact, she almost sounded like a bad actress with a duff line. Right on cue, everyone round the table turned towards her. Ettie wondered if this had all been scripted. They must have been chatting on a different WhatsApp group.

'What's that?' asked Jane in equally wooden tones.

'Yes, do tell,' said Ettie with a saccharine-sweetened voice, realising that this was an ambush. She didn't dare look at Dominic; surely he must have realised that this was a set-up.

'An open-water swim meet,' said Gracie, shooting a reproving stare at Ettie before holding up a hand. 'And before you say no, Dominic, let me finish.'

Ettie couldn't decide who was more shocked by Gracie's uncharacteristic autocracy. Dominic's mouth had actually dropped open.

With a clearly rehearsed patter, Gracie then went on to explain what the event would entail and listed in great detail all the safety measures that would be put in place, with ultra-helpful interjections from Grandad and Hilda, which made it obvious who the ring-leaders behind the plan were. It was a masterful performance and the result of brilliant strategy, as they'd pre-empted any objections before Dominic could even voice them.

When she finally came to the end of her speech, there was a momentary silence filled with apprehension, as if everyone was holding their breath as they waited for Dominic's reaction.

To Ettie's and everyone else's surprise, he began to laugh. The others looked at each other with consternation and Ettie began to smile. It kind of served them right for being so sneaky.

'You lot never give up, do you? What will you do this time if I say no? Fill the lake with goldfish? Bubble bath?'

'Now there's an idea,' said Hilda.

'And where do you fit in all this, Ettie?' asked Dominic.

She held up both of her hands in innocent surrender. 'I had nothing to do with any of this.' She glared at Grandad and Hilda.

'To be fair, she didn't,' said Grandad. 'She'd already said she wanted no part in it and that we had to respect your wishes.'

'You did?' Dominic stared at her in amazement.

She shook her head at him, disappointed that he was still so quick to assume the worst of her; but then again, she hadn't given him much reason in the past to trust her. 'Oh ye of little faith.'

'Well, I apologise, then.' He turned to the others. 'You're all a bunch of scheming reprobates. And about as obvious as a hippo in a swimming pool.'

'We are,' said Hilda with a satisfied nod.

He turned to Josh. 'I want to help, really I do, but you know it's the safety aspect that worries me.'

'Yeah, I get it,' said Josh with a laconic shrug. 'I told them you wouldn't change your mind. I guess if you could swim, you wouldn't mind so much.'

Dominic's eyes narrowed and then he shot Ettie a furious glare.

She opened her mouth to deny anything. She hadn't said a word to anyone about his fear of water.

'You can't swim?' said Rachel. 'How does that happen? Gracie said you were in the Navy.'

'I can swim,' Dominic said matter-of-factly.

'Can you?' Cyril sounded amazed.

'Yes.'

Ettie frowned.

'So why don't you want us in the lake?' asked Josh.

Dominic floundered slightly and Ettie couldn't help but come to his rescue.

'He's not allowed to swim until his leg has healed properly. There have been complications since his last operation.' The lie slipped out smoothly and he raised an eyebrow, but even as she said the words, she knew exactly what she had to do. It would involve another lie, but she'd just lied to save his pride and he hadn't seemed to mind too much. It meant she'd have to break the vow she'd made when he'd sacked her. What was one more lie in the scheme of things? He'd made it clear he didn't trust her.

'Oh,' said Josh with a wise, knowing nod. 'Of course. Well, once you're better and you've swum in the lake, you might change your mind.'

'Hmm,' replied Dominic, not giving anything away.

As everyone started to disperse, taking mugs to the sink as the dishwasher was already in full flow, and helping with the last of the tidying up, he wandered up behind her and murmured in her ear, 'Thanks for coming to my rescue. You have an uncanny ability to dissemble the truth.'

'You mean lie,' said Ettie bluntly.

'Yes,' said Dominic, but for once he looked thoughtful as he picked up a tea towel to dry up the last few items on the draining board, as did she as she pondered just how she was going to put her plan into action.

Chapter Twenty-Nine

E ttie had to wait a few days before she was able to put her idea in motion, and throughout that time she veered between thinking it was a good idea and a truly terrible one.

'We're in business,' said Dominic, punching the air the following Monday morning. Ettie had just returned after a weekend at home, having solicited Grandad's help for what she wanted to do. Impatience had taken over and she was determined to help Dominic, whether he wanted helping or not.

'We've just taken our first booking.'

'Wow! That's amazing,' said Ettie.

'And they want to do Nordic Walking and book a Prosecco date night in the tree house.'

Ettie preened for a second. 'And remind me whose idea that was?' As soon as the words left her mouth, she wished she could snatch them back, as they both stared at each other. A flush raced up her neck as she remembered the night in the tree house, her embarrassment made worse by the fact she knew that he was also remembering.

'That was a good night,' she said suddenly, refusing to feel ashamed of it. It was Dominic who had called time on things, not her, and she was fed up with pussy-footing around him. He wanted her to be honest, so she would be, and that included being honest about her feelings.

Dominic almost choked on his coffee.

'What?' she queried. 'You wanted me to tell the truth.'

'Uh,' he spluttered.

She hid a smile as she went back to her computer screen, feeling buoyed up by her decision to be her usual blunt self. Sometimes payback was sweet.

'How's the bookkeeping course going?' he asked abruptly.

'Fi— Actually, it's not. I sacked it off this weekend.'

'You did? Why?'

'I hated it. I was kidding myself. Lying to myself that it was the answer.'

He sat back in his chair, his eyes shrewd and assessing as he stared across the room at her. 'What is the answer? What do you want to do?'

She looked up at him. 'You want me to be honest?' she asked with an inward smile when he stilled in sudden apprehension.

He sighed. 'Yes. Always.'

She met his gaze head on. She might have given up on the bookkeeping course but she didn't give up on things she really cared about. And she cared about Dominic, whether he wanted her to or not. And whether he realised it or not, he needed her.

'What I'd really like to do is to stay here. I could run the gin tastings, organise and dress the Prosecco date nights, help Gracie, and if you ever change your mind about swimming in the lake, I could be the on-site lifeguard.' She stopped and lifted her chin with a now-what-do-you-have-to-say-to-that? challenge.

Dominic opened his mouth and then clearly thought better of it. His jaw tightened in that familiar stubborn way she'd become used to. 'I'm not sure it's a good idea, Ettie.'

'Of course it is,' she said, folding her arms. 'You're just scared.'

'Scared?'

'Of me.'

His head jerked back. 'What do you mean?'

'You know what I mean,' she said and turned to her computer monitor.

'For your information, Ettie Merman, I am not scared of you.'

'Yes, you are. You can trust me with your business affairs but not your heart.'

'We are not talking about my heart. And I can't believe we're having this conversation.'

'We *are* talking about your heart. You've got as big a phobia about feelings as you do about swimming.'

'Don't tell me you worked for a psychiatrist once,' he snapped, falling back on anger. Ettie now realised this was his defence mechanism when he was scared or unsure. That's why he'd got so angry with them swimming in the lake. It all made sense now.

'No, but I think that might have been interesting.'

'You have an answer for everything.' He stood up. 'I'm going out.'

With that he strode out of the room, leaving Ettie feeling that she'd won round one. Now all she had to do was get him to the lakeside that afternoon.

'I'm not wearing a swimming hat,' said Josh. 'I'll look a right twat.' He twisted one of his crutches in the sand on the lakeside beach and scowled. Across the lake a duck quacked loudly as if agreeing with him.

'You'll have to look like a twat then,' said Grandad, picking up his new training aid, the red-and-white megaphone Ettie had found in the stables. He put it to his mouth and the words 'You're acting like one!' came shouting through.

Ettie winced. *Not helping, Grandad.* She gave Josh a diplomatic smile and put a hand out to lower the megaphone from Grandad's lips. She'd thought out her plan carefully and for it to be convincing, she needed Josh to wear a cap. 'Look, you're going to have to wear one when you're competing. In fact, Olympic swimmers wear two caps.'

'Why?'

'For competitive edge. They wear a second cap over their goggles for additional streamlining.'

'I'm not in the Olympics, am I?'

Ettie studied him, debating whether or not to explain the real reason. Grandad jumped to the rescue. 'Josh, Ettie needs help. If you wear the cap, you're helping, all right? Don't ask anything else, but it will be obvious later. We're going to run a safety drill.'

'Providing Dominic turns up,' said Ettie, shooting an anxious glance over the hill towards the house. She'd seen his car return fifteen minutes ago. If she knew him as well as she thought she did, he'd be here to watch Josh, to make sure nothing went wrong rather than out of innate interest.

'I'll wear your pissing hat,' grumbled Josh. 'Are we going to get going or not?'

'Just another minute,' said Ettie, looking again for Dominic. Where was he?

Josh sighed with over-exaggerated teenage petulance and put one hand on his hip, balancing casually on one crutch, which made Ettie smile. He'd come a long way in the last couple of weeks, not just physically but emotionally.

'How was school?' she asked.

'All right,' he muttered.

'No problems?' asked Grandad, getting straight to the point, as always.

'Nah, some of 'em were a bit nosy but me mates, they were OK.' He snorted. 'I think they were pleased to see me, and so were them that don't know me so well. Some of the girls in my class were nice, but they were a bit embarrassed. Like shy. Dunno why.'

'Probably worried about saying the wrong thing,' suggested Ettie.

'You think?' Josh's voice pitched in disbelief.

'Yes. They probably worry about upsetting you. Although there will always be some people that don't care.' Ettie knew that not everyone would be kind but she prayed that most people would be.

'Tossers, you mean.'

'There are always tossers,' she agreed. 'But avoid them – you can't change them. And remember, it's *their* problem, not yours.'

Josh's forehead crumpled in thought. 'I guess you're right.'

'I'm always right,' said Ettie with a grin. 'But don't let the bastards get to you. Life isn't going to be easy – for you, for anyone. All you can do is be your best and be kind to other people.'

'And here ends today's lesson,' said Grandad. 'By the time you've trained up, built up your upper-body strength, you'll be able to punch the buggers in the jaw, and don't you forget it.'

Ettie lifted her eyes heavenwards. 'Thanks, Grandad.'

'Lad can't get by on platitudes. He needs to know he can defend himself and let others know he can fight back.'

Josh grinned. 'Ha! I reckon the teachers aren't going to give the disabled boy detention if he gets into a fight.'

Ettie huffed out a sigh. 'Grandad, you're a very bad influence.'

'I know, lass.' He winked at Josh. 'And here comes the boss. Don't look too happy.'

Ettie gave a twisted smile. 'I might have upset him earlier. Put him a bit off balance.'

'Excellent, girl. You keep him on his toes. You know he can't take his eyes off you. Gracie said she reckoned he pined for you.'

'Hmm.' Ettie wasn't so sure about that, but after today he'd either sack her once and for all or decide to keep her on.

'Dominic,' Grandad greeted him. 'Right, come on, Josh, we've got work to do.' He waved a blue float in the air and led Josh into the water.

Ettie sat down on the beach, her heart doing flips and tricks in her chest as she thought about what she was about to do.

Dominic paced for a little while before he finally came to sit next to her. She wanted to take his hand and stroke away his pent-up anxiety. Now she was aware of it, she realised it was coming from him in palpable waves. For a moment she wondered whether she should abandon her plan. Let sleeping fish lie. But then without a push, she suspected Dominic's stubborn determination would keep them in stalemate for ever, and she wasn't the sort of person to sit around and not take action. Crossing her fingers out of sight beneath her thigh, she prayed that this was going to work.

Dominic kept a steady gaze on Grandad and Josh. Today Grandad was focusing on increasing the strength in Josh's arms and had him keeping the float between his legs, so that his arms did all the work. Ettie remembered doing it herself when she was younger. As they neared the little knoll, the muscles in her shoulders tensed and her hand scratched small circles in the sand. Grandad and Josh got out of the water.

'What are they doing?' asked Dominic.

'Probably taking a breather. It's hard work swimming with a float like that.'

'OK.' But then Josh staggered forward before collapsing – with quite a lot of panache, thought Ettie. Grandad dropped to his knees beside the boy.

Dominic strained forward. 'Something's wrong?'

Ettie frowned and watched for a moment and then Grandad began to wave. She jumped to her feet and stripped off her T-shirt, pausing for a moment so that Dominic had the full effect of her bright-red bikini, before tugging down her shorts, kicking off her flip-flops and racing into the water.

With smooth, clean strokes she ate up the distance, enjoying the sunshine lighting up the water and the clear depths below, dappled with clumps of vivid green pondweed, and the silty sand patterned with rippled undulations on the floor of the lake.

In no time she reached the little island and rushed out of the water towards Josh and Grandad, breathing heavily. Gasping, she clutched her chest – it had been a long time since she'd put on such a sprint.

'You took your time,' said Grandad, beaming from ear to ear, still knelt next to Josh, who now propped himself up on his elbows.

'You're flipping kidding me,' wheezed Ettie.

'Are you two going to tell me what's going on?' asked Josh, as Grandad pushed him back down.

'Well done, lass. Do you want a quick breather before we head back?'

'What's going on? Cyril told me to play dead.'

'We're trying to get Dominic into the water,' explained Ettie.

'Well, it's not working,' replied Josh, squinting over the water. 'He's pacing and looking this way.'

Ettie stood up and gave him a wave and a double thumbs-up before sitting back down.

'Now what?' asked Josh.

'Take your hat off.'

'What? Why? You had a right cob on earlier, wanting me to wear it.'

'Ah well, I've changed my mind,' said Grandad with a tough smile.

Josh muttered under his breath and peeled off his cap. 'What do you want me to do with it now? Don't tell me I've got to swim with it between my legs.'

'Now there's an idea. But no, the float'll do fine. Just leave it here.'

Josh frowned and shrugged, clearly thinking Grandad was weird.

'Ready to swim back?' asked Ettie, now having caught

her breath.

'Yes,' said Josh, bristling with suspicion.

'All in good time, lad,' said Grandad. 'All in good time.'

They set off together, all three of them swimming breast stroke in tandem, and then, when they were three-quarters of the way there, Ettie spoke to Grandad in a very loud voice which surely carried across the water: 'Oh no, we've forgotten Josh's swimming cap.'

'But you told me—' Josh started to say.

'Shh, lad, you'll give the game away,' said Grandad before raising his voice. 'You'd best go back for it then.'

With that, Ettie turned around and swam back to the island, breaking into her speedy freestyle.

Deciding that Grandad and Josh were nearly back, she stopped. For a moment she trod water before allowing herself to sink below the surface. Holding her breath, she stayed there, looking at the underwater landscape brilliantly spotlit by the sunshine above. Then she surfaced, taking a leisurely breath before screaming, 'Help!' With that she let herself sink beneath the surface again, deliberately letting her arms thrash wildly above her, splashing about so much that when she dramatically surfaced again, she'd scared all the ducks into flight.

Through the splashes of water, she could make out Dominic on the beach. She held her breath and watched him as he stood frozen there. Guilt pricked at her as she imagined his fear. She waved her arms again and ducked under the surface. When she looked again, Dominic was still standing there. Her heart hammered in her chest. *Come on, Dominic!* She closed her eyes, feeling the taste of failure sharp in her mouth, and sank under the water again, with one last flail of her arms. How long could she or should she keep this up?

The next time she bobbed up, she sighed in a mixture of relief tinged with panic, as she saw Dominic rip off his T-shirt, scramble out of his shoes and tear into the water. This was D-Day. He might well kill her when he realised what she'd done. She allowed herself a tremulous smile as she watched his powerful crawl – crisp, clean, decisive strokes as his arms dipped in and out of the water. While he was coming to save her, she also hoped he was saving himself at the same time, although he might not thank her for it. She'd cross that bridge when he got to her.

As he neared, she went under once more just to keep up the charade. Hands grabbed at her shoulders, one smacking into her face, making her inhale a gulp of water, which added significant authenticity to her coughing and spluttering when he hauled her to the surface.

'Ettie. Relax. Otherwise, I'll have to slap you again.'

Again?

With textbook expertise and not without a little roughness, he hooked a hand under her chin, tipped her backwards and began to swim with powerful kicks towards the island. Still spluttering from her inadvertent mouthful of water, she allowed herself to be towed along, her heart fluttering and dancing with adrenaline, anticipation and just a touch of dread. This could of course go horribly wrong.

He reached the island and put his feet down and, without waiting for her to put hers down, scooped her up in his arms and carried her out of the water, which was rather romantic until he dumped her on the sand, kneeling over her.

'Dominic?' she asked uncertainly, looking up at him. With the sun behind his head, it was difficult to read his expression.

'You wretch,' he said, before snaking a hand behind her neck and dropping down next to her and hauling her into his arms.

His lips were cold and tasted slightly muddy, but she didn't care as she opened her mouth to his. His body was heavy on hers and she welcomed it, wrapping her arms around his cold skin, revelling in his hot mouth racing over hers with the most delicious desperation. She pressed her chilly body up against his, her pulse picking up and hope starting to burn bright. His hands moved down to caress the V between her breasts, one leg straddling hers, and she could feel desire stirring.

She moaned and pulled away from his mouth. 'You do know we've got an audience.'

'Mm,' he groaned and kissed her again quickly before rolling to the side and sitting up, pulling her with him. 'Serves you right.'

She caught her lower lip between her teeth. 'How did you know?'

'What? That you were faking? Give me some credit! I'm a professional rescuer. Your antics were decidedly amateur.'

'Oh,' said Ettie, a little chastened. 'But you got into the water.'

He kissed her gently on the mouth. 'I couldn't risk being wrong. And also, I realised if you were prepared to go to such lengths, I ought to at least try and rescue you.'

'Good choice,' she said.

'What am I going to do with you?'

'Give me a job, let me stay and love me.'

He smiled. 'Brutally honest.' He kissed her again on the corner of her mouth. 'I already love you, Ettie.'

'You do?' she squeaked, her heart ballooning in her chest, robbing her of breath.

He nodded. 'I've tried so hard not to. But I realised, you might tell lies—'

She pulled a face. 'I've been trying not to.'

'I noticed, but I'm not sure I can survive your bluntness.' He laughed and took her hand in his, rubbing his thumb over hers. 'But I realised that when you tell half-truths, fibs or whatever you want to call them, you only do it for good reasons. You never do it for yourself. It's invariably for other people. Ironically, you are one of the most open and forthright people I've ever met, and I've been too stubborn to realise that. I was so hung up on the concept of honesty, that I didn't see it. But, in fact—' he lifted her hand to kiss her knuckles '—you have an honest soul. You don't pretend to be anything you're not. You don't try and hide things from people, which is probably why you've had so many jobs.'

'That, and I've got a low boredom threshold.'

'You'd better not get bored with me.'

'That's unlikely to happen,' she said with a sudden grin. 'I'm very good at keeping you on your toes.'

'And do you think you could bear to work with me as well?'

'Of course, we make a great team.'

'And the job? Permanent lifeguard in situ?'

'I'll take it.' She paused and then said, 'Hang on. Does that mean you'll need a lifeguard?'

'Yes, you've worn me down. We'll let guests swim in the lake by arrangement. And we'll hold an open-water event once a month to raise funds for Josh. Happy now?'

'Oh, Dominic.' She threw her arms around him. 'That's wonderful. Thank you.'

'It's going to take a lot of payback.'

With a sultry smile she kissed him. 'You don't need to worry about that, I've got lots of great ideas about payback.' She pushed him back on the sand and lay on top of him to kiss him again. They would have stayed like that for quite a while longer if it hadn't been for a sudden shout through Grandad's megaphone.

'Will you put my granddaughter down!'

Dominic laughed. 'They talk about mothers-in-law, but I'm thinking a grandfather-in-law like Cyril is going to be a lot more trying.'

'It's all right,' said Ettie, 'you get used to him after a while.'

Epilogue

'**B**y the love that has brought you here today and by the vows you have pledged, it is my great honour to pronounce you married. You may kiss the brides.' The celebrant stepped back as a cheer went up on the beach.

Dominic squeezed Ettie's hand and they smiled at each other as Hazel and Jane, each clad in white bridal gowns, kissed each other.

The wedding party was quite small. In the end Hazel and Jane had decided to suit themselves. They'd quietly invited close friends and Hazel's immediate family, including her ex-husband, but had decided against inviting Jane's family. It had been a hard decision but in the end Jane decided that they would spoil the day and she would be happier without them. As she said, Hazel was family enough for her and all that mattered, which had made Gracie, Ettie and Rachel cry just a little bit. Rachel was here with her husband, looking radiant, and it was obvious he was very much in love with her, although, as he said, he didn't love her enough to swim in a lake at the crack of dawn on a Wednesday morning.

'Don't they look beautiful,' said Gracie with a happy sigh, clasping her hands together over the waist of her pretty floral tea dress.

'They do,' agreed Ettie, looping an arm through hers. 'And so do you.'

Gracie giggled. 'Don't be silly.' But she pinkened in pleasure at the compliment. In the last few weeks, she had blossomed, and to Ettie's delight had started bossing Grandad about, which, judging by the permanent grin on his face, he adored.

'What are they doing?' asked Gracie. 'Is this a lesbian thing?'

Ettie turned and began to laugh as Hazel unzipped the back of Jane's dress to reveal a jazzy pink-and-orange swimsuit.

'No, I think it's a swimming thing.'

As Jane's dress dropped to the floor, pooling around her sturdy ankles, Hazel turned to allow Jane to unzip her dress to reveal a matching swimsuit. They both stepped out of their dresses and waved at the assembled audience, who clapped and cheered. Linking hands, lacing their fingers together, they ran towards the lake, haphazardly throwing their bouquets behind them.

'Watch out,' yelled Rachel, tugging at her husband's hand and ducking out of the way as one of the posies of orange and pink roses came flying towards Gracie, who made an instinctive two-handed grab and, by some miracle, caught the bouquet.

'That's a sign,' said Cyril, putting his arm around her.

'Go on with you,' said Gracie, a bright-pink blush staining her cheeks.

'Now I understand the colour scheme,' said Ettie, nodding towards the lurid swimming costumes. 'I wondered where the orange and pink had come from.' Back in the house the morning room was festooned with orange and pink bunting which Gracie and Rachel had spent the last week making, in between bouts of cooking in the kitchen. After a few of Rachel's dishes had been tasted and she had submitted a suggested menu to Dominic for Haim, she had been appointed head chef and would be starting a week before the first guests arrived in two weeks' time.

Hilda, who was wearing a hat so large it nearly eclipsed the sun, began to clap as the two brides breasted the water and began to swim.

'What a thoroughly lovely occasion,' she said, coming over with her lover Harold (she insisted on referring to him as such, much to his delight). 'I got Adam to take lots of photos, so that you can advertise lakeside weddings. It'll be a real USP.'

'That was very kind of you,' said Dominic, nudging Ettie. 'Do you even know what a USP is?'

'Haven't the foggiest,' crowed Hilda. 'But it sounds good.'

'I'll bear it in mind, although I doubt I'll have any say in the matter.' He raised a brow at Ettie, who gurgled with laughter.

'I have been thinking about a package we could offer.' With a sweet smile she added, 'After all, I need to generate more income so that my boss will give me a pay rise.'

'I don't think he has much say in that matter either,' said Dominic in a dry voice. 'Poor hen-pecked chap.'

Ettie stepped closer to him as Hilda turned to talk to another guest, and murmured in his ear, 'Poor hen-pecked chap, my arse! You were quite masterful this morning when you carried me into the summer house.'

He glanced across the lake at the newly built summer house, which virtually filled the whole of the little island.

'I needed to be, it's the only place I could get you to myself – the whole house has been overrun with people for the last few days.' He paused before whispering, 'Has Cyril moved in?'

Ettie laughed. 'No, but I think you should be prepared for Gracie moving out. He's just had the cleaners in at his house and has filled a skip he's had delivered in the front garden.'

'All change,' he said.

'Yes, but it's a good thing, isn't it?'

'Yes,' he said, kissing her on her forehead. 'There's never a dull moment with you around. I've got a horrible feeling that in your dotage you might out-Hilda Hilda.'

'I certainly hope so. I'm hoping at that age you and I will still be swimming in the lake on a Wednesday morning.'

Dominic squeezed her shoulders and pulled her to him. 'I wouldn't expect anything else of you, Ettie. I somehow think the Wednesday Wild Swim is here to stay.'

Acknowledgments

This book was inspired by the wonderful women I've met since swimming regularly at a local pool. We're not best friends, in fact we rarely socialise outside the gym, but we've become confidants, supporters, friends and cheerleaders over the years. In the pool we are ourselves, women in swimming caps, swimsuits and goggles, all equal and not defined by our roles as wives, partners, mothers, employees or bosses. There's something about swimming together which is a great leveller and gives you a certain anonymity. It seems much easier to share things with people who don't know the background minutiae of your lives.

The wild water element of the book was inspired by my dear friend Alison Cyster White, with her six inch challenge of 2021, where each month she challenged herself to immerse herself another six inches into wild water.

As always there are lots of people to thank because

writing a book, while solitary in some ways, needs the support and back-up of lots of other people. I'd like to thank celebrant, Kate Morgan, based in Australia, who kindly shared with me the wording she uses to celebrate same-sex marriages and who suggested ending the celebratory note with, 'You may now kiss the brides.'

Also a big shout out to the fantastic team at One More Chapter and the fabulous rights team at HarperCollins, the unsung heroes of the publishing industry – thank you all for bringing my books to the readers. Special thanks to my much loved editor, the awesome and talented Charlotte Ledger, and to my utterly brilliant agent, Broo Doherty, who is endlessly patient with my author wobbles.

Thanks also to my wonderful writer friends, especially Donna Ashcroft, who is my absolute rock, along with Bella Osborne, Darcy Boleyn, Philippa Ashley and Sarah Bennett, all of whom keep me sane during the writing process. I'm so grateful to have found you all, my life is immeasurably richer for having you in it.

Finally the biggest thanks, go to my readers. Thank you for the support: the messages, emails, contacts and shares on social media. You really do make it all worthwhile and I thank every one of you for buying my books. I hope they bring you a little bit of joy and happiness.

YOUR NUMBER ONE STOP

ONE MORE CHAPTER

FOR PAGETURNING BOOKS

One More Chapter is an
award-winning global
division of HarperCollins.

Sign up to our newsletter to get our
latest eBook deals and stay up to date
with our weekly Book Club!
<u>Subscribe here.</u>

Meet the team at
<u>www.onemorechapter.com</u>

Follow us!

 <u>@OneMoreChapter_</u>
 <u>@OneMoreChapter</u>
 <u>@onemorechapterhc</u>

Do you write unputdownable fiction?
We love to hear from new voices.
Find out how to submit your novel at
<u>www.onemorechapter.com/submissions</u>